Restoration at River's Edge

Restoration at River's Edge

Susan R. Lawrence

Gannah's Gate

Restoration at River's Edge
by Susan R. Lawrence

This novel is a work of fiction. Characters, plot, and incidents are
products of the author's imagination, and any similarity to people
living or dead, is coincidental.

SBN-13: 978-1-946985-13-2

Cover design by
Lynn Edler
LE Design

Chapter 1

EITHER HIS WIFE had been delusional, or he was lost.

Jon Washington stared out his truck window at the dilapidated gray house. There was not the slightest resemblance between this monstrosity and the vivid pictures Angela had painted in his mind of her beloved uncle's home where she'd spent summers as a child. He compared the address on the GPS to the one on the deed he held in his hand. The deed that stated the property now belonged to him.

Jon dropped the paper on the seat and stepped out of his truck. When he slammed the door, an answering echo bounced back from the bluffs that rose behind him in a towering wall.

The house, its back to the hill, faced the river valley below. Like an aging dowager unaware that her beauty is gone, it still wore the architectural details of a grand Victorian mansion. But the once-white siding had faded to the color of early morning fog. The roof was crumbling, shingles and trim torn and missing. The entire front porch leaned slightly like a misplaced appendage.

When Uncle Bruce died, Angie became the sole beneficiary of his estate. She described the place to Jon in glowing terms, determined to convince him to quit his job as an insurance adjuster and move to Missouri to remodel the home and open a restaurant. They both enjoyed cooking and serving their friends and family, and Angie thought owning a trailside café would be perfect. Finally, Jon gave notice at Phelps Insurance Agency. Two weeks later, on an icy morning in Minnesota, he lost Angie under the wheels of a runaway semi. Now Uncle Bruce's home belonged to him.

Jon waded through waist-high weeds and brush and stepped over a fallen portion of picket fence. A faint pathway led through the unmown grass and weeds. From the porch, the yard sloped gently down toward the river. A wild tangle of bushes and trees grew unfettered to the paved edge of the bike trail.

The state-owned recreational path ran between the towns of Maple Grove and Benson, Missouri, on an abandoned railroad bed, a ribbon of asphalt threading through the timber along the edge of the Cadence River. River's Edge Farm. Jon gave a snort. That was the grand name Bruce had given this ramshackle property.

The lawyer who served as executer of the estate after Uncle Bruce died had mentioned the house was *a little run down*. An understatement. Jon fingered the key in his pocket. Might as well take a tour.

He followed the path and stepped onto the porch. The floor groaned in protest. In years past, families undoubtedly gathered here to catch the cool breezes from the river. A single length of rusty chain dangled from the ceiling. He pictured his wife as a child, bare feet dangling as she rocked on the porch swing. Now strips of peeling paint, broken railings and the sagging roof offered a bleak welcome. A tattered screen door hung by one hinge, creaking slowly back and forth in the breeze.

He unlocked the heavy wooden door and stepped inside. Layers of thick dust covered everything. Uncle Bruce's furniture, tall, dark, and imposing, stood like wooden sentinels as Jon stepped through a parlor and into the spacious dining room. Dishes were still stacked on the round oak table. At one of the tall narrow windows, Jon pushed aside heavy drapes, coughing in the cloud of dust that ensued. Sunlight spilled into the room, lighting up the dust in the air, but doing little to dispel the chill.

He stepped around a broken chair and into the kitchen. Signs of varmints were everywhere. They must have moved in like a furry army after Uncle Bruce's death. A box of crackers lay on the counter, one end chewed open and a string of crumbs trailing out. The floor was sticky with remnants of meals long past. A strong foul odor permeated the air. Jon covered his nose and stepped through the other kitchen doorway into the hall. A few steps later, he stood back in the entryway at the foot of the wide stairway. What disasters would he find upstairs?

As he put his hand on the massive banister, it wobbled dangerously. Missing spindles gave it the appearance of a gap-toothed dinosaur. Jon dropped his hand and moved to the center of the steps.

Upstairs he found five large bedrooms and an antiquated bathroom with an original claw-footed tub. He opened closets and surveyed boxes with unknown contents. He gagged at the musty odors. Two of the bedrooms had water-spotted ceilings, and beneath one large stain sat a faded blue plastic bucket. Jon trudged back down the stairs.

He turned in a slow circle in the main hall. Everywhere there were signs of disrepair. Nothing appeared to have been fixed or changed or updated since his wife had stayed here nearly thirty years ago.

Jon pushed back his hair and groaned aloud. "This place needs a complete overhaul. What am I supposed to do now?" His words echoed in the house, bouncing back to mock him. How, in all their conversations about this place, had Angie never managed to mention the fact that it was falling apart?

After her aunt died, the year she was eight, her summer visits had ended. But Angie remained kind and caring to Bruce, taking on the role of the daughter he'd never had. And he had rewarded her by willing her River's Edge Farm. Some reward.

He started a mental list. The small amount of money from the life insurance policy Angie received from Wells Fargo would scarcely repair one corner of the house. Even with his limited construction knowledge, he knew the house needed a new roof, siding, windows, paint, and flooring. To fulfill his wife's dream of a restaurant in River's Edge he'd need to knock out walls, install a cooler, purchase commercial stoves, fryers … the list seemed endless. It would be months before all that could happen. How could he make a living in the meantime?

Jon trudged out to the porch and sat gingerly on the top step. He watched the people pass by on the trail, some biking, some walking. The afternoon slipped into evening. Shadows deepened in the timber beyond the yard. A chorus of frogs chirruped from the direction of the river. Overhead, without city lights to dull them, stars glittered thick and brilliant. Still, Jon sat, reclining against a solid, faded pillar.

The trail disappeared into the night. The bicycle and pedestrian traffic ceased. There were no onlookers to see the tears on Jon's cheeks. There were no ears to hear as he whispered. "How can I do this without her?"

When he'd packed everything and come to Missouri, he had thought pursuing Angie's dream would bring peace and healing. But the first view of this money pit was salt, not salve, on the wounds of his soul.

Chapter 2

KIRSTEN DANIELSON FUMBLED with the key pad that unlocked the back door of the Furry Friends Animal Clinic. She'd been up for two hours, but she was nearly late again. Trying to get eleven-year-old Josiah moving in the morning was a monumental task. And then, when she dropped him off at her dad's house for breakfast, there was another delay. Dad loved to visit.

A chorus of barks, whines, and mews met her when she stepped inside. The overnight boarders and post-surgical patients demanded breakfast. She dropped her bag on the desk in her miniscule office originally designed as a closet and stored her lunch in the shared refrigerator in the hall. Then she stepped over to the sink to wash her hands before she greeted the wiggling bodies pushing against the wire cages.

Kirsten's dream was to own a clinic, but when the chance to work with Dr. Jennings in Maple Grove had arisen, it seemed like the perfect opportunity. Her dad was thrilled to have her and Josiah close, the church she'd attended growing up was welcoming, and her hometown seemed like a great place for healing from her failed marriage. But, even with Dad's help, juggling single motherhood and work hadn't been easy. Josiah's diagnosis of Asperger's meant additional challenges. And sometimes the loneliness was overwhelming.

She poured food into a stainless steel pan, and a sleek brown boxer wiggled with delight. "Good morning, Bobby." She gave him a quick pat before she closed the cage. She could wait for the assistant to feed the animals, but the pleading eyes and plaintive voices got to her every time.

A tiger-striped cat and an overweight, stand-offish dachshund were next in line for breakfast. In the last cage, a dirty ball of fur cowered in the corner, pressing against the far side as if it thought she would grab it and give it to the boxer for a second course.

"Hello, ragamuffin. Where did you come from?"

Dr. Jennings stepped out of his office, shrugging into a white lab coat. "Our little orphan pup? Darrel Stevens brought her in this morning. They went to clean up their rental property and found her abandoned in the house. If he hadn't started cleaning this morning, they wouldn't have found her until it was too late."

Kirsten opened the door slowly and laid a hand on the floor of the cage. The half-grown pup thumped a hesitant tail against the wire and wiggled forward to sniff her. "She's a girl? Have you given her any food?"

"No. Just popped her in a cage. Go ahead and check her over, give her a first round of inoculations, and start her on some puppy chow. When Elizabeth gets here, she can give her a bath. And we'll post her picture this week. We should be able to find a home for this one right away."

Space was limited at the city-owned pound, and they regularly euthanized strays. So Furry Friends often ended up with unwanted animals. Dr. Jennings rarely turned a refugee away. What the town needed was a no-kill shelter.

The pup evidently decided Kirsten was not a threat. Her whole body wagged, and she reached for Kirsten's face with a wet tongue. Gently, Kirsten wrapped her hands around the dog's midsection and lifted her from the cage. "Come on, girl, let's see if you're healthy."

She checked the pup's temperature, eyes, ears, and teeth and listened to her heart and lungs. No sign of fleas. Underweight. Ears in need of cleaning. A few cuts and abrasions on her legs. She made notations on the chart as carefully as if the dog belonged to a paying customer. Underneath the filth, the fur was a soft yellow, and her triangular ears and blocky body showed classic signs of Labrador retriever breeding. Why had she just been thrown away?

The pup blinked when the needle poked through her skin, but a minute later she placed her paws on Kirsten's chest and licked her chin. Josiah would love this dog, but she didn't need a pet to add to the chaos of her home. She'd better keep him away from the clinic until they found a home for the pup. She lifted the dog off the exam table and returned her to the cage. When she set a bowl of puppy chow in front of her, the pup began to crunch it down, her tail waving in pleasure.

Kirsten moved to the cages of the animals that had undergone surgeries, checking their vitals and incision sites. Most would be picked up by owners and taken home today. They were the lucky ones. She glanced at the cage with the little yellow Lab. Maybe she'd have a home soon too.

In the next hour, Furry Friends Clinic became busier. They opened for business at nine. Yvonne, the receptionist, and Jessica, the veterinary assistant, took preliminary information while Kirsten and Dr. Jennings met with patients and their owners in the exam rooms. Elizabeth, an older, part-time employee arrived, and Kirsten filled her in on the abandoned puppy. Next time she went by the cage, the pup had obviously been given a bath. Wet fur stood up in every direction, and when Kirsten stopped, the puppy shook, wet drops flying from the flopping ears.

"Hey, I had my shower before I came this morning." Kirsten laughed and hurried on to her office to fill out a chart.

At lunchtime, Kirsten pulled out the wrap she'd packed for herself when she fixed Josiah's lunch. Even when he spent the day at her dad's house, he took his lunch. It was easier for her dad than dealing with Josiah's finicky eating habits.

She nibbled on the wrap while reading information on a new flea-control medication. She rarely had time to just sit and eat, as clients used their own lunchtimes to bring their pets in.

"Kirsten?" Elizabeth stood at her office door. It must be important, or she wouldn't interrupt. Gifted in nurturing the two-footed creatures in the office as well as the four, Elizabeth frequently advised her to take care of herself.

"Umm-hmm." Kirsten wiped her mouth with a paper towel from the lab. She always forgot to pack napkins. "What's up?"

"There's a man up front who wants to know if we have any cats he can adopt. He's the new owner of the old River's Edge Farm out on the bike trail. And he's looking for help catching mice."

"Oh, good. Maybe Tiger will get a home." Kirsten tucked the wrap back into the plastic Ziploc bag she'd brought it in. It didn't look like she'd get to finish it any time soon. Then she followed Elizabeth up front.

For some reason she was expecting an older man, perhaps a sort of reincarnation of Bruce Rickert. She still missed the friendly, white-haired man. Every few months he would show up at the clinic with a stray cat or dog. Once it was a dog with a whole litter of pups.

But this was not an old man. He wore jeans and a pale blue

pullover shirt, but he would look good in any clothes. Tall, with brown hair that curled at his neckline. And the warm chocolate-colored eyes he turned on her could melt more than candy.

What was she doing? Ogling a man in the clinic? She tucked a strand of hair behind her ear, gave him what she hoped was a businesslike smile, and offered her hand. "Hello. I'm Dr. Danielson. I understand you're interested in adopting a cat."

His handshake was firm and brief. "I'm Jon Washington. I just moved, and I have a mouse infestation on my new property. I like animals and thought a cat would help. It'd be a pet, too."

"We have a lovely tiger-striped female. I don't know if she's a good mouser, but she's a sweetheart. Follow me, we keep the animals for adoption back here." Kirsten was acutely aware of Jon as he followed her down the narrow hall and through the swinging doors. She stopped in front of the row of cages. The tan and black cat looked up at them, blinked sleepy amber eyes, and curled up again.

Kirsten moved to the side so Jon could see the cat. "This is Tiger. Would you like me to get her out of the cage?"

Jon squatted in front and spoke softly. "Hi, pretty girl. Are you inclined to catch mice? I have more than a few I'd love for you to take care of for me. I can't promise posh accommodations, and you'll have to put up with lots of construction in the future, but you would be compensated fairly." The cat stood, stretched, and pressed her head against the cage where Jon's hand gripped it.

A sudden yip startled all of them. Across the room, the Lab puppy tried to get them to notice her. She stretched up full length on the wire mesh with her tail moving in frenzied circles. Her sharp baby teeth bit at the wire, then she yipped and bit it again. When Jon moved to stand in front of her cage, she shot around in a circle like a wind-up toy just released. She made a lap around the perimeter, stood up to lick at his hand, then dashed around again.

"Is this little guy up for adoption, too?" Jon poked a finger through the wire at the frantic tongue.

"She's a girl, but, yes, she's available. An abandoned puppy. But puppies take a lot of work." Kirsten still stood by the cat's cage.

"Could I take both of them? I mean, I need a cat to take care of the mice, but this little girl needs a home too. A place she can get out and run. I'd take good care of her."

The man looked like a taller version of Josiah when he was begging for something. She wasn't at all sure the man knew what the responsibilities of pet ownership entailed, but the clinic didn't have time for extensive screening of adoptive owners. Any home offered was better than life in a cage.

She smiled up at him. "I don't see why not. Our job is finding homes for them. And Tiger doesn't seem to be bothered by the dogs. Why don't we step into an open exam room? There's some paperwork to fill out, and I'll give you a copy of their immunization record."

Fifteen minutes later, Jon left his two new family members and went to purchase the necessary equipment for them from the local hardware store. When he returned, he looked as excited as a ten-year-old boy as he carried first the cat, then the Lab puppy out to their crates in his truck.

Later, as Kirsten swept and cleaned out the empty cages, her thoughts drifted to the tall, good-looking man. She'd noticed he didn't wear a wedding ring and wondered why he wasn't married. She stopped scrubbing the floor of the cage and scolded herself. When David confessed to his latest in a string of infidelities and then asked for a divorce, she'd made the decision to focus on her son and her career. She didn't have the time or the strength for anything or anyone else. That was God's plan for her, and she needed to stick to it.

✑

Chapter 3

✑

JON WATCHED FROM the porch as a battered tan Ford truck skidded to a stop in the driveway.

A short, wiry man stepped out. He wore Carhartt coveralls and a dirty red Ace Hardware cap. Gray hair poked out on either side.

Midway to the house, the man stopped and peered up at it. "Ain't much ta look at, is it?" He spoke around a wad of something Jon hoped wasn't chewing tobacco. When he reached the porch, he asked, "You Jon Washington?"

"Yes, sir, I am."

"I'm Paul Donovan, the contractor you called. Gonna redo this place, huh? Make it a fancy restaurant?"

Jon stepped down from the porch and shook the man's calloused hand. "Not really fancy. I plan to serve sandwiches, drinks—lunch for those on the trail. And I'll have a limited menu for dinner, which I'll serve family style."

Paul swallowed whatever he'd been chewing and, instead of coming inside, he circled the house. Jon followed. He wasn't sure what the contractor looked at, but the older man walked slowly, his eyes taking in every inch of the house. Every few steps, he'd stop and make a comment. "House is in pretty good shape for her age. Good bones, ya know? Little foundation repair needed there." He pointed to a spot where the brick had crumbled. "But overall it looks better'n I thought it would. Let's go inside, and you can show me what you want done."

Jon held the door, and Paul stepped into the old parlor. "Well, I'll be a monkey's uncle. Ole Bruce's stuff's still in here."

"Yeah." Jon ran his hands over an antique oak buffet. "Know how I can get rid of it?"

"McCullough's the name of the auctioneer in town. He always draws a crowd. He'd help you out. I got his number here somewhere." He rummaged in the roomy pockets of his coveralls and pulled out a handful of sawdust, a couple screws, a wadded-up receipt, three Laffy Taffy candies, and a dirty business card.

"Found it." He handed the card to Jon with a tiny bit of a flourish.

"Thanks. I'll call him this afternoon."

Paul leaned forward and lowered his voice. "Better call before six. Sometimes McCullough hits the bar fairly early, if you know what I mean." He paused and looked around. "Now, once you get all this cleared outta here, what're we gonna do?"

Jon swept his arm in a gesture that included the entire downstairs area. "This will all be the main dining room. I thought maybe we could take down the walls between the existing dining room, parlor, and hall, and open up the whole area."

"Umm." Paul rubbed a grizzled chin. "Maybe if we put a beam across. We'd need one or two support posts. But we could do it."

"Good. I want a counter here." Jon stood by the front door and patted an imaginary work surface. "For a cash register and reception area. The bathroom stays, but it needs updated, new fixtures and a wider door to be handicap accessible."

Jon moved down the hall to the kitchen. "This room needs a

complete remodel. I'm no designer, but I have a crude drawing of what I want."

Paul pulled out a candy, unwrapped it and popped it in his mouth. "Want a taffy?"

Jon shook his head. "No, thanks."

"I used to smoke, 'til the wife made me quit. So now I chew taffy." He looked around the kitchen. "Kinda smells in here, don't it?"

"Yeah. I think there's a dead mouse somewhere. Probably in the walls. They seem to have taken over after Bruce passed away. I adopted a cat today, hoping she'd help catch them, but she's in her carrier upstairs. I didn't want her underfoot or escaping outside while I showed you around."

"Well, when we gut the place, we'll probably find all kinds of things in these here walls." Paul chuckled and patted the flowered wallpaper. Jon shuddered.

Jon used one hand to brush debris off the wobbly kitchen table. He spread out the drawing of the proposed kitchen, and Paul peered over his shoulder.

Paul pointed across the room. "Sink over there? Stove across here? Counter against this wall?"

Jon nodded. "Is all that doable?"

"Sure." Paul swallowed his latest wad of taffy. "We're gonna hafta redo the plumbin' and 'lectricity anyways. Whatcha got is way outdated. It's a miracle ole Bruce never had a fire out here."

Jon moved across the kitchen to where an old door that once led to a sagging back porch was boarded shut. "I need a back exit, so I'd like to keep the door there and have it open to a small deck." He pointed to the back wall. "And I'd like a walk-in cooler and freezer here." He stepped to the far wall. "Then over here, a storage room with floor-to-ceiling shelves."

"I can jus' tear that porch right off, build a deck, and add a bump-out addition so's it can be your storage area."

Jon nodded approval and moved into the hall. "I want my washer and dryer in the storage room, handy to wash aprons and towels."

Paul nodded and chewed, occasionally making notes in a small spiral notebook with curling page corners.

Upstairs, Jon pointed out the water spots on the ceilings and the few changes necessary so he could live above the restaurant. Paul followed him, occasionally asking for clarification. When they stepped back out onto the porch, the sun had dipped behind the bluff, and the house cast her shadow clear to the bike trail.

"I think we can do you up right spiffy. I'll work these figgers and git you an estimate tomorry." Paul spoke around his latest wad of taffy.

"I'd like to do some work myself. I'm no carpenter, but I can wield a paint brush. And I'll be living in the middle of everything."

"Well, I'll just consider you part of the crew, then. Good way for you to keep the cost down, and all righty by me. We'll keep you busy until the diner's up and runnin'." He stuck out his hand and they shook again. A few minutes later the Ford truck roared to life and careened down the road, a cloud of dust billowing behind it.

Jon looked at his watch. Not quite six o'clock. He pulled out the auctioneer's business card and his phone. Marty McCullough agreed to meet him at the house the next morning.

He raced upstairs to the bedroom. "Sorry to shut you two up your first afternoon at River's Edge. I didn't want you to get lost when the contractor was here." The puppy yipped and pawed at the cage door. Tiger stretched slowly and yawned. He opened

Tiger's door, showed her where her litter box was, poured some of her cat food in a dish, and filled a second dish with water. She rubbed against his leg and he stroked her back before she wandered over to sniff the dish.

The puppy's yips were beginning to sound frantic. "Calm down, I haven't forgotten you." Jon unlocked the door of the large kennel and scooped her up in his arms as she bounded out. "It's downstairs and outside with you before dinner."

In the yard, the puppy raced in giant circles around him. She grabbed a stick, tried to entice Jon to chase her, and dropped it at his feet only to snatch it up again and race away. Jon laughed, a joyous booming laugh that echoed in the valley. It was the first time he could remember laughing in months.

Down the hill from his yard, the trail beckoned. Early spring sunshine had warmed the air, and the smell of wet earth and new growth tickled his nose. Jon grabbed the leash he'd bought and fastened it to the pup's new collar. But the little Lab either dashed on ahead, hitting the end of the leash and nearly pulling Jon's arm from the socket, or she lagged behind, pawing at the unfamiliar tether. After a short distance, Jon turned around and coaxed her back to River's Edge. He unfastened the leash and sat on the porch steps as she worked her nose back and forth across the yard.

"Here, pup. Here girl," he coaxed. When she came, he scratched behind her ears. Angie always wanted a dog, but they'd both been so busy with careers, he told her to wait. Now, he'd give anything to see her with this pup.

"Guess you need a name. I can't keep calling you *pup* or *girl*."

Her bright eyes gazed up at him, her head cocked to the side, her tail waving slowly.

"How about Maisy? You look like a Maisy."

Her tail wagged faster.

"Okay, Maisy. You ready to have some supper?"

She was on her feet now, not only her tail wagging, but her hindquarters too. Jon stood and went inside, and Maisy scampered after him.

After he fed her, Jon made himself a peanut butter sandwich. He'd picked up a few groceries in town and gotten the water and electricity turned on before his trip to Furry Friends. One bed was stripped and remade with his sheets. Cleaning supplies stood on the kitchen table. He was ready to make River's Edge his home.

Chapter 4

KIRSTEN LEANED HER head on the steering wheel. She hated sitting and waiting. But she and her dad agreed it was best for her to wait in the car when she picked up Josiah. If she went in, Josiah often had a meltdown in the transition.

The front door opened, and Josiah emerged, backpack hanging from one arm and his blue windbreaker jacket, half-stuffed inside, dragging on the ground. His sandy brown hair was rumpled. And he had a scowl on his face.

She rolled down the window. "Josiah, pick up your backpack. Your jacket's dragging."

He hitched it up an inch or two, but the sleeve still dragged. When he got to the car, he tossed the bag in the back and slid into the front seat.

Kirsten leaned over to give him a kiss on the cheek, which he tolerated without flinching. "How was your day, honey? Did you do okay on the science quiz?"

"I knew all the answers." Josiah's tone was conversational, but his blue eyes focused outside his window.

"We had a yellow Lab puppy in the clinic today. She'd been abandoned."

Josiah glanced at her. She'd caught his attention. "A Lab? They're the coolest. Can I go see her?"

"She already left for her new home, partner. A man came in and took both her and the tiger cat."

"Aw, Mom. I really want a dog." Josiah's fingers poked at a small frayed hole in the knee of his jeans.

"I know you do, Josiah. But with your schedule and mine, we don't have time to take care of and train a dog. A pet is a big responsibility."

"Sixty-two percent of U.S. households have dogs. I'm going to be twelve on November eleventh. I'll be old enough then."

Kirsten steered the car into their driveway. She didn't argue. Time with Josiah always meant dancing—making sure she was instructing and disciplining, but not doing anything that would provoke a meltdown. The tantrums seemed to be increasing, and she wondered if it was due to his age and hormones. Josiah was growing. She feared someday in the not-to-distant future, he would become too large and strong for her to control.

Josiah hung up his coat and pulled his communication folder out of his bag, while Kirsten set out fruit, crackers, and cheese for his snack. "Here you go, son. Would you like milk or water to drink?"

Josiah perched on the edge of the stool at the bar and slowly rocked his body as he reached for a piece of cheese. "Milk, please."

Kirsten handed him a glass of milk and opened the folder. His teacher had checked the box for *satisfactory* in every area. She noted the spelling test would be tomorrow, and he had a social studies assignment to complete.

"Looks like you had a good day, buddy."

"Umm-hmm." Josiah didn't pause his rocking. "I showed my class how to divide fractions. I'm the king at math." He carefully laid another piece of cheese across a cracker.

"Yes, you are king at math. Are you ready to study spelling or do you want to finish your snack first?"

"Did you know that a dog's sense of smell is ten thousand times better than ours?"

"I didn't know that. But Josiah, I asked when you wanted to study your spelling."

He pushed the empty plate across the bar and drank the rest of his milk before answering. "Now."

Kirsten read the words and listened as Josiah spelled each one aloud with no mistakes. Practice was probably an unnecessary chore, but it was still one thing they could do together, the familiar routine of homework. She checked *study spelling* off the list in his planner, tucked it back in the folder, then scanned the social studies worksheet.

"This looks fun. You get to study a state and make a report on it. All you need to do tonight is choose a state."

Josiah rocked just a little faster. "I want to do a report on dogs."

Kirsten forced a smile. "That's not a choice. Think of all the fun states you could choose. Maybe Florida or South Dakota—you've gone on vacations there."

"All right." Josiah slid off the stool. "I choose Wisconsin. That's where my dad lives, right?"

Kirsten took a deep breath and puffed it out. "Yes, it is. You remember living there, don't you? Wisconsin will be great. Maybe your dad will even send you some information. You need to fill out the sheet and then you're done."

Josiah took the sheet and the pencil she handed him, filled in the blanks, and returned it to the folder. "Now can I play Lego Super Heroes?"

"Sure, sweetie. I'll have supper ready at six." He dashed off to the game room while Kirsten opened the fridge and pulled out vegetables for a salad. The routine of their evenings never varied. Letting Josiah play his favorite game gave her time to fix supper, toss a load of laundry in the washer, and perhaps do some personal emails or calls. As soon as supper was ready, the video game would be turned off. After eating, he could read, play a game with her, or play outside when the weather permitted. Occasionally, they would watch a movie together.

She turned on the radio and upbeat, contemporary Christian music filled the kitchen. She hummed along softly as she chopped vegetables and put some chicken in the tabletop grill, wishing it were warm enough to use the outside one. Their meals were simple. Although Kirsten loved to try new recipes, an unfamiliar food could easily result in one of Josiah's outbursts. She put plates on the table, wondering how Tiger and the little Lab were adjusting to their new home. She often became attached to their orphans. Although she was delighted when one of them got a forever home, she worried they wouldn't get the loving care they deserved. She felt a little foolish, but she often prayed for the animals.

She grabbed silverware from the drawer and placed it beside the plates. Josiah would invariably rearrange his silverware and rotate his plate so that his meat was on the right.

"Josiah, time for supper. Turn off the game and wash your hands," Kirsten called.

There was no reply. The beeps and noises of the video game continued. She walked down the hall to the small bedroom they'd converted to a TV and game room. Josiah sat in his rocking game chair, the control in his lap, his lips pursed and his eyebrows drawn together.

With effort, she kept her voice calm and even. "Josiah, I

called you for supper. Turn off the game and wash your hands." The game screeched and something flew apart on the screen. "I'm doing the second chapter, Enter Magneto. I'm on level five. I need to finish level five."

Kirsten inhaled and let her breath out slowly before responding. "No, Josiah. Supper is on the table." The timer on the oven beeped. The rolls were warm. "Come now," she added before hurrying back to the kitchen.

A few minutes later, Josiah slid into his chair opposite hers and bowed his head. Kirsten prayed and thanked God for the food, Josiah's good day, and the home for the cat and pup. As soon as she said "amen," Josiah began eating, his eyes on his plate, one bite after another as if devouring the meal was a mission to be accomplished.

As a single parent of an Asperger's child, one thing that Kirsten missed and longed for was the give and take of dinner-time conversation. She asked Josiah a few questions about school, but he grunted replies around mouthfuls of food. She told the story of the little yellow Lab shaking water all over after her bath, but Josiah gave no reaction that indicated he'd even listened.

In a few minutes, Josiah's plate was clean. "May I be excused?" Josiah blurted the question as if it were a single word.

"Sure, sweetie. Put your dishes in the dishwasher." Kirsten finished her chicken, grabbed a second roll, and buttered it. She tried to eat healthy, but sometimes what she called the stress diet took over.

After stuffing most of the roll in her mouth, she began cleaning the kitchen. "Josiah, are you picking a game for us?" There was no answer. Kirsten added detergent to the dishwasher, started it, and wiped off the grill and counters. Then she walked down the hall.

Josiah sat in his game chair, the sound on Legos Super Heroes muted, the action on the TV screen frantic.

"Josiah James Danielson!" Kirsten regretted the shrieking tone as soon as it left her mouth.

Josiah, who rarely reacted to his mom's emotions, jerked around to face her, dropping the game controls. Then his face contorted into a familiar scowl. "I'm on level five. I have to finish this chapter."

Kirsten forced her voice to return to a moderate range, one that wouldn't set off a tantrum. "No. The deal is, you may play video games while I fix supper. The game goes off before supper and you are not to turn it back on."

"I didn't turn it back on."

"Then you didn't turn it off before supper. Josiah, your choices now are to read or play a game with me. Or you could use the treadmill downstairs for some exercise."

"I have to finish this game. I'm on level five."

It was like he hadn't heard a thing she'd said. Kirsten bowed her head and rubbed her temples. Then she walked across the room and unplugged the TV. The reaction was instantaneous. Josiah screamed, a high-pitched keening wail. His body rocked the chair wildly.

Kirsten stepped over beside Josiah, but she was careful not to touch him. "I'm sorry Josiah. Our rule is: no video games after supper. Now, if you are going to throw a tantrum, you need to go to your bedroom."

She might as well have been talking to the blank-screened TV. She stepped over his feet and moved toward her bedroom. Josiah's howls followed, surging around her like a Missouri thunderstorm. Behind her closed bedroom door, she sat on her bed and picked up a romance novel she'd started last week. She flipped through the pages, but she knew she couldn't concentrate with Josiah's tantrum rocking the house. If only she could take him in her arms, wipe away his tears, and comfort him. But her touch only escalated his tantrums. All she could do was wait and pray for him to calm himself.

It was nearly eight-o'clock when she heard the crying subside and the bathroom door close. She laid down the book she'd been holding and went into the hall. When Josiah came out of the bathroom, his face was red and swollen.

"Go get your pajamas on, son, and I'll come in to talk."

Josiah moved woodenly toward his bedroom. He didn't acknowledge her, but she could tell the storm had passed and the sun would shine again.

Later, Kirsten sat on the edge of Josiah's bed. She held his hand and prayed for him. As soon as she said amen, he pulled his hand away.

"You know we have to follow rules. Whether you're at school, or home, or at a job, there are rules. When you don't follow them, there are consequences."

"I know." Josiah pulled the blanket up to his chin. He looked like a very little boy, his eyes large and dark in the dim light. "I'm sorry I screamed, Mom."

"I am too. I missed our game time together."

"I'll turn the video game off tomorrow."

Kirsten brushed a brief kiss on Josiah's forehead. "Night, son. Sleep tight and wake up bright. I love you."

"Night, Mom." Josiah rolled over to face the wall.

Kirsten stepped into her bedroom and flung herself across her spacious queen bed. She felt as drained as if she was the one who had screamed and cried for an hour.

Chapter 5

JON MANEUVERED AROUND two boxes of dishes and a table strewn with embroidered dish towels, handmade afghans, and all kinds of fancy little cloths. What did people do with things like that, anyway?

Marty McCullough's men scrambled everywhere, pulling things out of boxes, hefting furniture out of the house, and arranging tables of collectables on his front lawn.

Four women had set up a food stand in his kitchen, and the smells of hotdogs, beef burgers, and coffee floated outside. Marty, a small, soft-spoken man, had introduced them as members of a local church. Fellowship something or other. They sold food at the McCullough auctions as a fundraiser for their missions. A second cup of coffee sounded good. He flipped the cold remnants of his first cup on the grass and went inside.

In the kitchen, a silver-haired woman with piercing gray eyes bustled up to him. "You must be Jon. I'm Margaret Hanson. I'm glad to see someone finally taking care of Bruce's estate. We miss him around here. He was a good man. He and his wife went to our church, you know. And Hazel, that was his wife's name, was one of my closest friends." She laid a hand over her heart and her gray curls bobbed as if she was certain Jon knew this information.

"Your wife is Bruce's niece, is that right?"

"Yes." Jon nodded, looking sideways for an opportunity to escape.

Another woman entered the kitchen through the hall door and set down a plastic container. Margaret turned away to address her. "No, no, Debbie, the cookies need to go over there, by my pies." She motioned toward a card table they'd set up by the window.

Jon took a step backwards toward the door into the dining room.

"Oh, here." Margaret reached for his coffee cup. "You need some coffee, don't you? We just made a fresh pot." She turned the tap and a fragrant stream ran into his cup.

"Thanks." Jon took it from her and sipped. He took another step toward the door.

Margaret waved her hand at him. "It's the least we can do. We took over your kitchen. Here, have some cookies to go with that." She wrapped a couple chocolate chip cookies in a napkin and handed them to him. "You can come back later for a meal and have a piece of my cherry pie."

Jon took the cookies and balanced them on top of his coffee cup. "I'll do that. And is it okay to pay you later for these? I need to go upstairs and check on my dog."

"Oh, don't worry about paying. Those are on the house. You go right up and take care of your dog. And welcome to Maple Grove. After you get settled in, we'd love to have you come to Fellowship Church. We're on Timmons Drive, out near the high school. It's a great place to worship – good preaching, good music, lots of young folks like you."

"Thank you." Jon smiled, backed out of the kitchen, and hurried upstairs. He knew Maisy and Tiger were fine. He'd put them in their kennels that morning, and both of them had curled up for a nap. He stood on the landing and looked out the little square window at the top of the stairway. Cars lined both sides of the gravel road as far as he could see.

When he opened the door of the bedroom, both animals lifted their heads hopefully, and Maisy's tail sounded like a percussion instrument on the side of the kennel. "Sorry, girls. You were just my excuse. It'll be a few hours before I can let you out." He closed the door. Outside, an expectant murmur rose as people jostled for a position close to the auctioneer.

Marty stepped up on a small ladder and spoke into a portable loudspeaker. "Welcome to the estate sale of Bruce Rickert. If you don't have a bidding number, you can get one from Kim inside. She's in the old parlor. As usual, the ladies from Fellowship Church have a food stand. Just walk through the house to the kitchen at the back. Don't worry about tracking something in, because the new owner's going to remodel this place. We'll be starting in about fifteen minutes."

Jon didn't have a bidding number and wasn't going to get one. He was trying to clear this stuff out of his house. He'd kept some bedroom furniture, one desk, and the kitchen table out of necessity. After the sale of his home in Minnesota, he'd moved a few things into a rented storage area and sold the rest. He didn't want reminders of Angie and their great life together.

Next week, he would drive up to Minnesota and bring back a truckload of the things he'd stored. It would be enough to fill the rooms upstairs where he, Maisy, and Tiger would live until the house was renovated and the restaurant opened.

Marty held up a glass dish and called, "Who'll give me twenty-five for this gorgeous cut glass bowl?"

Jon watched from the porch, sipping coffee, and munching

the chocolate chip cookies.

An older man stepped out of the house, the lop-sided screen door banging behind him. Probably a farmer with his weathered skin and the seed corn cap. He held a card with the number eighty-nine written on it in large black numerals. He carefully slid it in his front shirt pocket with the number facing out. He looked over at Jon. "You the fella that bought this place?"

Jon nodded and swallowed the last of his cookies. "I am. My name's Jon Washington." Jon reached out and his hand was swallowed up in the strong grasp of the older man.

"Jus' gonna tear it down?"

Jon nearly spit out his mouthful of coffee. "Oh, no. I plan to renovate the house and make the downstairs into a restaurant."

"A restaurant? That's crazy. Who'd drive all the way out here, when there's a couple perfectly good places to eat downtown?"

Jon opened his mouth and shut it. He tried to think of a polite response. But before he could, the older man stepped off the porch and wove his way among the spectators.

Marty was in full swing now, his rapid sing-song chant booming through the loudspeaker above the clusters of on-lookers, most of them doing more chatting than bidding. This seemed to be a social outing for the people of Maple Grove. Potential customers, though. Jon set his cup on the porch railing and stepped into the crowd.

He introduced himself to several people and was met with polite disinterest when he talked about opening a restaurant at River's Edge. There were over a hundred people here, and the majority of them were probably from Maple Grove. They liked to eat, he could tell that by the number of beef burger dinners and pieces of pie coming out of the kitchen. But no one wanted to hear his plans. Would he create this thing and have no customers?

As the afternoon wore on, the clutter on the front yard began to disappear, a box here, a chair there, and armfuls of new-found treasures loaded into cars. By three o'clock, most of the crowd had dispersed.

Marty climbed down from the ladder and mopped his brow with an oversized handkerchief. "A good sale, Jon. Some of the furniture didn't go as high as I would have liked, but the dishes went like hotcakes. We'll load up the leftover boxes and the PA system in my van, and by suppertime we'll be out of your hair. I'll cut you a check sometime next week. You can start your renovations Monday, if you want."

"Thanks, Marty. I'll tell Paul I'm ready. I kind of thought I'd see him today. It looked like everyone else in town was here."

"He's probably working. If the sun's shining, Paul never misses an opportunity to work. Except Sunday. That man wouldn't work on Sunday if his own house was falling in on him."

Marty's assistant stopped and spoke around a cardboard box full of newspapers he was carrying. "Paul goes to Fellowship Church. I do, too. You're welcome to join us tomorrow."

There it was again. Why was this whole town trying to get him to church? "Thanks for the invite, but I've got stuff I need to do around here." He wasn't sure what, but it wouldn't be church. He would never again have anything to do with the God who had taken Angie from him.

Chapter 6

MARGARET HANSON LIMPED out to the kitchen. She loved working the food stand at Marty's auctions, but the next day her feet hurt, her hip was sore, and she was just plain tired. And this morning she'd woken with a headache.

Perhaps a strong cup of coffee would perk her up, so she could enjoy church. She measured the water and the coffee, pushed the button to start the brewing, then lifted her worn blue Bible from the shelf. God's word would perk up her soul.

By the time the coffeemaker beeped, she'd read a Psalm and a chapter in 1 Peter. Now for her breakfast with God. She took a blueberry muffin out of the pantry and an orange from the refrigerator and laid them on a plate. Ever since her husband, Nathaniel, died, she spent breakfast conversing with her Lord. Today, she talked about her daughter, Melanie, a fashion designer in New York City. *Watch over her. Protect her. Help her to depend on You.* God's comfort and assurance warmed her heart as much as the coffee warmed her stomach.

On the counter were the leftovers she'd unloaded last night – an empty crockpot that had held beef burgers and still needed to be washed, one piece of peach pie, and a whole strawberry rhubarb pie. She'd have the peach for her dessert today, but what was she going to do with a whole pie? She sipped her coffee and nibbled on the muffin and a segment of the orange. *What would You have me do with this pie, Lord?*

The young man at River's Edge. He liked desserts. After church, she could drive out and give him the pie as a welcome gift. The thought cheered her, and she finished her breakfast and prayer time.

After church, Margaret's feet no longer hurt. The headache had subsided some, too. The praise music and uplifting message were good medicine. She changed from her flowered dress to a pair of slacks and a blue knit shirt. Then she fixed a salad, topped it with some leftover chicken, and buttered a homemade roll. She put her plate on the table, sat down, and unfolded the Sunday newspaper.

When she'd finished her meal, she took the newspaper into her living room and leaned back in her recliner. Within a few minutes she was asleep, the newspaper spread over her chest.

She woke with a start. When her eyes opened, she saw two couches across the room and two front doors. She rubbed her eyes, shook her head, and her vision cleared. She was supposed to be somewhere, do something, but what? The pie. She hoisted herself out of the comfy chair and hurried to the kitchen. It was almost four o'clock, and she hadn't even put away her dishes from lunch.

She stuffed them in the dishwasher, slipped into a jacket, and carried the pie out to her faithful blue Buick. Before turning onto the highway, she pulled into Casey's. She filled up her car with gas and made a mental note to get the oil changed within the week. Her beloved Nathaniel had been gone for many years now, and she'd had lots of practice in car and house maintenance.

She remembered going to River's Edge when Nathaniel, Hazel, and Bruce were all alive. They'd had such great times—

playing croquet in the backyard or cards in the kitchen, laughing and solving all the problems in the world. Now she was the only one left.

Her car tires rumbled as she crossed over the Cadence River on the old iron bridge, and she reached out with her right hand to steady the pie. Then she turned into the driveway of River's Edge. Without the clusters of people around, it looked even shabbier than yesterday.

As she stepped out of the car, a yapping, yellow blur tore around the corner of the porch and raced toward her. She almost jumped back into the car, but then she saw the wagging tail.

"Why, hello." She reached down to pet the dog and was almost knocked over when the pup planted two huge front paws on her and reached for her face with her tongue.

"Maisy! That's no way to greet a visitor." The lop-sided screen door banged behind Jon. In a minute, he was beside them, and he pushed the dog into a sitting position. "I'm so sorry. I haven't had her long enough to teach her manners yet. You're Margaret—one of the church ladies, right?"

"Yes." She smiled, pleased he remembered her. "I brought you something. I don't know why I didn't just leave it with you yesterday. But I was so tired after working that auction I couldn't even think." She stepped around to the passenger side and pulled out the pie. "Just a little welcome gift."

"I thought that's what the cookies were." Jon took the pie from her. "Oh, this looks delicious. Do you want to come up and sit on my porch? You're my first official visitor. I don't think I can count the contractor or people at the auction."

"I'd love to. It's such a beautiful afternoon. I think spring may be right around the corner from Maple Grove."

Jon released Maisy, and she galloped off across the yard, her nose to the ground, her tail waving. Margaret followed Jon to the porch.

He motioned to two old lawn chairs perched on the sagging porch floor. "Sit down. I'll put this pie in the kitchen. Can I get you something to drink? I still have some of the iced tea you made yesterday. Someone left a container, and I've been enjoying it."

"That sounds wonderful." Margaret sank onto one of the chairs. It wobbled slightly but didn't collapse. In a few minutes, Jon appeared with two tall glasses filled with iced tea.

Margaret took the glass he held out to her and sipped. "So, tell me about your plans for this place."

A slightly crooked smile lit up his face. Something about his smile, the way his eyes crinkled, reminded her of Nathaniel.

"It was my wife's dream, really. She used to spend her summers here with her uncle. When he died, and she inherited the place, she wanted to turn it into a restaurant. She talked me into it. I quit my job and everything." The smile faded, and he paused and gazed away down the bike trail.

Margaret took a drink of tea and waited for him to continue. When he didn't, she asked, "Is your wife moving here soon?"

His quick intake of breath told her the question was somehow terribly wrong. "I'm sorry, Jon. I didn't mean to pry."

His gaze dropped to the porch floor and he shook his head. When he looked up, his eyes were brimming with tears. "You weren't prying. I'm sure lots of people in town are wondering. Angie was killed in a car accident last November. River's Edge became mine when she passed away. And it just seemed right for me to go ahead with the project. I couldn't save her, but I could save her dream." His head dropped into his hands.

Margaret set her glass down and reached over to lay a hand

on his knee. "What a strong man you are. I'm sure your wife would be proud of you."

Jon didn't raise his head. His voice was muffled. "Thanks. But I had no idea the house was in such disrepair. It's going to take far more money than I thought to get the restaurant going. I'm feeling pretty stressed out about it right now. If there was a way I could run back to Minnesota, I think I would. Problem is, there's nothing for me back there, now."

Margaret stood up. "Give it some time. Things have a way of working out. Just try to tackle one problem at a time. Would you like to show me what the restaurant's going to be like?"

Jon looked up. A smile spread slowly over his face and erased the lines of worry. "Really? You want to see?"

"Sure. I love old houses, and this one in particular. My husband and I were good friends with Bruce and Hazel. And I appreciate people doing things to preserve the past."

Jon held open the screen door with a tiny bow and a flourish of his arm. "Welcome to River's Edge Restaurant."

The next half-hour Jon gave the tour, painting Angie's dream in Margaret's mind. He showed her where the tables would sit, what he wanted in the kitchen, and where the walk-in cooler and pantry would be built. He answered her questions with well-thought-out answers.

"You certainly seem knowledgeable about restaurants," she commented when they made their way back to the porch.

"My Aunt Georgia had an Italian restaurant in Kansas City. While Angie was a kid spending summers here in the country, I was in the city helping at the restaurant. Never imagined I'd own one, though."

An idea kept poking into Margaret's mind. She stuffed the ridiculous thought back down. "Jon, I have enjoyed this so much.

I'm excited about what you plan to do. I will certainly be praying for the success of River's Edge."

"Thanks." Jon took the glass she held out to him. "I was rather discouraged yesterday when I talked to people. No one seemed interested."

"People around here don't get excited about ideas. This is Missouri, remember? The Show-Me State. There'll be plenty of excitement when it opens. A restaurant on the bike trail? What a wonderful plan." Margaret talked fast, but the idea kept popping up. Finally, she asked, "Have you given any thought yet to employees?"

Jon frowned. "I'm not sure what I will be able to afford. It may be a one-man-show for a while."

"Would you like someone to help with the baking?"

Jon's frown brightened into a grin. "Do you mean what I think you mean?"

"I'd love to help you get started. I could bake a day's worth of cookies, cakes and pies in just a few hours. It would be a part-time job for me, just what I need to get me out of the house. You wouldn't have to pay me much."

"Margaret, that would be wonderful. You're the first good thing that's happened since I got here." At that moment, Maisy bounded up on the porch and nosed her way between Jon and Margaret. Jon bent to ruffle her ears. "Oh, yes, Maisy. You and Tiger are good things, too."

The sun had dropped behind the bluff, and a chilly wind gusted across the yard. Margaret clutched her jacket closed. "Brrr. I better get home and let you get inside. You keep me updated on the remodeling, okay?"

Jon pulled out his phone. "I need your number." She gave it to him, and he punched it into his contact list.

"I'll be in touch. Thanks, Margaret. For the pie and the offer to help in the restaurant."

She stepped off the porch, then looked back. "Don't forget. We'd love to have you at Fellowship Church. Services are at ten."

Jon waved but didn't respond to her invitation. She hurried to her car. *Baking pies for a restaurant. What have I gotten myself into?*

Chapter 7

JON WOKE TO a cold nose nudging his arm. He rolled over and opened one eye to peer at Maisy. "Can't you wait?"

At the sound of his voice, she pranced beside the bed. Her tail thumped against the nightstand. Then she twirled. The answer was obviously no.

Jon sat up, stretched, and reached for the paint-splattered jeans he'd left on the floor last night. He shook the dog hair off and slipped them on, pulled on a clean tee, and padded downstairs in his bare feet, Maisy bumping his heels. Downstairs, she raced to the front door and stood waiting. Jon opened the door for her and she shot out. He maneuvered around the saw horses in the dining room and into the kitchen.

Paul had arrived with his crew early Monday morning after the auction. By that night the dumpster was half full of plaster and lath, the narrow boards sticking out of the pile like monster-sized porcupine quills.

Inside, the house took on an odd, old-wood smell. The odor in the kitchen, however, improved after they removed the inside wall and swept away three decomposed mice and remnants of several nests. Jon brushed plaster dust off the table, took the can from the refrigerator, and started brewing coffee. Then he stepped out on the porch. Tiger, who preferred being outside most of the time, rubbed against his ankles, and Jon reached down to stroke her. For the first few weeks, she'd rewarded him daily with a mouse. She always laid it by the front door and seemed to relish his praise of her hunting prowess. Jon hoped the occasional lack of the daily offering now meant the mouse population of River's Edge was diminishing rather than Tiger's interest in the sport of catching.

Maisy trotted around the corner of the house, her tail waving. When she saw Tiger, she bounded up the steps of the porch and washed the side of the cat's head with her tongue. Tiger gave a disgusted look and leaped onto the narrow rail. Maisy looked at the door and then up at Jon.

"I'm so sorry, girl. No breakfast for you. We're going to visit Dr. Danielson for a little surgery." He opened the door and Maisy waggled inside.

Tiger jumped off the rail and followed them in. She found a spot where the early morning sun warmed the dusty old floor and curled up.

Maisy raced into the kitchen looking for her breakfast. She stood in the place where Jon placed her dish, looked at the empty spot and then up at him, her dark eyes pleading. Jon filled a to-go cup with coffee and screwed on a lid.

"Come on girl, let's go," he called.

With one last look at the empty spot where her dish should be, Maisy trotted after him. Jon slipped his feet into a pair of flip-flops, pulled a leash off the hook by the door and snapped it on her collar.

Outside, Maisy leaped up into the truck without even being coaxed, the disappointment over missing breakfast apparently forgotten with the thrill of a ride. After the day at the vets, she might not like truck rides so much. Jon cracked the window so she could enjoy all the delicious scents on the spring breeze. She stood on the seat, her nose pressed to the crack and her tail thumping against the back.

"Poor girl. You won't be so peppy after Dr. Danielson fixes you up. Part of the adoption agreement, though. No pups to get abandoned like you were." He pulled into the clinic and turned off the car. Maisy pulled her nose away from the window to give him a quick kiss on the ear. When he opened the door, she scrambled out after him. Dr. Danielson stood in the reception room when they entered, her curly hair pulled into a tidy bun.

"Good morning. Oh, look at you. You're growing into a beautiful dog." The vet stroked Maisy's back, and the pup wiggled in delight. Dr. Danielson pushed a curl off her forehead and smiled at Jon. "You're obviously taking great care of her."

"Thanks." Jon was suddenly aware that he hadn't put on clean jeans this morning, and in his hurry to bring his dog in, he hadn't shaved, brushed his teeth or combed his hair. He felt his ears grow warm and he knelt and rubbed Maisy's golden head. "You be good and do just what Dr. Danielson says." He handed the leash to the vet.

She coaxed Maisy to her side. "We'll keep her overnight, but I can call you this afternoon and let you know how she's doing if you'd like."

Jon nodded. "Yes, I'd appreciate that."

Dr. Danielson turned and gave a little tug on the leash. "Come on, Maisy. Let's get you ready for surgery." They moved down the hall, and Jon returned to his truck.

Back at River's Edge, the construction crew had arrived for the day and already was hard at work. New thermal-paned windows were to be installed today, and they were already hauling old windows out of the downstairs rooms. The sound of splintering glass pierced the morning as the men heaved them into the dumpster. Jon hurried inside. He went into the upstairs room he used as an office and TV room. Last week, Jon had stripped the floral wallpaper and repaired the rough patches in the plaster. He'd painted his bedroom yesterday and could easily finish the office today.

For a minute, he thought he heard Maisy, but it was the high-pitched whine of the saw downstairs. He wondered if Dr. Danielson had started the surgery. He tried not to think of the risks, or what he would do if anything happened to that flop-eared clown of a dog. Right now, she and Tiger were all the family he had.

He shook his head and picked up the paint brush. Two hours later, he stood back and looked at the office with satisfaction. One wall was a deep navy blue. The other three were a pale creamy color. When the paint dried and he got the room cleaned up, he could move in his comfortable red leather couch and a small walnut desk that had belonged to Bruce. His home was taking shape.

He rinsed out the paint brush in the kitchen sink, not even worrying about paint splashes. A new large sink would replace this one. The whining of the saw had stopped. Paul's men must be taking a break. Maybe one of them could help him move the couch and desk out of the upstairs hall and into his office.

He walked toward the old parlor where he could hear the murmur of voices. Paul squatted by the far wall near a gaping hole that waited for one of the new windows. His familiar Ace Hardware hat was off and his gnarled hand scratched the full head of grey-brown hair.

"What's up?" Jon asked.

Paul used the window frame to pull himself to his feet. He put his hat on and turned the brim to the front. "We got a problem. Nothin' we can't fix. Jus' a little detour." He pointed to the wall beneath the window. "Got some termite damage. I don't see no signs of active termites, but we gotta get it checked out. Need to replace some of those two-by-fours in that wall, too."

Jon's head swam. Termites? He might have known the construction would result in more setbacks and problems. Nothing seemed to go right in this place. "I'm too far into this now. Just do what you need to do to get it cleaned up."

"I'll phone Dirksen tomorry. He's an honest bug man, he'll let us know if we have to treat. But we're gonna jus' board this window up till we know for sure."

Jon surveyed the crew. "Could I borrow Caleb for a few minutes to help me move furniture into the office upstairs?"

"You bet." Paul nodded as he fished a piece of taffy from his pocket, unwrapped it, and popped it in his mouth.

Caleb followed Jon upstairs, and between the two of them, they got the couch, chair and desk arranged in the room.

"Thanks," Jon told him.

"No problem." Caleb's heavy boots pounded down the stairs.

Jon had just gotten his laptop computer laid out on the desk when his phone rang. His heart lurched, and he fumbled in his pocket. It was Furry Friends.

"Hello, is Maisy okay?" he blurted.

Kirsten's voice was calm and reassuring. "She's fine, Jon. The surgery went as expected. She's awake, she's eating, and beating the cage with her tail." The smile in her voice came through clearly.

Jon puffed his breath out. "Great news!"

"You can pick her up tomorrow any time after eight."

"I'll be there." Jon dropped his phone back in his pocket. He turned back to the computer and brought up Quicken. His joy over Maisy's successful surgery faded as he viewed his accounts. The money he'd carefully saved from Angie's life insurance was melting faster than a snowstorm in April. He'd taken out a construction loan from the bank, but would it cover all the additional costs that were popping up? What if he had to treat for termites? What if construction took longer than expected?

His upstairs apartment was nearly finished. He needed to find a job to last him until the restaurant opened. He scrolled through the Maple Grove want ads on the internet. Two jobs in construction. He already had done more of that than he wanted. One job as a dishwasher at a local sandwich shop. A skilled craftsman at a cabinetry shop. An assistant in the meat department of the local grocery store. The salaries from any of the listed jobs would be less than one-fourth what he made as an insurance agent. But beggars couldn't be choosers. And at this point he was a beggar. He would apply at the grocery store first thing tomorrow before he picked up Maisy.

Chapter 8

Jon stood at the door of the Maple Grove Foods store as a young man unlocked it for morning business. The clerk swung the door open and waved Jon in with a cheery, "Welcome to Maple Grove Foods."

Jon nodded and smiled. "I came to apply for the job in the meat department."

"You'll need to talk to Andy. Go on back. He's the big guy behind the counter." The man motioned toward the back of the store before taking hold of a stray cart and pushing it toward the line-up of carts awaiting customers.

Jon walked through the produce aisle, mentally purchasing items for the restaurant that was still weeks from opening. The meat counter stretched the length of the back wall, with a small area where customers could select prepackaged fresh meat and a large area with a glass case displaying meat that could be weighed and sold as customers requested. The piles of pork chops, beef, and poultry made Jon's mouth water for a grilled steak, but he backed away from the counter. His budget had no room for steaks.

A large man in a white shirt covered with a white apron stepped through a door from a back room. "May I help you, sir?" he asked as he reached for a box of latex gloves.

"I'm here to apply for the job you had listed. Is it still open?"

"Yes, it is. Come through the door there at the end of the display case, and I'll meet you in the back. You ever worked with meat before?"

Jon shook his head as he moved toward the door. "No, sir, I haven't." He pushed aside the rubber strips and entered the back room. The dimly lit area smelled of raw meat and produce and was cluttered with pallets of canned goods. One corner held a small table with a cannister of napkins set in the middle. Probably for employees on lunch break.

The aproned man waited beside the table. "Have a seat. I'm Andrew Brown."

"Jon Washington." They shook hands, then Jon pulled out a chair and sat.

Andrew handed him a form and a pen. "Just fill this out. I'll be back in about ten minutes, and we can talk."

Jon filled in the spaces, chronicling his personal information, education, and employment. A few minutes after he'd finished and laid down the pen, Andrew lowered his large frame into the chair opposite. He studied the form for a minute, then looked up. "Tell me a little bit about yourself. You're not a native Missourian, are you?"

Jon laughed. "I can't shake that Minnesota accent, can I?" He gave Andrew a brief overview, how he'd moved to River's Edge and was in the process of construction for a restaurant. He felt he owed it to an employer to be honest. He didn't expect to be working more than a few months before he'd be ready to open his own business.

"Are you married?" Andrew asked.

No matter how much time passed, the shock of that question always felt like someone had knocked him into an icy Minnesota lake. He took a deep breath. "My wife passed away."

"I'm sorry. You're so young."

Angie had been young. Too young. And their marriage had been too short.

There was an awkward pause, then Andrew tipped back in his chair and rubbed his chin. "I'd really hoped to find someone more permanent. But we hire some college students knowing they'll leave in September." He glanced at the form again. "No experience that would qualify you for this job, but your education makes you over-qualified. We could train you, I guess."

Jon waited, wondering if he should say something, then Andrew stood up, nearly tipping the flimsy folding chair backwards. "Let me show you what the job entails, and if you still want it, it's yours."

Twenty minutes later, with his head swimming with the names of various cuts of meats, Jon walked out the doors of Maple Grove Foods. Tomorrow he would be the assistant to the manager of the meat department. He smiled briefly as he imagined Angie's reaction to his new occupation. He made a quick stop at Walmart for white dress shirts for work, then he turned the car toward Furry Friends Clinic. The anticipation of seeing Maisy again overshadowed thoughts of his new job.

At six the next morning, his alarm jolted him awake. Even Maisy seemed confused. She yawned noisily as if annoyed to be woken. Then she stretched, shook, and followed Jon downstairs. She seemed to have recovered completely from her surgery, and she was eager to go.

After a short run on the trail with Maisy, he fed both animals, showered, and dressed. If Angie were here, she would insist on ironing the white shirt. But they would have to take him with wrinkles. He smoothed the front of it with his hand.

"Come on, Maisy. You need to be in your kennel today. But I promise a long walk on the trail tonight." As he closed and latched Maisy's kennel door, he felt a pang of guilt. What would Dr. Danielson think of him shutting her in a cage for the day? Would she revoke the adoption?

But if he didn't become gainfully employed, he might not be able to afford the dog food Maisy was gulping down on a regular basis. He ruffled the fur pressed against the cage before hurrying down the stairs and out to his truck.

He arrived at Maple Grove Foods ten minutes early. Hoping for a cup of coffee and maybe a fresh donut from the bakery department, he parked and went inside the employee entrance using the card Andrew had given him to unlock the door.

As he stood inside, his eyes adjusting to the dim back room, Andrew greeted him. "Good morning, Jon. Good to see you can be punctual. Let's get started learning the ropes before the store opens and it gets crazy in here."

Two hours later, Jon slumped in the chair at the small break table with a cup of lukewarm, stale coffee from a Mr. Coffee coffeemaker. His empty stomach rumbled. He'd never gotten that fresh donut, but after inhaling the odor of meat all morning, he really didn't want to eat.

He took a last swallow of the coffee, tossed the cup in the wastebasket, and pushed through the rubber strips to the meat department. Andrew was behind the slicer cutting a hefty chunk of cheese.

"May I help you?" Jon asked the middle-aged woman on the other side of the counter.

"I'm picking up steaks for my husband. Would I be better off getting the ribeye or the T-bone?"

"My personal preference is the ribeye. But I don't know your husband and what he likes. Why don't you give him a call?"

"Good suggestion." The woman pulled her phone out of her purse and stepped away from the counter as she spoke into it for a few moments. Then, she dropped it back into her purse and stepped up. "I'll take two of the bigger ribeyes."

Jon selected two, weighed and wrapped them. "Thank you very much. Hope he enjoys them."

At least he didn't need to worry about getting bored at this job. When there was a stretch with no customers, he cleaned the area, and Andrew trimmed, sliced, or wrapped meats. During his thirty-minute lunch break he grabbed a sandwich and drink from the deli counter and leaned against the back wall to eat, wondering how Maisy was doing in her cage.

The afternoon was a little slower at the counter. Andrew showed him how to use the slicer and the shrink wrap machines. When a young man showed up at four to take his place for the evening shift, Jon was surprised at how quickly the day had gone.

"You're a great addition to the meat department, Jon." Andrew gave him a slap on the back. "You have a way with the customers. I hope you'll be back tomorrow."

"You bet. I need this job. See you in the morning." Jon tossed his dirty apron in the tub and pushed the door open into the sunshine.

Chapter 9

TWO WEEKS LATER, Jon and Maisy were used to the routine of his job. Jon showered and dressed while Maisy did her business and ate breakfast on the deck. Then, with a cup of coffee and a bowl of cereal, he joined her outside.

Signs of the construction were everywhere. Stacks of new lumber and a dumpster full of old wood filled the yard. Tarps covered the table saws used outside. Jon missed being a part of the work. By the time he arrived back from Maple Grove Foods, the saw was silent, and the crew was packing up to leave. But he needed the income, small as it was, from this job.

He called to Maisy, and she bounded into the house and up the stairs. A small dog treat enticed her into the kennel. As Jon knelt to latch the door, he felt a stab of guilt about adopting a dog and then leaving her alone all day. He stuck his finger through the wire for her to lick. "Don't worry, Maisy. You won't be caged all your life. This job is just temporary, so I can pay the bills until the restaurant gets going."

Once he arrived at Maple Grove Foods and stepped into the meat department, he was too busy to think about home. Andrew and Jon worked more as a team than a boss and employer. Jon felt competent in most areas of the job, but he loved connecting with customers best. He had worked there long enough that they recognized him. He even knew some of their habits and could say, "Tim, I think you'd really like this brisket in your smoker," or, "Hello, Mrs. Nelson. Is your husband feeling well enough for some of your meatloaf? We have a special on ground beef."

Yesterday, Andrew commented, "Sales of meat have increased since your start date. I don't think that's coincidence." Jon's cheeks warmed at the praise.

This morning, Jon arrived before Andrew. He made sure the area was clean and everything was ready to go before the arrival of customers. He pulled out the long roll of salami and noted they were almost out.

Then Andrew arrived, and he needed help stocking the counter with ready-to-purchase items. When the store opened, there was a rush of people. "Early-morning shoppers," Andrew called them. Jon sold a package of four pork chops, some kabobs, and two pounds of hot Italian sausage. He was just ready to grab the salami and slice it, when another customer approached. She looked familiar, but it took him a moment before it hit him.

"Dr. Danielson, how are you?"

She looked up from the meat case. "Jon, I didn't know you worked here. You're not scrapping your restaurant plans, are you?" She sounded genuinely concerned.

"No, no. I'm just working here to pay the bills while the construction is going on. I still hope to open in August. How about you? Aren't you usually hard at work at this time of the morning?"

"I took a couple days off for the end of school. My son has field day today." She glanced at her watch. "I need to get some ground beef and get going. I promised him tacos tonight. And I have to be at the school in thirty minutes."

Jon tore off a piece of butcher paper and placed it on the

scale. "Do you want the eighty-twenty, or the ninety-ten?"

"I'll take two pounds of the ninety-ten, please."

Jon scooped out a pile of ground beef and checked the reading on the scale. "Two and three-tenths. Too much?"

"No. Just wrap it up."

Jon folded the paper tightly over the meat, taped it shut, and stuck on the tag the scale printed off. He handed Kirsten the package. "Thank you very much for your purchase. Good luck to your son at field day, and I hope he enjoys his tacos."

Kirsten smiled before she laid the meat in her cart. "Thanks, Jon. I'm looking forward to visiting your restaurant."

Jon watched her walk away down the aisle and wondered why he felt a little sad knowing she had a son. He imagined her and her husband, eating tacos and discussing field day with their child. He turned with a sigh.

The roll of salami still lay beside the slicer. He glanced up the aisle to make sure there were no customers he would need to serve. He flipped on the power to the slicer and lay the roll on the holder. Using the handle, he pushed the roll past the blade and caught the round, even slices. When he was finished, he turned off the machine and wrapped the slices of salami for sale. Still no customers at the counter. Andrew was in the back room ordering meat from the processing plant.

Jon straightened the work area. Little bits of salami were stuck to the slicer. He unplugged the machine and tried to remember Andrew's instructions for cleaning it. He moved the meat holder and removed the protective cover over the blade. Using a cloth, he swiped at the blade trying to dislodge the salami.

He saw the drops of blood before he felt the searing pain. He quickly wrapped the cloth around his hand, but not before seeing the deep cut in the outside fleshy area of his palm. Not good.

"Andrew. Could you come here?" Jon leaned against the table that held the slicer, his legs turning into rubbery raw meat.

A moment late Andrew pushed through the doorway. "Yes?"

Jon held up his hand and grimaced. "I had a bit of an accident."

"Oh, no." Andrew's look of annoyance faded to concern.

"I tried to clean the meat slicer and it sliced me."

Andrew took hold of his hand, peeled back the edge of the cloth, then quickly wrapped it up again. "You need to get that stitched up. You weren't wearing the cut resistant gloves?"

Jon shook his head. Why hadn't he remembered that detail from Andrew's instructions?

An older man hobbled past the counter, leaning on his cart as he pushed it.

Andrew gave Jon a little push. "Go back and sit at the break table. Keep pressure on it. Do you have someone you can call to take you to the doctor? Who's your doctor?"

Jon started toward the back room. "The only doctor I've seen in Maple Grove is the vet at Furry Friends. Maybe she could stitch me up?"

Andrew shook his head as he turned to help a young woman approaching the counter. "Don't think so." He called over his shoulder.

Jon sat at the table and felt like sobbing like a small boy. He knew no one who could take him to a doctor, he didn't even know where the doctors were in Maple Grove, and he knew he didn't get paid if he wasn't working. And an injured hand could prevent him from working on River's Edge and delay the opening.

As his mind ticked off the people he knew in Maple Grove, he remembered Margaret, the older woman who wanted to bake pies for the restaurant. She was retired, she might be home, and she might not mind taking him to the doctor.

Andrew hurried in the back room. "Shall we call 911, or do you want someone else to drive you?"

"I thought of someone that might be available." Jon pried his phone out of his pocket with his left hand. Using one finger he found Margaret's contact information and pushed the button.

"Margaret? This is Jon Washington. I have a bit of a problem. I'm working at Maple Grove Foods and I cut my hand on the slicer. I need someone to drive me to a doctor and then bring me back here after he stitches me up."

Margaret's voice, soothing as his mother's had been, came on the line. "Why, Jon. I would be happy to drive you. Who is your doctor?"

"Well, I don't have one. I haven't lived in Maple Grove long enough to need one."

"I can take you to mine. You'll love her. Give me five minutes to get there. I have a blue Buick and I will pull up front."

Andrew had already pulled forms out – accident report, a paper for filing for workers' compensation. Jon awkwardly scribbled his signature. Then Andrew, who had asked someone from the deli to watch the counter, walked him to the front of the store where Margaret already waited in her Buick.

Several hours later, Jon sat on the front porch of River's Edge cradling a bulky bandaged hand in his lap. It had taken seventeen stitches to close the wound, and because the cloth he'd wrapped around it wasn't sterile, there was a real danger of infection.

After Margaret returned him to the store, he had gone in to the meat department and turned in his resignation to Andrew. As tempting as it would be to collect workers' comp for lost wages, he couldn't wait the two weeks suggested for his hand to heal, and then quit when River's Edge opened. He would live on his meager savings, and perhaps push Paul to move the completion date ahead.

His hand throbbed, but not as badly as his head. Jon looked down toward the river. The great oak and hickory trees were leafed out and everywhere the landscape had greened up and was budding. But not him. He still felt as cold and lifeless as winter.

Chapter 10

JON STOOD ON the front porch with a cup of coffee. Maisy had disappeared around the corner of the house, but he wasn't worried. She never went far, and she came running when he whistled. He scratched at the frayed bandage around his hand. The wound was healing nicely and Dr. Nancy, the general practitioner Margaret had taken him to, had okayed him helping with the construction again.

A sudden yelp sounded from the brush behind the house. Jon stepped off the porch and whistled. Once, twice, three times. Maisy appeared, but she limped, stopping to lick at her back left leg.

Jon covered the distance between them in a few running strides. Blood streamed down Maisy's leg from a deep cut on her flank. She'd probably run into an old barb-wire fence. Jon parted the fur to examine the wound and got blood on his bandage in the process.

Instead of compassion, Jon felt frustrated. "It needs to be stitched, Maisy. Couldn't you just stay out of trouble for a few minutes?"

Her eyes searched his face. Her ears flattened and her tail waved slow and low. She sensed his displeasure.

"Awww, come on. Let's go see Dr. Danielson."

Kirsten watched Josiah until he opened the door of her dad's house and went inside. Summer months without the structure of school were challenging. Josiah qualified for summer school services for two weeks, but after that ended he stayed with his grandpa for the entire day. She knew there was too much screen time and too little physical activity, but she couldn't find another solution.

She pulled into her parking lot at Furry Friends and hurried inside. No time for a leisurely start to this day. There were already clients waiting outside. As she washed her hands, she heard Yvonne unlock the front door and greet the pet owners. The caged dogs and cats would have to wait for Elizabeth to give them their breakfast this morning.

She dropped her lunch bag in her tiny office and entered exam room two. Bella, a rather pudgy Boston terrier, needed flea and tick medicine. Kirsten drew blood for the required heartworm test and handed the packages of medicine to Bella's owner, Gabby.

"Wait until you hear from Yvonne that her test is negative before you start these," Kirsten reminded her.

She barely had time to wash her hands before Yvonne announced a dog waited in Room Three for probable sutures. She pushed open the door. Maisy lay on the exam table. When she saw Kirsten, her tail began thumping the metal surface. It sounded like an audition for steel drums.

"Why, Maisy. I didn't expect to see you so soon again." Kirsten looked up at Jon. His rumpled hair and tee shirt smeared with blood made her wonder if his start to the morning had been a little rushed as well. And then she noticed the bloody bandage on his hand.

"Are you hurt, too? What's going on?"

"No. I mean I cut my hand two weeks ago working in the meat department of the grocery store. This is Maisy's blood. Mine is nearly healed, but I keep it bandaged so I don't reinjure it working."

"So, how did Maisy get hurt?"

Jon ran a hand through his hair, messing it further. "First thing this morning she took off into the brush. She was gone for a bit, then she yelped and came out with this cut." He pointed to her leg, bandaged with what looked like a strip from an old tee shirt.

Kirsten undid the strip carefully and examined the wound.

"Maybe a barb wire fence?" Jon asked.

"Could be. It's deep, but in the fleshy part of her leg. It should heal all right if I put a couple stitches in. Hold her here on the table for a minute while I get things together."

Within minutes, Kirsten returned with Jessica. She cleaned the area thoroughly, deadened it, and then, while Jon and Jessica held Maisy, she stitched it closed. She placed a cone around Maisy's neck to keep her from bothering the stitches. "She'll need to wear this for at least two days. I'll give you some antibiotic cream to prevent infection. Especially since we don't know what happened." She handed a clipboard with the details of today's visit to Jon. "Just take this up front and give it to Yvonne."

Jon nodded. "Ummm. Dr. Danielson?"

She stopped in the doorway.

"I should have said something right from the start. I'm really low on funds. Can I make payments on this bill?"

"Yes, we can do that. Just tell Yvonne that I okayed it. Pay what you can today. We'll send you a monthly bill after that. And Jon, maybe you need to keep Maisy on a leash after this. At least keep her contained until she's healed. Bring her back in a week and let me check it."

Jon nodded, and he and Maisy exited the exam room. Just like a man to be so irresponsible. He couldn't keep himself safe, and he couldn't keep his dog safe either.

Chapter 11

JULY SIZZLED INTO Maple Grove. The temperatures rose into the triple digits and sweat was standard. Because the reconstruction hadn't been completed and doors and windows often stood open, Jon hadn't turned the air conditioning on. Leaving it off kept the costs down on bills he was unable to pay. He slept with the windows open and a fan on, but sometimes it was so unbearable upstairs he slept on a cot in the middle of the construction debris. Both his hand and Maisy's leg had healed. Jon returned to helping Paul where he could. And Maisy returned to mad dashes into the woods when Jon didn't have her on a leash.

Paul's crew, faithful to show up every day, finished a little bit more of the work each day. So, Jon was surprised when Paul announced, "We won't be around tomorry, ya know."

Jon twisted his office chair away from the computer to face Paul. His face must have registered confusion.

"It's the Fourth. The town always has a lil' celebration. I don't make the boys work on the Fourth. They can spend time with their families."

"Of course." Jon stammered. He'd completely forgotten about the Fourth of July. It would have been a good time to have a restaurant up and running.

"You should come into the park. There'll be some good eatin'. The Methodist church has a funnel cake booth, and I bet Margaret's pies will be at the Fellowship Church stand. Now, it's not as big as Maple Festival, but jus' a nice lil' town party. Fireworks at dark, of course."

"Sounds like fun. I'll be there."

The sound of firecrackers woke Jon, and then the bed heaved as Maisy jumped up with him. "Maisy, you haven't done this since you were a small puppy. What gives?"

Another blast of fireworks, and Maisy tried to burrow her fifty-five pound body under the covers. Jon put his arm around her trembling form. "Nothing to be scared of, girl."

He rose and dressed, and Maisy followed him downstairs. He snapped the leash on as a precaution. Outside, another blast of fireworks sent Maisy dragging him back toward the house. Jon dug in his heels. "Not yet, Maisy. You need to use the grass."

There was a brief lull in the noise, and Maisy obeyed, then they hurried back inside. Jon brewed coffee and fixed a bowl of cereal. Maisy paced between the front door and the kitchen while he ate. When Jon sanded the sheet rock in the dining room, she finally flopped down in the hall. But rather than roll to her side and sleep, she kept her eyes open, and her ears twitched at every little bang outside.

At eleven o'clock, Jon laid down the sanding block and went upstairs for a shirt without sheetrock dust streaked across it. Maisy followed.

"What am I going to do with you, girl?" He hadn't used the kennel since he'd cut his hand and resigned from Maple Grove

Foods. And she'd almost outgrown it. He stroked her great, golden head. "I won't be gone long. You can just curl up somewhere and take a nap."

Jon made sure her water dish was filled, refused to look at her sad eyes, and pulled the door shut behind him.

When he arrived at the park, it looked like the entire population of Maple Grove was crowded into the small green space. There was a softball game on the baseball field, a musical group performing on the stage, a ring of ponies giving rides to children, and food stands everywhere.

Jon bought a hot dog, decorated it with ketchup, mustard and pickle relish, and walked around as he ate it. At least twice he had to stop and wipe ketchup off his chin. Several people spoke to him. He wondered if they'd been to the auction, and if he should remember their names, but he didn't.

At the Fellowship Church stand, he spotted Margaret, fanning herself with a printed program with one hand and serving a customer with the other. She waved to him, and he walked over.

"Jon. It's so good to see you. How's the renovation coming?"

"We're almost ready to paint the interior of the dining areas. Hopefully, there will be no more delays and we'll still have an opening in August."

Margaret pushed a wet curl off her forehead. "I can't wait to see it finished. Do you want a piece of pie?"

"Sure. Why don't you give me a slice of the cherry? And put a scoop of homemade ice cream on it, please."

He paid her and took the Styrofoam bowl and spoon. He sat at the picnic table in front of the stand savoring the tart cherries and the chill of the sweet ice cream melting in his mouth. After he finished, he wandered over to watch the men on the baseball field. They were playing slow pitch softball. Jon had played baseball in high school, and this looked like fun. Maybe next year he would join the group.

The day slipped away. He sampled some nachos and a piece of peach pie while watching the group on stage sing a mixture of country and rock and roll. Then, the crowd moved toward the baseball field where the fireworks would be set off. Jon didn't have a chair or a blanket, but he leaned back against an oak tree. After all the beautiful explosions had ended, he headed to his truck. Memories swarmed around him like mosquitoes. The last time he'd watched fireworks, he'd had his arm wrapped around Angie as they watched from the window of their Minneapolis apartment.

The house was quiet as he parked his truck. He unlocked the door and swung it open. Maisy hurled herself at him, a slightly crazed look in her eye and her tail wagging furiously. A strip of sheetrock paper hung from her mouth. As he pushed the door shut, he could see the devastation. In her frantic attempts to flee the noise of the fireworks, she had scratched the door, her nails raking long furrows in the wood. She had bit at the unpainted sheet rock around the door, tearing gigantic holes and shredding the paper.

"Oh, Maisy, what have you done?" Jon held his head in his hands. When she leapt at him a second time, he lost it. "Get down! Look what you've done. Bad dog, Maisy."

Maisy stopped and lowered her head and her tail. Then she turned and crept toward the kitchen.

Jon looked again at the destroyed entryway and could only see dollar signs and further delays. He grabbed Maisy's leash from its hook and hauled her outside. When she'd finished, they went upstairs and Jon pulled out the kennel from the closet where he had stored it and pushed her inside. He ignored her soft whines.

He dropped onto the bed without undressing. But sleep was a long time coming.

Chapter 12

JON PUMPED HARD on the pedals of his Trek. The timber lining the trail whizzed by in a green blur.

The August sun warmed his shoulders. His jersey didn't wick all the sweat away, and he felt it trickle down the middle of his back. Beneath his helmet, the headband felt damp against his forehead. He left the paved trail, swung through the ditch down a well-worn path to his yard, and coasted to a stop. He pulled his water bottle from its holder, took a long drink, and gazed at the nearly completed River's Edge Restaurant.

Paul and his crew had done a great job. The July Fourth incident had been cleaned up and rebuilt. The rest of the new windows were installed after termite treatment. New pewter-blue siding covered the house and a dark-gray roof capped it. All the gingerbread trim had been repaired or replaced and painted maroon and bright white. Maroon shutters framed each window. Inside, the house had been rewired, replumbed, and sheet rocked. And Jon was deep into debt.

He needed to set a date for the grand opening, and it couldn't come soon enough. He took another big swallow of lukewarm water and walked his bike to the shed behind the house. Then he slipped in the back door and upstairs to shower.

As he dressed, Maisy paced between him and the bedroom

door, her tail waving. She knew all his clothes. Bicycling shorts meant she would be left in the kennel, work clothes meant she would be allowed to roam the house by Jon's side, hiking boots meant they would explore outside together, and khakis or dress pants meant he was going to town and she probably would not be invited. Today's jeans and a tee shirt caused her four feet to dance with joy.

"Hang on, girl." Jon ruffled the soft ears. "Let me get the gate." Jon had installed a baby gate, so Maisy could have the run of the upstairs during River's Edge's operating hours.

In the kitchen, Jon poured a cup of coffee from the large Bunn coffee maker. The soft gleam of the stainless-steel appliances made the expanded room look clean and fresh. And the only odors were the smells of paint and cleaners. Tiger, the traps, and the new siding had done their jobs. No mice. Where the unused back porch had been, there was a new entrance with a small deck just big enough for his grill, a table, and dishes for Tiger and Maisy. The new walk-in cooler and pantry were stocked with supplies Jon had picked up from Kansas City. A corner of the pantry held a washer and dryer, handy when they needed to wash aprons or cleaning cloths.

The dining room, more than triple its original size, was still empty. The tables and chairs would be delivered this week. The original oak floors had been refinished and now shone golden. The staircase rose from the entry like a centerpiece, the banister solid and complete again with the missing spindles replaced. Views of the yard sloping down to the river could be seen from almost every window.

Jon stepped outside with his mug of coffee. The new door glided shut. Maisy leaped off the porch and rolled in the grass, legs and paws waving in the air. After a few mowings, a dousing of fertilizer, and a treatment of herbicide, the yard actually looked decent. He'd planted marigolds and zinnias in front of the porch. And today, the crowning touch would go in place.

"This the spot, Jon?" One of Paul's men, Jared, called out.

Jon stepped down off the porch and walked toward him. "It better be. You've already started." Jon peered down at the hole in the corner of his yard.

"We could always fill it in again." Jared stopped and leaned on his shovel.

"No, it looks good. Right here, a sign can be seen from both the trail and the road."

"Good thing. Cause if it weren't, I'd fill it in, but I'd clobber you with my shovel first for changing your mind." Jared chuckled at his own joke as his shovel bit another chunk of dirt and lifted it out.

The sign Jon had picked up yesterday lay on the ground nearby. It was made of cedar and painted to match the house with a blue-gray background and maroon lettering.

River's Edge Restaurant
Serving lunch and dinner

Jared tossed another shovelful of dirt to the side. "The holes will be deep enough, and it'll be cemented in. This sign won't move even if there's a tornado."

"Thanks Jared. I'm going to head back in and get some more painting done downstairs." He raised his voice and shouted, "Maisy." He couldn't see his dog anywhere. She was generally good about staying within the boundaries of River's Edge. He walked past the gazebo-like curve of the porch and behind the house. In the brush beyond the mowed portion of the yard he could see the grass moving. "Maisy." He called again, and she trotted toward him. A foul odor preceded her. She'd rolled in something. Again.

"Maisy. How many times do I have to tell you? If you want to live in the house, you can't roll in stuff like that."

Maisy's head drooped and her tail slowed and tucked between her legs.

"Come on." Jon led her to the outdoor hydrant where a hose he'd used to water the recently-planted flowers was attached. Holding Maisy by the collar, he squirted and rubbed until there was no brown stain and most of the odor had dissipated. He found a shovel in the shed, searched for the offending dead racoon carcass and shoveled it into a garbage sack, so Maisy wouldn't find it again. Then, leaving her to dry on the porch in the sunshine, he went in to paint.

Two hours later he stood back to admire his work. The dining room walls were a soft beige. Everything looked and smelled clean and fresh, including Maisy, mostly dry and stretched out on the porch napping.

Jared had the sign in place, and the cement that held it was hardening. He still had a lot to do, but it looked like an opening date the middle of August could be a reality. Twelve days away.

Jon rinsed out his paint brush, careful not to splatter the new sink. He laid the brush it on a newspaper to dry and stepped out on the porch. Maisy looked up, and her tail thumped on the wooden floor.

Paul loaded a battered metal tool box into his truck. The man never looked like he was in a hurry. When he worked, his movements were measured and deliberate. Jon was amazed that the work on River's Edge had gone as quickly as it had. He guessed Paul's meticulousness paid off, and there were few times he had to redo anything. Paul waved at him, then walked slowly across the yard, past the new sign and up on the porch.

He swallowed the last of a wad of taffy. "So, what do you think? Is it shapin' up like you thought?"

"It looks great. The sign's the final touch. Makes it a reality."

"Yup. Looks purty with all them red letters. We're about finished here. I have a few more tools to pick up and I hafta wait for that one door handle to come in 'fore I can install it. But," he stuck out his hand, "it's been fun. And you're a great crew member. I can't wait to taste your fried chicken."

Jon shook Paul's hand firmly. He was going to miss having the taffy-chewing old man around. "You come on out when we open, and the first meal's on me."

Paul smiled and nodded. "I can pay for my own plate." He pulled on the brim of his cap and gazed out toward the river. When he turned back, his eyes no longer sparkled with mischief. "I hope an' pray God'll give you peace an' healin' here at this place." He raised his hand, almost as if he were giving some sort of benediction, then turned and went to his truck.

Unexpectedly, Jon's eyes filled with tears. He was about to accomplish Angie's dream. Surely that would bring peace and healing, wouldn't it?

Chapter 13

MARGARET FLATTENED THE ball of dough with her rolling pin, back and forth and around, until a perfect circle formed. She draped one side over the rolling pin and with a quick flip, the dough rested on warm cherry filling. She crimped the edges with her fingers, then cut a vent hole in the dough in the shape of the letter C. She paused for a moment to admire her work, then popped all four pies into the oven and set the timer.

She probably didn't need to take four pies to a potluck. There would be more than enough desserts. But it seemed impossible to make just one. She rinsed her hands at the sink and wiped them on a towel hanging on the handle of her oven door.

The pies would bake for almost an hour. She had time to shower and change clothes. She rubbed her arms. Maybe a hot shower would ease the aching. The warm water felt wonderful, and she relaxed and just stood for a minute or two. Then she washed her hair and lathered a bright pink loofa. Her arm was certainly tender. Surely not from baking pies. She could roll out pie dough in her sleep. She raised her arm and began scrubbing her arm pit. Ouch! That seemed like an odd place to have sore muscles. Gingerly, she poked at the tender spot with her finger. It seemed swollen. Maybe it was time to make the appointment for her annual check-up. She finished scrubbing up and stepped out of the shower onto a fuzzy pink bath mat.

She dressed in a pair of bright blue capris and a soft white knitted top with a row of embroidered flowers around the neck. A warm sweet fragrance drifted from the kitchen. Opening the oven door, she checked to make sure the pie crusts were browning evenly. The air conditioner would probably run extra this afternoon, but a Fellowship potluck just wouldn't be right without her pies.

Her cell phone rang, and she glanced at the caller ID. "Hello, Melanie. What a treat! Nothing's wrong, is it?" Her voice rollercoasted from joy to motherly concern.

Her daughter's cheerful voice came through the phone like music. "No, Mom. I knew you had a potluck at church tomorrow, so I called today."

Margaret eased into her chair and leaned back. "Great! Tell me about the fabric show you went to. Was it wonderful?"

Melanie went into a detailed account of the show, describing fabrics, people who were there, and the importance for her company. Margaret listened, interjecting questions and "ahs" and "um-hmms" at all the right spots.

When the oven timer went off, she quickly stood up. "My pies are done. Can you hold a minute while I pull them out?"

"No, I'll let you go. I'm going to a movie tonight with Martie. She's the girl in the apartment next door. So, I need to clean up my place and do laundry beforehand. Now, don't forget to turn the oven off after you take the pies out."

"Okay, sweetie, I won't. I love you. Thanks for calling." Margaret held the phone to her cheek for a moment, as if it were her daughter's hand. Then she hurried to pull the pies out of the oven and onto the cooling rack. And turn off the oven. When had the roles reversed, that her daughter worried about her?

Next was the grocery store. She didn't need much to make meals for just herself, but it seemed there was always something she needed.

As she backed her car out onto the road, she decided to take a little detour. She hadn't been to River's Edge for a while, and she loved to watch the changes as the renovation continued. Maybe Jon would have a date for his Grand Opening and she could start thinking about her baking schedule. And, of course, she could invite him to church. Again.

She'd just turned off the highway when she saw the sign. *River's Edge Restaurant.* That really looked nice. She didn't know whether to get excited or nervous about baking pies for an honest-to-goodness restaurant. She waited to get out of her car to see whether Maisy was in the yard. She loved that pup, but her greetings could be quite exuberant.

When she saw no sign of her, she eased out of the car and walked up to the porch. The heavy wooden door was open, and she could see Jon behind the counter with a new cash register. She knocked softly on the glass storm door.

"Margaret, come on in." A broad, welcoming smile spread across Jon's face. "Did you see the sign as you drove up?"

Margaret opened the door and stepped in. The patter of large paws sounded on the steps, and she just had time to brace herself before Maisy greeted her with wildly wagging tail and little huffy whines of pleasure. Margaret bent to stroke her back where the summer sun had deepened the color to gold. Standing, she turned back to Jon. "The sign looks lovely. Does this mean we have an opening date?"

"I just talked to Paul this morning. He has a little clean-up work to do, but he's finished for the most part. The tables and chairs will be delivered on Monday. How does August fifteenth sound? Can you have pies baked for the whole county by then?"

"Not sure about the whole county, but I can do Maple Grove for sure. This is good timing. We get a lot of leaf watchers through town and on the trail in the fall."

"That's what I've been told." John closed the cash register and stepped around the counter. "Want the grand tour?"

"Sure. I didn't come all the way out here just to see Maisy."

Tail waving in response to her name, the dog led the way as if she were the official tour guide.

"Oh, I love the color in here." Margaret waved a hand at the dining room walls. She stepped to a window and peered out. "Still the amazing view of the river. Okay, what have you done with the kitchen?" She followed Maisy and Jon to the large room with the stainless-steel appliances. Her hands brushed lightly over the gleaming surfaces. She opened the large, commercial oven, peeked in the walk-in cooler, then entered the storage area, built where the old porch had been. Her eyes took in the supplies Jon had already stocked. "This is wonderful. You've thought of everything."

"I'm sure I'll forget some things, but I'm trying to be more like Angie and make lists and check them off." Jon still winced whenever he said her name. He opened the fridge. "How about a glass of ice tea?"

Margaret looked at her gold wristwatch. "Oh, my. It's almost noon. And I still have to get to the grocery store. No, thanks for the offer, but I need to get going." She reached down to pet Maisy, sitting quietly beside her. "Oh, Jon. Our church is having a potluck after services tomorrow. Kind of an end-of-summer celebration. You could come as my guest." She gave him what she intended as her sweetest smile.

"Not tomorrow, Margaret." Jon shook his head. "I'll be

working to get ready to open here." He smiled back at her, but his eyes had a kind of steely resolve, and she wondered if she should ever ask again.

"Just call if you happen to change your mind." She hurried down the hall and out to her car. Why was such a nice young man so set against coming to church?

Chapter 14

EARLY MORNING SUNSHINE teased Jon's eyes awake. He stretched and sat up, plunking his feet down on the wood floors. Maisy watched with interest from her round fleece dog bed and when he stood, she bounded up too.

Jon pushed aside the towel he'd hung in the window for a make-shift curtain. "Looks like a good morning to have tables and chairs delivered, huh, Maisy? Things are really falling into place."

He followed her waving tail downstairs, let her out, and started a pot of coffee. When it finished brewing, he stepped out on the small back deck. The air was warm and heavy, even this early. It would be a hot afternoon. Tiger stepped delicately onto the deck, weaving her way around the chair. Jon bent to pet her. "Better hide today, Tiger. There's going to be a lot of activity."

Tables and chairs delivered today. Tomorrow, another trip to the restaurant supply store in Kansas City. And Saturday, the grand opening. He'd had notices printed up and posted them everywhere in town they allowed him. The Maple Grove Courier had run ads for a month. He took a deep breath. It was a good thing the restaurant was about to generate some income. He was more than broke. He was up to his eyeballs in debt.

At nine, Jon heard the rumble of a large truck. He saved and closed the spreadsheet of menus he was working on and looked out. The furniture had arrived. He fastened the upstairs gate so

Maisy would stay out of the way, then went downstairs to supervise.

⌇

When the dining room was full of assembled tables, Jon stood by the truck as the last box of chairs was being unloaded. A lone bicycler, a young boy, had stopped to watch. Jon waved to him and he lifted his arm in reply, then took off down the trail toward Benson, pedaling like his life depended on it.

"Nice morning for a ride," Jon remarked, slightly envious of the young boy's freedom.

The man in the back of the truck folded up the padding and wiped a sleeve across his dripping forehead. "Yeah. But it's heating up. The heat'll bring in a storm."

"Nothing in the forecast."

The man trundled down the ramp. "Mark my words." He pointed to his knees. "These are more accurate than any meteorologist."

After signing the invoice, Jon set the tables and chairs in their spots. The replica pressed-back wooden chairs and round oak tables were perfect. It finally looked like a restaurant.

He let Maisy out, fixed a sandwich and went out on the porch to eat. The man who unloaded his furniture was right. Dark clouds were building in the west, moving fast, and looking like some overweight, angry poodles. He took a bite out of the ham and cheese and wondered if he needed to put anything away before the storm.

With a sickening lurch of his stomach, he remembered the boy on his bike. Had he gone back by while Jon was in the house? Was he already safe in Maple Grove? Or was he still out on the trail?

Jon stuffed the last bite of sandwich in his mouth and grabbed his truck keys from behind the counter. With a sharp call to Maisy, he ran to the truck, his dog sprinting along behind. When he opened the door, she leaped into her spot on the blanket in the back seat. At the place where the gravel road crossed the trail he peered down it. No bike or boy in sight. If he took the road, he could see parts of the trail but not all of it. Abruptly, he turned the truck onto the trail. Although just barely wide enough to accommodate the four tires, he began driving toward Benson. About a half mile beyond River's Edge, Jon spotted him. The boy was pedaling fast and heading toward the truck. Jon eased to a stop and got out. The wind had picked up and bits of leaves and dirt swirled around his feet.

As the boy got closer he slowed, eying Jon and the truck. His feet left the pedals and dragged his bike to a stop. The boy was slender with almost delicate features and sandy-blonde hair poking out of his helmet. Something seemed a bit odd about the way he glanced at Jon and turned away.

"My name's Jon Washington. I live down the trail in that big gray house. I saw you go by earlier, and when the storm came up, I thought you might need a ride back into town."

The boy shook his head. "No. I don't ride with strangers."

Jon glanced up at the darkening skies. A few drops of rain were now spattering across the hood of the truck. "That's a great rule. But I think this is one time you need to trust a stranger." He took a step forward.

The boy's hazel eyes widened in fear and he scooted backwards pushing the bike with his feet. "No. I don't ride with strangers."

Suddenly the wail of a siren split the air. Tornado alarm. The boy clapped his hands over his ears and screamed.

Jon had to do whatever it took to get this boy to safety. He waited until the siren had stopped and the screams subsided to a moan. "I know your mom," he lied. "So, I'm not a stranger. Those sirens mean a tornado may be coming. Please, just get in my truck."

The boy looked up at him briefly. His feet pushed the bike back and forth. "You know my mom?" At that moment Maisy leaped out of the truck and trotted up to the boy. "Hey, you," he said as he reached out to Maisy. She washed his fingers with her tongue.

Jon moved next to him and grasped the handlebars of the bike. "Okay buddy, you get into the truck and my friend Maisy will follow you in."

The boy drew away from him. "My bike?" he whispered.

"I'll put it in the back. Go on, she'll follow you."

"Come on, come on, dog." He stepped off the bike and grasped Maisy's collar. Jon couldn't tell who was leading who, but they both climbed into the back seat of the truck. Jon lifted the bicycle into the bed and hopped into the driver's seat. He slammed the truck into reverse and began backing, looking for a place he could turn around.

The boy began rocking and singing in a kind of chant, "Come on, come on, dog." Maisy watched him for a moment, then wiggled closer, wedging her upper body across his lap. He stopped rocking. "Do you take your dog to see my mom?"

What could he mean? Why would he take Maisy to see his mom? Jon spotted a field entrance and backed the truck in, turned it around, and sped up. Sheets of rain were sweeping across the trail in front of him. Even with the wipers going full blast it was hard to see.

Suddenly he had a thought. Maybe he hadn't lied after all.

"You mean at the Furry Friends Veterinary Clinic?"

"Yeah. That's where she works, you know."

"That's where I got Maisy." Jon skidded into the gravel parking lot of River's Edge and turned off the truck. "We're going to go into the house and to the basement until the storm passes. We'll call your mom, so she knows you're safe."

The boy wrapped his arms around Maisy's neck. "What about her?"

"She'll come with us." Jon stepped out and opened the narrow door to the back seat. The rain pelted his back, soaking his clothes. He reached out his hand, but the boy flattened himself against the seat, so he stepped back. Maisy leaped down, and after a moment, the boy scrambled after her. They all raced for the porch. Inside, they stood dripping on the large entryway mat.

Jon shook the rain from his hair. "What's your name?"

"Josiah." He laced his fingers under Maisy's collar.

"Hold on to her, and I'll get us some towels. Then, we'll go down to the basement. We can call your mom from there. Do you know her number?"

Josiah rattled off a string of numbers. "That's her work number. And her cell phone is…" He started with a new string of numbers.

"Wait till I get the towels." Jon slipped out of his shoes and raced upstairs. He pulled three towels out of the linen closet and a small radio from the office. Downstairs, he looped through to the kitchen and grabbed a box of granola bars.

Josiah and Maisy still waited by the front door. He handed a towel to Josiah and used a second one to wipe off Maisy. "Come on." Jon led the way to the hall where a small wooden doorway opened to the basement. Downstairs, the old brick foundation formed the walls and the floor was packed dirt. A bare light bulb hung from the ceiling. Jon spread out one of the drop cloths he'd used for painting. "You can sit on this."

Josiah looked around his eyes wide. "Are there spiders down here?"

"Maybe. But I don't see any on the drop cloth. Go ahead, sit down."

"I want to go home."

Jon tried to keep his voice calm and even. "We'll stay here where we can be safe until the storm passes."

Josiah sat down. His body began to rock back and forth, slowly at first and then faster. He hummed, and then his mouth opened and the hum increased to a wail. Maisy, who'd been thoroughly enjoying the smells in this new place, padded over to Josiah. She sniffed his ear and then lay across his lap. Almost immediately, the wails stopped and the rocking subsided. Josiah wrapped both arms around Maisy.

Jon pulled out his phone. "Let's call your mom. Tell me her phone number again." He punched in the numbers as Josiah called them out. The phone rang several times before a woman's voice answered.

"Dr. Danielson."

So, Josiah's mom was the vet. "This is Jon Washington out at River's Edge. I have Josiah here with me. I saw him on his bike earlier today going toward Benson. When the storm came up, I went out searching for him, and found him on the trail. He's safe. We're waiting out the storm in my basement. His bike is in my truck."

Kirsten's voice squealed over the phone. "I thought he was at my dad's house. Out on the bike trail? At River's Edge? He's not even allowed to go that far. Oh, thank you, Jon." She paused and seemed to take a breath. When she spoke next, her voice was more composed. "Josiah has … umm … special needs. Do you need me to come out? Is he upset?"

Jon looked over at Josiah who had his head buried in Maisy's fur. "Maisy's keeping him calm right now. We're okay. Are you in a storm shelter?"

"Yeah. I'm here at the clinic, and everyone's in the surgery room where there are no windows. I need to call my dad. If he knows Josiah's gone, he's probably frantic with worry."

"I'll keep Josiah here with me and call you back as soon as the storm has passed. Then you can tell me where you want me to take him."

"Thanks, Jon." Her voice seemed taut with concern.

Jon ended the call and looked at Josiah. "Do we need to call your dad, too?"

Josiah's head jerked up and he glanced at Jon, then put his head on Maisy again. "My dad's in Wisconsin. He divorced Mom and we had to move to Maple Grove and I don't get to see him anymore."

There was no sorrow in Josiah's voice, but Jon ached for the young boy without his dad. And for Kirsten, raising her son alone.

The old house creaked and groaned overhead as the wind picked up outside. Jon turned on the little radio and sat down gingerly on an overturned bucket that had held sheetrock mud.

"Would you like a granola bar, Josiah?" The boy's head lifted, and he reached out with one arm. But the other he kept wrapped tightly around Maisy. The energetic pup, who never liked to be confined, hadn't moved a muscle.

Chapter 15

KIRSTEN'S FINGERS TREMBLED as she dialed the phone. "Dad, did you give Josiah permission to go on the bike trail this morning?"

She cringed and held the phone away from her ear as her dad's voice boomed back. "No, I didn't say he could go on the trail. Have you seen him? Is he with you?" Kirsten could hear the fear behind the angry tone.

"He's safe, Dad. Jon Washington, the new owner of River's Edge, picked him up. They're staying out there until the storm is over. Do you want me to have him bring Josiah back to your place or just to me here at the clinic? He'll need consequences for breaking the rules, you know."

Kirsten could picture her dad running his fingers through his thick, silver hair. "Yeah, tell Mr. Washington he can bring him back here. I'll let you take care of the punishment. But, Kirsten?"

"Yes, Dad?"

"Something's got to be done about that kid. He can't just take off and not tell me where he's going. I was about to call the police."

"I know, I know. We'll talk about it later, okay? I need to get back to work. I'll tell Jon to bring him to your place. Let him watch TV or something until I get there. He may be really upset."

Kirsten dropped the phone on her desk and covered her face with her hands. She wanted to collapse in tears, but that wouldn't help. When she looked up, Dr. Jennings, the assistants, even Yvonne, were looking at her.

"Is Josiah okay?" Dr. Jennings asked, the journal he'd been reading lying open on his lap.

"Yeah. He took off on his bike and was out on the trail when the storm struck. The owner of River's Edge picked him up. He's safe, now."

"The kid needs some buddies to ride with," Dr. Jennings commented.

Kirsten agreed with him, but it was more complicated than that. "It's not so easy to find buddies when you have no social skills."

Dr. Jennings picked up his journal and thumbed through it. "Why don't you hire one?"

Kirsten gave a short laugh that held no humor and turned back to the records she'd been filling out.

Elizabeth moved over to stand beside her. She was holding a Chihuahua puppy that trembled with fear. "It's not a bad idea."

"To hire someone? I don't have extra money. And who would I hire anyway? Another eleven-year-old? I don't see how that would work."

"How about a college student? Someone who likes to work with challenging children."

"And where would I find someone like that?"

"Do you know Jessica McHale? She goes to Fellowship."

Kirsten nodded. "We were in the Easter choir together."

"She has a boy who goes to school at KU. Erik is home right now, between summer school and his senior year. He loves kids, and I bet he'd be willing to spend some time with Josiah. He could take him bike riding or play basketball, get him out of your dad's hair for a couple hours and wear him out. Want me to call and see if he'd be interested in doing that?"

Kirsten didn't know what to say. Did she have enough to pay someone in addition to what she insisted on paying her dad? How would Josiah react? Would her dad resent someone helping him?

She took a deep breath and blew it out. "Sounds perfect. Go ahead and call." She grabbed a sticky note and jotted down her phone number. "Here's my number if Erik wants to call me."

Dr. Jennings stood and waved his phone. "The radar shows that the storm has moved through. I think it's safe to get back to work."

"I'm going to let my kid's rescuer know he can take him to my dad's house." Kirsten walked to her office as the Furry Friends employees scattered to their various duties. Outside, she could hear the town's alarm system sounding the all-clear.

That afternoon, Kirsten left the clinic as soon as it closed. There had been very few patients today. Everyone had kept their families, including pets, close at home. Except for her son, out riding on the bike trail. She shook her head and hoped nothing like that would happen again.

The tornado hadn't touched down, but storm debris lay everywhere – broken tree limbs, garbage cans that had rolled into the street, and even a few signs bent or blown over by the wind. She prayed silently, thanking God again for Josiah's safety.

When she pulled into her dad's driveway, she hopped out. They needed to have a family discussion, and it should involve all three of them.

Josiah stepped outside, his clothes, as usual, in disarray. "Time to go home." He tried to step around her, but Kirsten blocked him.

"No. I need to talk to both Grandpa and you."

"Time to go home." Josiah protested, but when Kirsten didn't move, he turned and went back in the house.

"Hi, Dad." Kirsten gave him a kiss on his cheek. "May I talk to you for a minute?"

Josiah stood by the door, his body rocking slightly. "I went on the bike trail, but Jon picked me up and I was safe with Maisy. Can we go home now?"

Kirsten sat on the edge of the sofa and her dad sank into his recliner. He used the remote to turn off the TV. "I'm so sorry, honey. I told him he could ride his bike. I thought he was just going around the block. Then, when the storm came up—"

"Dad," Kirsten interrupted. "You do a great job watching Josiah. I appreciate you and your help so much. Josiah disobeyed, broke the rules—" Kirsten looked at her son, but he was staring out the window. "And there will be consequences. But Elizabeth had an idea, and I think it might be a great solution for the rest of the summer. Erik McHale is a college student who's home on break. I talked to him, and he'd be willing to come every afternoon and take Josiah bike riding or to the park—something to burn off some energy. What do you guys think?"

Josiah continued to stare out the window. "Jon has a dog named Maisy. She's a Labrador retriever."

"I know, buddy. Would you like to spend some time with a college guy named Erik?"

"Mmm."

Josiah's noncommittal answer was better than nothing. At least he wasn't screaming *No*.

"I think that's a great idea." Her dad beamed at her. "I'd love to get out and go biking, but with the arthritis in my hip, I don't think I could keep up with the youngster. Josiah and I can still have our card games and watch TV, and he'll be able to get some exercise, too."

"Okay. I'll call Erik and tell him he can start tomorrow. I'll leave money with you, Dad, so they can get a snack or go to the pool. After lunch, about one, okay?"

Her dad nodded. "Tomorrow's fine."

"Josiah, I need eye contact." She waited while his eyes drifted to her face. "There will be no bike riding on your own. You have lost the privilege of riding by yourself for two weeks. You may go with Erik, but not by yourself. Understand, Josiah?"

"I went on the bike trail. But I was safe."

"Yes, you did go on the trail. You broke the rules. So now you can't ride your bike by yourself."

Josiah scowled. "I was safe with Maisy. She's a Labrador retriever. But they're really from Newfoundland."

Kirsten was satisfied. She knew Josiah changed the subject to end the discussion, but he understood what was expected. "Thanks, Dad. Let's go, buddy."

She hurried out to her car with Josiah straggling behind. It wasn't until hours later, after Josiah had been safely tucked in bed, that she realized there had been no conflict the entire evening. Despite the trauma of being out on the bike trail in a storm, being picked up by a stranger, and confined in a cellar, Josiah was calmer and more focused than usual.

Chapter 16

BETHANY ALCANTER STOPPED at the wooden bench and stared out at the slow-moving waters of the Cadence River. She slumped on the seat and pulled the little plastic stick out of her jean short's pocket. There were still two lines on it. Two lines that meant her life was over. She laid her head in her hands, her elbows braced on her knees, and let the tears come.

She was still sobbing quietly when something nudged her arm. She lifted her head, and a big yellow dog poked her with a wet nose. She wiped her face with her hands, wishing she had a tissue. She reached out to stroke the dog's head. The velvet ears slid through her fingers and the dark eyes gazed up at her face.

"Where did you come from, doggie? Do you know I'm sad?" Bethany buried her head in the thick fur of the dog's neck.

"Maisy. Maisy." A man's voice called from down the trail. A few minutes later a tall, thin, dark haired man in running shorts jogged up the trail.

"I think she's here." Bethany lifted her head from the fur, but the dog remained by her side.

"Sorry." The man puffed. "We were jogging, and she just took off. Usually she stays right with me."

"I think she knew I needed a hug." Bethany tried to laugh, but the laugh got stuck and came out more of a sob. Then the tears began again.

The man looked up and down the trail, then down at his feet. He stuck his hands in the pockets of his lime green shorts. Then, as she tried desperately to get her emotions under control, he asked softly, "Is there something I can do to help?"

"No. Nobody can help. It's my own mess." Bethany looked down. Right under the edge of Maisy's paw was the early pregnancy test.

The man's eyes followed hers and a knowing look spread across his face. He gazed down the trail, then back to her. "My name's Jon Washington. I bought the old River's Edge property near here. I don't know what you're going through, but you're young. Your life isn't over. You just have some decisions to make."

"And how do you make decisions when every choice is wrong?"

Jon shrugged. "I guess you have to trust your own instincts. Or ask others for advice."

"Well, I sure need some good advice." Bethany stroked Maisy's back, smoothing down the gold fur. "She's pretty."

"Yeah. She's kind of an amazing dog. She seems to really care about people."

"She sure made *me* feel better." Bethany stood up, sliding her own foot over the plastic stick.

"Tomorrow is the grand opening of my restaurant at River's Edge. Come out, and I'll treat you to a free sandwich. What's your name?"

She attempted a smile. "Bethany. I just might take you up on that. I never turn down free food."

"Come on, girl." Maisy trotted over to Jon's side. He took her by the collar and guided her back on the trail. "Bye, Bethany. I hope to see you tomorrow."

Bethany picked up the offensive stick and put it in her pocket. Nothing had changed. Her life was still over. She still needed to tell her mom. And Kyle.

When she got back to the trail, Jon and Maisy were far ahead, jogging side by side. She looked for the golden dog as she passed the restaurant, but the yard surrounding River's Edge was quiet and empty.

Loneliness and fear streamed over Bethany. She stared at the river where it lapped over the fragile willow saplings. They bent under the current but didn't break. She hoped she could bend, too, and that the current sweeping her away wouldn't break her.

～

Jon stripped off his clothes as he climbed the stairs. He probably shouldn't have gone for a run, but he and Maisy both needed it. He wondered how she would cope with being locked upstairs when the restaurant opened. Maybe there would be a break between the lunch and dinner crowd and she could go for a run.

After a quick hot shower, Jon got busy in the kitchen. Maisy lay on her rug by the back door watching his every move. If he dropped a morsel of food, she was ready. He did all the prep work he could, chopping vegetables, washing salad greens. His menu was simple and basic – sandwiches, salads, and soups for lunch. Dinner would be different each night, but only two entrée choices, served family style with sides in bowls. Of course, Margaret's homemade pies and cakes would be the dessert options.

Maisy grunted and stretched out on her side. "Worn out from our run this morning?" Jon laughed.

Then he sobered, remembering the young girl they'd met.

Pretty, with her long brown ponytail, big brown eyes, and petite features. Probably even prettier when she smiled. What a heartache. Angie had tried and tried to get pregnant, but some high school girl gets pregnant at the drop of a hat. He wished he'd had some wisdom to share with her, something that would make her feel better. But he couldn't ease his own pain, let alone someone else's. She'd loved Maisy, though. He smiled over at the dog.

A knock sounded on the front door. Maisy rose to her feet, barking as she raced down the hall. Jon rinsed off his hands and dried them before going to the door through the dining room. When he got there, Maisy was dancing and wagging. A boy's face peered in. Josiah. Had he slipped away again?

But when he got closer, he could see a very tall, broad-shouldered young man behind Josiah.

Jon spoke through the screen. "Why, hello, Josiah."

"Can I see Maisy?" Josiah kept his eyes on the waggling dog inside.

Jon opened the door, and Maisy bounded out and off the porch. Josiah leaped after her. She turned, nearly knocked him over, and his arms went around her neck.

The young man stuck out his hand. "My name's Erik McHale. Josiah's mom hired me to do activities with him, kinda give his grandpa a break, I think. Anyway, every day when I pick him up, he asks if we can come here. I didn't want to bother you, but then I saw your grand opening was tomorrow, so I thought we'd better come today."

"Josiah's always welcome, but you're right, today is better than tomorrow."

The men paused to watch Josiah rolling around on the grass with Maisy. Suddenly, she raced around the corner of the house.

Josiah tore after her.

Jon shook his head. "They seem to have a strange connection. Maybe because they're both young. Do you think Josiah will be satisfied with just one visit?"

Erik sighed and shook his head. "This may have been a mistake. Now he'll really want to come every day."

At that moment Maisy came from the other side of the house, Josiah close behind. The dog looped around the front yard in big circles and Josiah dropped to the grass giggling. Then she was beside him, licking his face. Josiah roared with laughter.

"I've never heard him laugh like that," Erik said in amazement.

Jon turned to him. "There's no reason you can't come whenever you want. I'll just show you where the leash hangs, and you can come in, take Maisy out the back door, play with her, then put her upstairs again before you go. It would be great for her to have a time outside in the afternoon, and it looks like it's a good thing for Josiah, too."

"Well, yeah. That would work." Erik called to the boy, now chasing in circles around the yard. "Hey, Josiah, come here a moment."

Josiah stopped running and stood for a moment, as if processing the request, or perhaps deciding if he was going to obey. Then he trotted up on the porch.

Erik waited until Josiah was standing in front of him. "Mr. Washington says we can come to River's Edge and play with Maisy, even after the restaurant opens. Let's go inside and see where he keeps the leash."

"Cool." Josiah didn't look at Jon, but an expression of pleasure spread across his face.

All of them, including Maisy, trooped inside. Jon showed

them Maisy's gated domain upstairs and the leash by the back door. "You two can stay as long as you like, but I need to get back to my kitchen. Just put Maisy inside before you go."

"Tell Mr. Washington thanks," Erik prompted Josiah.

"Thanks." Josiah mumbled, his eyes still on the dog.

Jon went back to the vegetables. About thirty minutes later, he heard the back door open and close. When he checked on her later, Maisy had emptied her water bowl and was stretched out on her rug in the hallway, sound asleep.

Chapter 17

SATURDAY MORNING WAS hot, even for central Missouri. Jon hadn't slept well, waking often to mull over details for the day ahead. He rolled out of bed before his alarm sounded and took Maisy for a short run down the trail, hoping he wouldn't run into any sobbing teenagers.

After their run, he showered and dressed in khakis and a short sleeved, plaid shirt. In the kitchen, he wrapped a white denim apron around his middle. He couldn't waste time running upstairs to change if he spilled something.

In the dining room, the old wood floor gleamed from his polishing. He'd kept a few antiques out of the sale and the enamel pans, washboard, and rug beater looked at home on the walls, while the butter churn stood in the corner as if awaiting fresh cream to churn.

Satisfied all was in order, he spun into action, baking frozen bread for the subs, brewing coffee and making gallons of sweetened tea that he anticipated being consumed by thirsty customers. He was preparing salads when he heard the front door open.

Margaret breezed in, her arms full of containers. Jon took some of them from her. "Is this it?"

"Heavens to Betsy, no, dear. My back seat is full. Remember

you asked me to make enough pies to feed the whole county?"

Jon laid the pie-carriers on the counter. "Let's put the ones we want to serve first over here." He indicated a small portable unit of stainless steel wire shelves near the swinging doors. "Then the rest can go in the pantry. I kept a shelf open for desserts. I'll go out to your car and get the others."

When he returned, Margaret had the containers unpacked and pies stacked neatly. She pointed to the shelves. "Cherry, raspberry, rhubarb, banana cream, and chocolate. And that's a chocolate cake on the bottom."

"I thought we agreed we only needed two choices."

"Well, this being the grand opening, I guess I got carried away."

"I'm not complaining." Jon grinned. "Thanks, Margaret. I'll update the menu board." On the dining room wall behind the counter, a white marker board listed the day's choices. Jon squeezed in the pie choices under the listings for sandwiches, salads, and soup. A separate area of the board listed the dinner choices served after four-thirty.

Shortly before eleven, Jon ushered Maisy upstairs and closed the gate. As he came down, he heard the crunch of tires in the gravel parking lot and looked outside. A familiar beat-up tan Ford truck was pulling in. Had Paul forgotten to do something? Jon brushed the crumbs off the front of his apron and stepped behind the counter.

"Welcome to River's Edge Restaurant," he sang out as Paul and three of his crew stepped through the door.

Paul grinned at him. "I heerd tell this was the place to get the best eatin' in Cadence County."

"Not sure if we rank as the best. Guess I'll see what today brings. Are you here to eat or inspect?"

"Oh, we're here to eat." Paul squinted up at the board. "Whatcha got that's good?"

Jon felt giddy with excitement. His first customers. "I'm partial to the buffalo chicken sub. But I like spicy." Jon rattled off the choices for Paul. "How about a table there by the window?"

"So I can reminisce 'bout findin' them termites?" Paul chuckled as the four men followed Jon to the table.

Jon took their orders, jotting them down in a small notebook that fit in the front pocket of his apron. "Your orders will be right out." Jon smiled broadly as he hurried out to the kitchen.

Neither he nor Margaret stopped or sat down for the next three hours. He hadn't planned on Margaret helping in the dining room, but she refilled tea and soft drinks, took dessert orders, and even ran the cash register. Jon had posted the luncheon hours as eleven to one-thirty. At two o'clock he rang up the last sale and closed the door behind two well-dressed young women he thought he recognized from the bank. In the kitchen, Margaret had loaded the dishwasher with the last of the pots and pans and was wiping off some ketchup containers.

"Our agreement was that you would leave at one," he scolded her.

"I'm just finishing up here, Jon. This has been so much fun! I got a few things ready for dinner to make it easier for you."

"Well, it wasn't my plan to have you wait tables. I really didn't think we'd be so busy."

"Pshaw. I loved every minute. And God is blessing River's Edge right off the bat. I think I will be up for a nap this afternoon, though. Do you have enough pie to last through dinner?"

"I have no idea how large a crowd there will be. But we have several pies still in the pantry. And most of the cake is left, too. The pies seem to be the favorite."

Margaret rubbed her shoulder. "You sure you don't want me to stay and help out tonight? If you have half as many as we did for lunch, you won't be able to keep up by yourself."

"No, I don't want you to stay." Jon thought of his own mom and how he wouldn't want her to be overworked. "You have to take care of those skilled baking hands. If something happened to my pie-maker, I'd probably have to close my doors."

Margaret giggled like a schoolgirl. "Then I better grab my things and get home."

"And I need to let a certain dog out. She's been very patient."

Jon raced up the stairs and opened the gate for Maisy. He rubbed her golden ears. "You were so good, Maisy. No barking, no bothering the customers. Come on, want to go out for a few minutes?"

She followed him downstairs and he let her out the back door. Then he went to the kitchen where Margaret was stacking empty pans. Jon lifted some from her arms. "I'll carry these to your car for you."

"Sure." Margaret grabbed a large handbag from the pantry and headed for the door. When they stepped outside, Maisy charged toward them. Then, as if she suddenly remembered, she skidded to a stop and stepped daintily toward Margaret.

"You're a good girl." Margaret rewarded her by stroking her back as Jon stashed the containers in the rear seat.

After Margaret left, Jon let Maisy sniff about the yard for a few minutes, and then called her to come in. He had less than three hours to get ready for the dinner hour. It would be difficult cooking, serving, and clearing tables. If things went well, he hoped to hire more people soon. But first, he wanted to make sure he could pay them.

Back in the kitchen, he saw Margaret had peeled potatoes for him. Jon turned the stove on under the pot so they would boil. His menu had two choices for dinner: fried chicken or country ham. Coleslaw, green beans, mashed potatoes, applesauce, and a dinner roll would be served family style with either entree. Later, he could expand the menu to include more options but still specialize in home cooked meals from scratch.

Jon worked steadily, mashing potatoes, heating the green beans, checking on the hams in the oven, and preparing the chicken to fry. He seasoned the chicken just as Angie had taught him. He knew if she were here, she would insist on baking the bread and rolls from scratch, but he was not as accomplished a baker as she'd been, so he'd opted to purchase them frozen and ready to bake.

At four-twenty-five, he again flipped the sign in the window to *open*. He left the wooden maroon door ajar. He wished he could open windows and let the breeze from the river blow through the room, but he knew his customers would appreciate the air conditioning more. It was still very warm.

At four-forty-five the first group arrived, a family with two kids. Then his parking lot began to fill. When one group of customers left, another group arrived to occupy the table. He flew between the dining rooms and the kitchen, greeting people, balancing huge trays with plates of steaming food, and thanking people as they paid their bills and left.

Midway through the evening, as Jon hurried from the kitchen to clear more tables, he heard the small tinkle of the bell he'd installed on the door. Still holding the cleaning towel, he went to greet the arriving customers. A familiar pony-tailed figure bounced through the door carrying a small blue backpack.

"Why, hello, Bethany." Jon glanced behind her to see if she'd come with her mom, but she appeared to be by herself.

"Hi, Mr. Washington. I remembered that the restaurant opened today, and I came to apply for a job." She glanced around the room, taking in the several groups of diners. "It looks like you could use someone."

"Bethany, I…tonight…uh," Jon fumbled for the right words to say. He nodded to a farmer in overalls and his wife as they left the restaurant. Then he turned back to Bethany.

"See, there's another table that needs to be cleared." Bethany reached out and took the cloth he was holding. "Fact is, Mr. Washington, I really need a job. And you have to admit, you need me."

Jon didn't have time to argue. "Okay, I'll let you clear tables tonight and I'll pay you for it. At eight o'clock, when I close, we'll talk about it."

Smiling broadly, she took the towel from his hand. She set her backpack behind the counter and began wiping the table he'd cleared previously. The second hour went much more smoothly with Bethany bussing tables. Without being asked, she also expertly rolled clean silverware into the napkins and set the tables.

The crowd was more than Jon had expected. He almost ran out of chicken, and he served all of the ham that he intended to use in a ham and bean soup the next day. After the last of the diners waved at Jon and strolled across the lawn to their cars, Jon filled two plates with the leftover chicken and handed one to Bethany. Then he led the way to a clean table and they both sank into their chairs.

For the next several moments they were quiet as they ate. Then Jon sat back and wiped his mouth with a napkin. "You were a big help tonight, Bethany. But I'm a small operation. I can't pay much. I need someone I can depend on. And someone I can trust."

"Mr. Washington, if you hire me, I'll work so hard." Bethany's pony tail bounced emphatically. "I've been a waitress before. I worked last summer at the truck stop. And I never missed a day. Some of the truckers were kinda rude, but I stuck with it. I really need a job." She glanced down. "Because, well, just because."

"Want a piece of pie?" Jon asked.

"Sure," Bethany looked up at him, her eyes hopeful.

Jon's mind whirled as he went to the kitchen. Bethany could be a lot of help. But would there be enough to pay her a salary and Margaret, too? And still have enough left for dog food? Dog food! He'd left poor Maisy upstairs. He raced up the stairs to let her out. When he returned to the dining room with two pieces of banana cream pie, he'd made his decision.

"Okay, Bethany, let's try it for a couple of weeks. School will have started by then. We'll see how many people we're averaging, and how it's working for you and go from there. You can come in at four and work until eight. You can eat dinner here, too. I can only pay you minimum wage, but you should make some tips. Sound like a deal?"

"Oh, thanks, Mr. Washington. You won't regret it. I'll be the best waitress you ever had."

"Ha. That's a record that won't be hard to beat. I've never had a waitress before. Now, do you want to call your mom for a ride home or do you want me to take you in the truck? How'd you get here anyway?"

Bethany looked down for a moment. "I walked," she said. "I can walk back. It isn't far."

"Too far to walk this time of night," Jon said firmly. "I'll get my keys."

Jon dropped Bethany off in front of a small, slightly shabby, yellow house. She waved to him, then wandered toward the back yard, her backpack slung over one shoulder. She'd refused his offer to go inside and meet her mom.

"She goes to bed early," Bethany explained.

Maisy squirmed from behind the front seat to her customary place beside him. "Hello, girl," Jon absent mindedly scratched her ear. What had he done? Rather than the solitary venture he thought he'd begun, he now had two partners. A gray-haired pie-maker and a pony-tailed teenager. What other surprises would River's Edge bring?

Chapter 18

"JOSIAH. ARE YOU ready?" Kirsten called down the hall.

There was no answer. When she poked her head in his room, he was sitting on the bed, backpack strapped on his back, reading *101 Facts About Dogs*, a book her dad had gotten him last week.

"Josiah, we have to go."

His eyes drifted up and focused somewhere behind her left shoulder. "Can I take my book?"

"Sure. Just don't be looking at it when you're supposed to be listening to the teacher." When there was no answer, she prompted, "Josiah, do you understand?"

"Yes, Mom," he mumbled as he slid the book in the new stiff backpack and rezipped it. "I'm ready."

Although he didn't show it as other boys his age might, she knew Josiah was nervous about his first day at middle school. She was glad she was able to take him and make sure he was settled in before she headed to her duties at Furry Friends.

Josiah was quiet as they drove to the sprawling, multicolored brick building at the edge of town. Her questions: *Do you remember your locker combination? What is your locker number? What's your teacher's name?* and reminders: *Remember that we already put money in your lunch account, Please use your coping skills,* were all met with a bored "Mm-hmm."

She'd been to orientation for the parents last week, but Josiah hadn't visited the building since his fifth grade class took a field trip to the middle school last spring. Her stomach was in knots thinking about all the changes for him and opportunities for the stress and frustrations that led to meltdowns.

When they arrived, the parking lot was jammed with parents who had brought their kids. But in most cases, the kids hopped out of the car and skittered off to groups of laughing and chatting preteens. A few stood, embarrassed, as their moms used phones to snap a first-day-of-school picture. And two or three gave their parents a quick hug before dashing off. At least that was one way Josiah looked normal. None of the middle schoolers wanted parental affection.

Kirsten stepped out of the car and walked beside Josiah up the sidewalk. She pointed to the front curb. "The bus will drop you off here tomorrow. Remember, it's bus number five."

"Why can't Grandpa bring me?"

"We already talked about this. It's hard for Grandpa to get around. The bus picks you up just two houses down the street from Grandpa's house and lets you off here."

She held the door for Josiah and bit back a rebuke as two boys elbowed past him and dashed through the door as if he weren't even there. Inside, several staff members were greeting the children and answering questions. She recognized Mr. Patterson, the principal, joking with a group of girls and wondered if he would joke with Josiah.

"May I help you?" A stern-looking older woman approached them as they walked in.

"We're looking for Gloria Sanchez, Josiah's associate." Kirsten looked at Josiah, whose hands were fluttering by his side. "She said she'd meet us outside the office."

"I haven't seen Gloria this morning. There's the office." She pointed across the hall to a large windowed room. "Why don't you stand over there by the wall? I'd hate for you to get run over by a group of these middle-schoolers." She gave a dry, mirthless chuckle.

Kirsten stepped around the stream of kids and watched Josiah to make sure he followed her. When they reached the opposite wall, she suggested, "You could take out your book while we wait." It might help to distract him from the noise and confusion in the hall. She wished she'd remembered his head phones. But they would only make him look more conspicuous.

Josiah shrugged off his backpack, unzipped it, and pulled out the book. In a minute he had it open and was reading a page on dew claws. She wondered what he would think if he knew it was part of her job to clip those off young puppies. At least his hands were no longer fluttering.

A short woman with large glasses wove in and out of the stream of kids as she hurried down the hallway. Her neatly-trimmed short dark hair framed a face almost covered with large, dark-rimmed glasses that magnified her eyes. "Are you Mrs. Danielson?" she asked as she skidded to a halt in front of them.

"I am. Are you Gloria?"

"Yes. Sorry I'm late. I had to take my two kids to the elementary first. This is my first year working at the middle school. The parking out there is a mess."

Kirsten tapped Josiah's book with one finger and waited while he looked up. "Josiah, this is Mrs. Sanchez. Put your book away now and listen to her."

"You probably should just take that book home with you. Miss Taylor told us that everyone has an approved reading list, and at school they need to spend their time reading from books that we're certain are at their level. You know, so they're challenged." Gloria nodded, her eyes on Kirsten.

Kirsten wanted to reply that Josiah had enough challenges, but didn't think that would be an appropriate response. Instead she told Josiah, "Did you hear Mrs. Sanchez? She'd like me to take your book home."

Josiah clutched the book. "You're not going home. You're going to the clinic."

Why did he have to be so literal? "I'll keep it safe for you until I pick you up from Grandpa's. And then it won't be a distraction."

Josiah's fingers tightened around the book. Why had his associate told him to do something that was so difficult in the middle of this stressful transition? But she couldn't back down now. She held out her hand. "Hand me the book."

Slowly Josiah handed it over, his fingers reluctantly releasing the cherished item. She could see his eyes, wet with unshed tears as he struggled to maintain control. She tucked the book under one arm, picked up Josiah's backpack, and handed it to him. "Good job, son," she praised him. "Show us where he's supposed to go, Mrs. Sanchez."

"Oh, would you take him? I want to run to the teacher's lounge and get a cup of coffee before the bell rings. It's just straight down the hall. Room 130. The door on the left. Miss Taylor will be there." Gloria pointed the direction they were to go and then bustled off.

Kirsten and Josiah stared after her for a second, Josiah's hands fluttering at his sides again.

"Well, let's go meet your first teacher." Even though she was fuming, Kirsten kept her voice cheerful.

On the way to his homeroom, they stopped at his locker.

Because of the practice she'd insisted on before school, Josiah easily locked, reopened, and locked it again with the backpack and most of his supplies inside. In room 130, it was a little quieter. Kirsten introduced herself and Josiah to his teacher, and he even managed a mumbled hello with no prompting. Miss Taylor asked Josiah about his summer, but before he had an opportunity to reply, the bell rang and the classroom began to fill up with chattering students.

"Thanks for coming, Mrs. Danielson. We'll take good care of Josiah." Miss Taylor moved to the front of the room and began greeting the students.

Kirsten bent over the desk. "All right for me to leave now, buddy? You okay?"

"I'm okay. Dogs sweat through their paws."

"Yes, they do. But we sweat all over. See you this afternoon." Kirsten forced herself to move away from his desk and out of the classroom. She could see Gloria, carrying a Styrofoam cup as she moved down the hall toward the classroom.

Gloria hadn't even spoken to Josiah. How was she going to keep him calm when she didn't even speak to him? She gripped the book she'd taken from her son and strode out into the warmth of the early September morning. She expected she'd get a call from the school before the day was over.

Chapter 19

MARGARET STUDIED HER planner. The quote at the top, *Commit your plans to the Lord*, was meant to be reassuring, but today it only added to the pressure she felt. And the fatigue. Surely baking ten pies a day, something she could do in her sleep, and helping Jon out through the lunch hour was not that strenuous. Something else must be going on. Maybe she needed some vitamins. She'd ask Dr. Nancy today.

She took a last sip of coffee from the flowered cup she loved, the one with a favorite verse from the Psalms. Melanie had given her the cup for Mother's Day, and it served as a reminder to pray for her daughter whenever she used it. "God, you know Melanie loves you, but she gets so distracted. Help her to remember you, and what's important in this life." She rinsed the cup and put it in the dishwasher.

The timer beeped, and she pulled the last of the pies, fragrant and golden, from the oven. She put them on racks to cool while she dressed for the day. Should she wear her white capris or the dark blue ones? White would be better. She always took time to greet Maisy before she left River's Edge and ended up with a dusting of dog hair across her legs.

When she arrived at the restaurant, Tiger sprawled in front of the door, and she had to nudge him away with her foot. He shook his head indignantly and moved under the swing where he promptly sank down. Customers seemed to love the relaxed atmosphere of the restaurant, including the cat sleeping on the front porch.

As Margaret maneuvered inside, Jon appeared wiping his hands on his apron. "I didn't hear you drive up. I'll get those." He set the pie containers on the counter and hurried out to her car to bring in the rest.

Jon and Margaret had settled into a routine that suited both of them. She generally arrived about ten, after her pies were baked. She helped him with any last-minute prep work. During lunch time they worked together, waiting tables, preparing food, and cleaning up. She left by two and had her afternoons to herself. It was a perfect retirement job. She'd been saving her earnings to take a trip to New York to see Melanie, maybe over Thanksgiving. Her arms ached to hold her daughter.

Margaret stacked the pies on the shelves as Jon brought them in, one shelf for cherry, one for coconut cream. She used Jon's pie slicer to cut each of them into eight equal pieces.

"How's your little waitress doing?" she asked as he brought the last load in.

"She's doing okay. I told her I was hiring her on probation, just to see if it would work out. But I'm making enough to pay the bills and a salary for the two of you."

"God is blessing River's Edge." Margaret reached for one of the bright flowered aprons she'd made and slipped it over her head.

"Mmm." Jon's response was noncommittal as always when she mentioned God.

She watched him stir a large metal pot on the stove. "Those

soups are going to become a whole lot more popular in about a month when we start getting some fall weather."

"It's already getting cold in Minnesota where I used to live. I'm enjoying this Indian summer. Cool enough at night to open up the house, but still warm enough for lots of bike traffic."

"Are you hiring extra people for the Maple Festival?"

Jon turned and looked at her, the spoon held up in the air. "The what?"

"You haven't heard about the Maple Festival?"

"Margaret, I haven't lived here for forty years like nine-tenths of the community."

"I know. But I thought somebody would have mentioned it. It's held the second weekend in October. People come from all over central Missouri. It's a big thing. There's a parade, a carnival … small town at its best. It's way bigger than the Fourth of July celebration. I bet you'll have customers lined up and waiting on the porch."

Jon laid down the spoon and lowered the heat under the soup. "Maybe I need to get some more advertising up in town. And you're right, I'll need extra help that weekend. I'll see if Bethany can work the entire day on Saturday and Sunday. Will you make extra pies?"

"Sure." Margaret smiled at Jon. Could she find the additional energy? Maybe she'd feel better in three weeks. "I have a doctor's appointment today at two. I hope you don't mind if I scoot out of here right away."

"Of course not. Go whenever you need to. Nothing serious, is it?"

"Oh, no. Just a checkup. I have to get one every hundred thousand miles."

Jon chuckled as he pushed through the swinging doors into

the dining room. She heard him open the door and greet some early arrivers.

At one forty-five, Margaret hung up her apron and hurried out. Jon had let Maisy out and she greeted the dog briefly, patting the golden head. "You get back in the yard, girl. I have to go today. No time to throw a ball for you." Maisy trotted back towards the porch, her green tennis ball tucked in her cheek like a grotesque tumor.

Dr. Nancy's waiting room swarmed with toddlers, moms, and moms-to-be. One elderly gentleman looked like he was hiding behind a newspaper in the corner. Margaret held her purse on her lap and watched the children, smiling at their antics, and wondering if she'd ever have the blessing of being a grandmother. One mother tried to settle a fussing baby, while her toddler slipped away and used crayons to decorate the glass window.

"Margaret." The nurse stood at the door with a clipboard. "How are you today?"

"I think I'm fine. Just want Dr. Nancy to confirm it." Margaret followed the nurse, who recorded her weight, then led her to the claustrophobic exam room.

The nurse took her blood pressure and her temperature. "What brings you in today, Margaret?"

"Well, I thought it was about time for a check-up. I've been feeling a little lethargic. Probably this heat. And I have a little tender area here in my armpit." She rubbed the spot gently.

The nurse nodded. "Something to get checked out. Why don't you get undressed, put on this lovely gown, and the doctor will be in shortly." She handed Margaret a faded cotton gown that tied in the front.

After a short wait, Dr. Nancy knocked on the door, then opened it and stepped inside, followed by a nurse. "It's good to see you, Margaret. I hear you're working at River's Edge Restaurant. We went there last Saturday night and I had the best fried chicken dinner since my grandmother died. Then I threw my diet entirely out the window for a piece of your raspberry pie."

Margaret smiled. "Glad you liked it. I think Maple Grove has just been waiting for a place like River's Edge."

"Ever since Findley's Deli changed hands, it's not quite the same. There's the truck stop, but it's, well, a truck stop. It's wonderful to have a place you can actually feel like you're going out to eat. The view of the river is lovely out there."

"Yes, it is." Margaret agreed. "And I love working with Jon. He's polite, kind—as well as a good cook."

Dr. Nancy sat on a stainless steel stool and swiveled closer. "Now, tell me what's going on with you."

Margaret told her about the tender area she'd noticed in her arm pit.

"Let's take a look. Lie back here on the exam table." With gentle fingers, Dr. Nancy did a breast exam. Then she closed the gown and helped Margaret to a sitting position.

"Go ahead and get dressed. I'll be back in and we'll talk."

Margaret put her clothes back on. Dr. Nancy would probably tell her it was nothing. She needed to remember to ask about vitamins for her lack of energy.

When Dr. Nancy returned, she was alone. She sat on the stool again and faced Margaret. "I'm scheduling a diagnostic mammogram for you as soon as we can get one."

"I had one less than a year ago," Margaret protested.

"This swelling may be nothing," Dr. Nancy continued, "but we're going to get it checked out. Someone from our office will call you this afternoon. You go to Lutheran Hospital, don't you?"

"Yes." Margaret nodded.

"I'm requesting a radiologist be present at the mammogram so it can be read immediately. If necessary, they may order an ultrasound, too."

"Do you really think I need another mammogram?."

"I do. And don't be wearing yourself out with all that pie-making." Dr. Nancy gave a broad smile as she hurried out of the room.

Margaret picked up her purse and made her way to the desk to check out. The test was just precautionary. They wouldn't find anything. She'd always been healthy as a horse. But, she'd forgotten to ask about vitamins.

Chapter 20

MARGARET SHUFFLED TO the car with the last of the pie containers. It might be easier to bake pies in the large, shiny new oven at River's Edge. But then she couldn't call Melanie while they baked or take a little nap. She'd been napping a little more frequently. The heat must be wearing her down. She dotted at her forehead with a tissue before sliding into the driver's seat.

At least this was Saturday, and tomorrow she had nothing planned. She could nap all afternoon if she wanted.

A steady stream of customers kept the dining room full through the noon hour. A few minutes before one, Margaret's friend, Elizabeth Sorenson, entered with the new vet.

Margaret, who'd been clearing tables, laid down the cloth and went over. "How did you two escape the puppy and kitten business long enough to have lunch out?"

Elizabeth smiled up at her. "Hi, Margaret. Have you met Dr. Danielson?"

Margaret looked at the apple-cheeked woman with brown ringlets and sparkling green eyes. "You've been here to eat before, right? And I think I've seen you at church with your handsome boy. I guess we've never been introduced."

Dr. Danielson reached out her hand. "Please, call me Kirsten. And yes, to both questions. My son and I attend Fellowship

Church. And this is my new favorite place to eat. Although for lunch, I usually eat a sandwich on the run at Furry Friends. It saves time and money. Elizabeth and I decided to treat ourselves today. Dr. Ewing is holding down the fort."

Margaret reached in her apron pocket for the pad and pencil. Jon didn't always use one because he could just remember the orders, but she couldn't rely on her memory. "What can I get for you?"

They both ordered the Sante Fe chicken salad, a crunchy blend of southwestern flavors topped with tortilla strips. When Margaret brought their meals out, most of the tables were empty. Jon stood behind the cash register with a group of customers.

As she set the plates down, Elizabeth nodded at the chair next to her. "Sit down for a minute. I haven't had any time lately to visit with my old friend. How's Melanie?"

With a glance at Jon, Margaret eased into the chair. She didn't think he would mind if she visited with customers, but she didn't want to shirk her duties, either. "I'll sit down for a minute or two. When we first opened, I left at one. But we have a late crowd, so I stay until two most days."

They chatted for a few minutes, sharing news of children and, in Elizabeth's case, grandchildren. When Jon appeared to clear the table next to theirs, Margaret stood up. "I can do that."

"No, you sit down and visit with your friends." He wiped the table clean with a damp towel and went back through the swinging doors into the kitchen.

Elizabeth leaned forward. "Have you invited him to church?"

"Jon?" Margaret sighed. "Yes. More than once. He always declines, but never gives a reason."

"We've got that guest band playing during worship tomorrow. Why don't you ask him if he'll come? It'll be the kind of music the younger people like. Right Kirsten?"

"I like their music." The younger woman agreed.

Margaret smiled and nodded. "That's a great idea. I will. Now, I better get back to work before I get fired. You two need pie?"

Kirsten made a face. "Please, don't tempt me. I stepped on the scale this morning and resolved to make it through one week eating healthy."

"None for me either, dear." Elizabeth smiled at Kirsten "My boss is dragging me back to work."

Margaret stood and picked up their empty plates. "Good visiting with both of you. See you in church on Sunday." She hurried out to the kitchen.

Jon had already stacked her empty pie containers and cleaned off the counter. "Did you give them their ticket?"

"No. I got so carried away visiting I forgot entirely. Want me to get it?"

"I'll do it."

Jon disappeared behind the swinging doors, and Margaret straightened up her area before taking a load of containers to her car. Elizabeth and Kirsten waved to her as they drove away. Maisy scampered out the door and Margaret walked over to greet her. The dog waggled all over, then dropped a slimy green tennis ball. It rolled against Margaret's foot and Maisy watched expectantly.

Margaret picked it up and threw it across the yard. Maisy galloped after it, scooped it up in her mouth and redeposited it at Margaret's feet.

Jon came out the door and leaned on the porch railing, watching them and chuckling. "You know better than to start that. Now she'll never let you go."

Margaret ignored the ball and walked up to the porch. Jon's

tall glass of sweet tea looked refreshing. "That looks good. Mind if I help myself to a glass before I go?"

"Not at all. You know you're allowed a meal every day, and all the drinks you want. And pie." Jon grinned.

"Just some tea." A few minutes later Margaret stepped back onto the porch carrying a glass. She sank down on the swing, and for a few minutes both of them were quiet. "That breeze from the river is nice." Margaret's foot pushed the swing gently.

"It's not as hot as I thought it would get today. Maybe we're in for some cooler weather. Do you have any plans for the weekend?"

Great. A perfect opening. "We have a guest band playing in worship service tomorrow. They're supposed to be really good. I'd love to have you be my guest."

Jon gazed out toward the river without speaking for a long moment. When he turned back to face her, his face was twisted with pain. "Angie loved her church. She taught the kids and sang on the praise team. I went nearly every week, mostly just to please her. But that night … I got the call … about the accident," Jon's voice broke, but he continued, "I pleaded with God, 'Let her live.' He didn't. She died. What kind of a God would take someone like Angie? The kindest, gentlest, most loving woman I've ever known. If there is a God, he obviously hates me. I don't want anything to do with a God like that." Jon covered his face with his hands and his shoulders shook.

Margaret sat quietly, tears filling her eyes. What could she say to comfort this young man she'd grown to love? She pleaded for wisdom, some words to say to him that wouldn't shut the door. "I understand your pain. My Nathaniel was taken too soon, as well. I won't ask you to church again, Jon. But I will pray for you. I'll pray for your healing, and pray that you come to see that

God does love you, more than you could ever believe."

She stood, the swing bumping against the back of her legs, but Jon didn't reply. Margaret took her glass inside. When she came out, Jon was wiping his face on his sleeve.

"Sorry for the outburst," he muttered.

"Don't ever be sorry about honest feelings. I'm big enough to hear them, and so is God. I'll see you Monday." Margaret laid her had gently on Jon's shoulder for a moment, then reached down to give one last pat to Maisy, who was lying on the porch, her tennis ball between her front paws.

Chapter 21

KIRSTEN DROVE HOME from church the long way around the town. The sun warmed her arm through the open car window, and a soft breeze lifted her hair from her forehead. The kind of day that made one delighted to live in central Missouri. It was much too pretty of a day to waste inside.

She'd started a meal in the slow-cooker before they left, and when they entered the house, the wonderful aroma of food hit their nostrils.

"Go change your clothes," she directed Josiah. Then she slipped out of her skirt and into a pair of jean capris and a soft purple top.

In the kitchen, she finished preparing the meal. She laid Josiah's orderly plate on the table. Then she filled hers with a couple slices of roast beef, potatoes, carrots, and a helping of apple salad. She wasn't worried if food touched, she was hungry. "Josiah. Lunch is ready," she called.

Josiah wandered out from his room with a book about dogs in one hand. "Mom, did you know that dog's eyes contain a special membrane that allows them to see in the dark? It's called the tapetum lucidum. The tapetum lucidum." He giggled.

"No, I didn't know that. Did you wash your hands?"

"No." Josiah went to the sink in the kitchen and began

scrubbing his hands. "Don't you wish we had a *tapetum lucidum?*"

"I do." Kirsten smiled at her son.

Josiah slid into his seat and bowed his head.

"Do you want to ask the blessing today?" Kirsten tucked her folded napkin in her lap.

Josiah's head bobbed. "Dear God. Thank you for our food. And please give my mom and me a *tapetum lucidum*. Amen."

Kirsten laid her napkin in her lap and picked up her fork. "You know, sometimes God says 'no.' That may be a prayer he says 'no' to. We don't need to see in the dark like animals do. We have flashlights and nightlights."

Josiah chewed a piece of meat and swallowed. Then he gave her one of his rare smiles. "I know, Mom. But wouldn't it be cool if he said 'yes'?"

"That would be cool." Kirsten knew the blessing of God saying yes, but she also knew the blessing of Him saying "no." *All things work together for good, for those that love the Lord.* Even Asperger's.

When Josiah was almost finished eating, Kirsten asked, "Would you like to go for a ride on the bike trail today?"

Josiah didn't look up from the potato he was spearing with his fork. "You don't have a bike."

"I do. When we were at Grandpa's the other day, I saw the old bike I had in high school hanging up in the garage. Grandpa said he'd get it down and make sure the tires were okay, so I could ride with you. I know you've missed riding since Eric went back to college."

"Okay. Can we go now?" Josiah pushed the last bite of carrot in his mouth, hopped out of his chair and carried his empty plate to the dishwasher.

"I need to put the food away, but it will only take me a few minutes." Kirsten was eager to go, too. She loved the idea of doing something with Josiah they would both enjoy.

Thirty minutes later, they pedaled down the bike trail. It had been years since Kirsten had ridden, but the old adage, *just like riding a bike*, proved true. After a few wobbly moments, she felt almost as confident as if she were the same age as her son.

She let Josiah lead, as the Sunday traffic on the trail was too busy for riding beside side by side. She greeted several customers, people from church, and townspeople. Josiah rode past like he didn't even see them. When they reached the first gravel crossroad on the outskirts of town, Kirsten called to Josiah, "Hold up, buddy. Time for a break." They pulled their bikes off the trail. Kirsten slipped off her bike and rubbed her backside. She certainly wasn't used to sitting on a tiny triangular seat.

Josiah straddled his bike and rocked it back and forth. "Can we go now?"

"Give your mom a minute or two. I haven't ridden for fifteen years."

"We're almost to River's Edge. We can stop and see Maisy."

Kirsten shook her head. "Today is the only day Mr. Washington has off. I don't think we should bother him."

Josiah's chin jutted. "Mom, he wants me to come so Maisy can get exercise."

Kirsten looked at Josiah's determined face. She always had to pick her battles. Maybe this was one she didn't want to fight. "We'll see if they're home."

At that, Josiah shot off on his bike. Kirsten mounted her bike and kept up with his pace only by pedaling as fast as she could. A well-worn path dipped through the ditch and up to River's Edge. Josiah veered down through it, bouncing as he went. Kirsten dismounted and pushed her bike across.

By the time she reached the yard, Josiah had disappeared. His bike was parked at the side of the house and his helmet hung from the handlebars. Suddenly, from behind the house came a yellow blur with Josiah in pursuit. Maisy saw Kirsten, skidded to a stop, and woofed.

"That's my mom." Josiah came up beside the dog, resting his hand on her shoulders. She glanced up at him, her tail waving.

Kirsten laid her bike down and knelt in front of them. "Maisy, you get more beautiful every time I see you. I bet you remember me, probably not fondly, though. I was the one who gave you all those shots."

"Come on, Maisy." Josh took off across the yard again and the dog loped after him.

Kirsten stood up and brushed off her pants. Jon stood on the porch and waved at her. Her cheeks warmed. "Sorry to barge in on you like this. We were on the trail, and Josiah insisted that we stop to see Maisy. We'll get going."

"It's fine. Let them play a while. Can I get you a sweet tea or water?"

Kirsten walked toward the porch. "Sure. An ice water would be good. My old bike doesn't even have a bottle holder."

Tiger was stretched out in the shade of the porch. She blinked up lazily at Kirsten, who bent to pet her.

Jon returned with two tall glasses and handed her one with lots of ice, just the way she liked it.

"Thanks." She perched on the swing and took a long drink. "This is such a pretty view. I didn't take the time to notice when we came to eat." Out on the lawn, Maisy and Josiah played tug of war with a rope that Maisy had dragged up from somewhere. Kirsten spoke softly. "I really appreciate you letting Josiah play with Maisy. He's crazy about your dog." She sighed. "All dogs really. I wish I could get one for him. But I don't think it would be fair to the dog when we're gone all day."

"Josiah is welcome to come see Maisy any time. I think she's missed him since school started." He turned and looked at the boy and dog. "They appear to have a special bond."

Kirsten followed Jon's gaze. Josiah grabbed the rope and raced away with it, heading for the gravel parking. Maisy galloped behind, biting at the rope. Josiah held it high and the dog leaped for it. She caught one end and planted her feet, jerking and spinning Josiah around as he clung to the other end. Suddenly he lost his balance and tumbled down, scraping against one of the larger rocks that outlined the parking. He dropped his end of the rope, grabbed his knee and screamed.

Kirsten bolted off of the porch, but Jon reached Josiah first.

Jon's voice was gentle. "I'm going to take you up to the porch, Josiah. Hang on." He scooped him up.

Kirsten examined the knee. He'd scraped it good, but nothing that would require more than cleaning and a bandage. "You'll be okay, you'll be okay." She spoke soothingly, but Josiah continued his shrieks.

Jon set him down on the porch. "I'll get my first aid kit." The door closed softly behind him.

Kirsten longed with every fiber of her being to hold Josiah and comfort him. That was one of the hardest things for a mom of a child with Asperger's—when your child is hurt or sad, you can't offer comfort with hugs or even words. She sat down by Josiah but didn't touch him.

Maisy had followed them to the porch. She nudged Josiah's ear, but he didn't respond, just continued screaming. Maisy stepped over him and lowered herself onto Josiah's lap, her front paws across his legs, her back against his midsection. His screams lessened in intensity, then trailed off into a whimper. He draped one arm over Maisy's back.

Jon reappeared holding a white plastic first aid kit, a bucket of water and some clean cloths.

Kirsten reached for the bucket. "Maisy's doing her part to make this easier."

Jon looked at the dog stretched out over Josiah. "That's what she did in the basement the day of the tornado. Is she too heavy for you, buddy?"

Josiah's head shook, his fine blond hair flying. He whimpered again as his mom started to gently clean the abrasion, but he didn't scream. Kirsten gently blotted the clean knee with gauze and put two Band-Aids across it.

"There you go, son. Good as new." She rubbed Maisy's ears. "And thank you, girl, for calming him."

Josiah reached over Maisy to gingerly touch the Band-Aids. "Maisy is a coping skill."

Kirsten was always amused when her words came out of Josiah's mouth. She'd been trying for years to teach him what a coping skill was and how to use them. "Yes, Maisy is a good coping skill. But she isn't always around."

Josiah wiggled a little, and Maisy stood up and moved off of him. She trotted down into the yard and Josiah followed, favoring the leg with the scraped knee.

Kirsten snapped the first aid kit shut. "Thanks, Jon. This came in handy."

"Is he okay? Do you need a ride back into town?" Jon's face showed genuine concern, and Kirsten felt like hugging him. So many people wanted to keep themselves away from Josiah, as if Asperger's was contagious.

"He's fine. When he gets a scrape or cut, anything where he

sees blood, he really loses it. What I can't believe is how he calmed when Maisy lay on his lap. It's like she did it intentionally."

Jon pushed the dark hair off his forehead and shrugged his broad shoulders. "Maybe she did. Do you need more water?"

"No, this is fine." Kirsten tipped up her glass. "We'd better head back to town anyway. Let you have some peace and quiet."

"Josiah. Five minutes." Kirsten held up one hand, the fingers spread.

"Aww, Mom." Josiah whined, but he turned to the dog. "I have to go on my bike now, Maisy."

Kirsten handed her glass to Jon. "This is twice now you've taken care of my son for me."

"Anytime. I like Josiah. I like watching him and Maisy play."

Kirsten thought he might say something about enjoying her company, too, but he didn't. She strapped on her helmet and got back on the trail with her son. She watched Josiah, the trail, the river, and the town as it neared. But in her mind, she saw Jon's kind face and warm brown eyes.

Chapter 22

MARGARET SHIVERED AS she sat in the hallway of Lutheran Hospital's mammography unit. The appointment had been scheduled for the afternoon, so she left River's Edge at one, not staying to chat or throw the ball for Maisy.

When the technician called her name, Margaret followed her, clutching the thin cotton cape around her shoulders.

"How are you, today, Margaret?" The girl's pink highlighted hair hung in sheets on either side of her face. She looked younger than Melanie did when she was in high school.

"I'm fine." Margaret stepped inside the room the technician indicated. "How are you? You look rather young to be doing this job."

The girl laughed, her hair sliding back as her head tipped. "You made my day. I'm nearly thirty. I have two little ones at home, and most days I feel pretty old."

A tall thin man stood at one side of the room. The technician introduced him as the radiologist, Dr. Berkenbosch.

"Step up here, please." She motioned Margaret in front of the machine and helped her slide the cape off her shoulders. "I understand you found a lump? In your left breast?"

"Yes. It was the left one." Margaret watched as the technician keyed something into the computer attached to the machine.

"Now let me know if anything is too uncomfortable." She positioned Margaret for the first x-ray.

"Two little ones? And a job, too. That keeps you busy." Margaret made small talk to distract herself from the discomfort of the procedure.

The technician took several pictures, more than Margaret remembered from previous mammograms. She and the radiologist studied each one on a screen before she proceeded with the next. Finally, Margaret asked, "Do you see anything that looks abnormal? Can you tell what that lump is?"

"I just take the pictures. That's why we have Dr. Berkenbosch here to read them." She smiled at Margaret from behind her computer screen. "That's all for now. We have some good clear shots."

Dr. Berkenbosch looked over the screen. "Go ahead and get dressed. Then we can visit a little and I'll share with you what I'm seeing."

"Okay." Margaret pulled the cape back around her and hurried back to the little cubicle where her clothes hung on a hook. The lump was probably just a harmless cyst, or a lump of fat from eating too much of her own baking. The doctor would reassure her, and she could be on her way.

Margaret was brushing her hair when the technician appeared. She led the way to Dr. Berkenbosch's small, cluttered office. His hands were folded, resting on a messy stack of papers. "Sit down, Margaret." She sank into the chair and crossed her legs.

"The mammogram shows an area in your left breast that appears highly suspicious. We need to schedule a sterotacic biopsy. We'll use a needle to remove a small amount of breast tissue from the lump and examine it for cancer cells. I want to schedule the biopsy as soon as possible. Now, what questions do you have?"

Margaret's mind seemed as full of fog as the river bottom on a fall morning. She couldn't even think of a question, let alone articulate one. Cancer? Surely not. They were just being overly cautious.

<p style="text-align:center">~~~</p>

Bethany slung her backpack on her bed. A chemistry test to study for and a paper due next week for English. But homework would have to wait until she got home from River's Edge. Between school and her job, her life was pretty busy right now. But that was good. She had less time to think about The Problem. Her hand covered her belly. Poor baby, to be thought of as The Problem.

Bethany knew she couldn't put off telling her mom forever. But her mom didn't deserve this. She'd worked hard to provide a good life for Bethany after her dad died in Iraq. Her mom was an attractive woman, but she'd never remarried. So it was just the two of them. It wasn't that Bethany was afraid of angering her mom. She was afraid of disappointing her.

She changed into black jeans, stuck her phone in her pocket, and slung a bag containing a light jacket over her shoulder. As she passed through the kitchen, she stared longingly at the fridge. She wished she had time to fix herself a snack. It seemed she was always hungry. But if she didn't leave right now, she would be late. The red Huffy bike she'd used in junior high had been dusted off and put into use as her transportation to and from work. A new tire and a high-powered light were affordable. A car was not. She wheeled the bike out of the garage and took off. Twenty minutes later she parked in the bike rack Jon had installed for his customers.

When she walked up on the porch, Tiger leaped down from his spot on a wicker chair. Bethany tickled under her chin. "How's the mousing today, Tiger?"

Inside, Maisy leaped from her rug and greeted her with a waving tail. Bethany bent and rubbed the floppy ears. "You're not in puppy prison yet, huh?" Maisy looked upstairs as if she knew what Bethany was saying.

Bethany smelled chicken frying and her stomach flopped. She could tolerate most smells with no nausea, but the smell of Jon's great fried chicken nearly did her in every night it was on the menu. She took a deep breath and swallowed.

"Hello, Bethany?" Jon called from the kitchen.

"Yes, it's me."

"Would you put Maisy upstairs?"

"Sure." She coaxed Maisy, and although the dog followed obediently, her tail hung between her legs. Once the gate was closed, she flopped down on the floor and poked her nose through the slats, watching Bethany go downstairs.

Bethany pushed through the swinging doors, hung her bag on a hook by the back door, and washed her hands. "What needs done first?"

Jon answered without turning, his attention on the fryer. "We need more silverware rolled in napkins, get two cherry pies from the pantry and cut them, and make the sweet tea."

"Gotcha." Bethany pulled out the tray from the dishwasher, wrapped each setting of silverware with a napkin, and fastened it with a little adhesive strap. She kept her face averted from the fryer, but her stomach still felt like it had gone ten rounds on the Mamba at Worlds of Fun. When the tub was full of silverware, she pulled out the large circular cutter that made seven cuts with one press. The cherry pies oozed red syrup and her mouth watered. How could she feel sick and hungry at the same time? She promised herself a piece for supper and restrained her fingers from swiping a taste as she would have done if she was home.

She turned from the pies just as Jon lifted another basket of crispy golden chicken from the fryer. Her stomach flipped again, and she dropped the pie cutter on the counter and raced to the small unisex bathroom off the dining room. She barely got the door closed before she emptied the contents of her stomach in the toilet. She grasped the rim, holding on until her stomach stopped heaving.

The cool water she splashed on her face revived her a little. She wiped her mouth with a paper towel. Her strength spent, she leaned against a wall and breathed slowly in and out. Her stomach actually felt better. And she was hungry. She wondered if Jon would mind if she took one of the small packages of crackers they served with the soups at lunch. After one last glance around to make sure she was leaving the bathroom in pristine order, she opened the door.

Jon stood in the hall in front of her. "Are you okay?"

"I'm fine." She tried to give him a bright and reassuring smile.

"I can manage by myself for tonight. I think you'd better go home. We don't need you to share your germs with our customers."

"Really. I'm okay. I'm not sick."

Jon tipped his head, frowning at her. "Someone who's not sick doesn't race for the bathroom. Unless…" There was a pause and Jon glanced at the front door. It was almost time to open. He looked back at her. "Bethany, I need to know what's going on."

Tears pricked at her eyelids. She wanted desperately to share this burden. But once it was shared, it became real. More real than she wanted.

"I'm pregnant." She whispered it, but to her ears it was if she had shouted, and the words seemed to echo again and again from the walls of the stately old home.

Jon looked down and his hand massaged his neck. When his eyes met Bethany's again, she thought she could see a glimmer of compassion. "Let's talk tonight before you leave, okay?"

Bethany nodded, and then asked, "Could I have a few crackers? They'll settle my stomach."

"Help yourself." Jon waved towards the pantry. The front door opened and the first customers entered, a young couple still in full biking gear. Jon smiled at them, but spoke to Bethany. "I'll take their orders."

When he returned to the kitchen, Bethany had munched through the contents of two packages of crackers and was feeling much better. She made a mental note to always eat something before she came to work. If she still had a job at the end of the evening. What if Jon didn't want a pregnant high-school waitress?

The doors swung inward and Jon hurried in. "Two sweet teas."

Bethany grabbed two glasses, filled them, and began serving. A family of four was the next party, and from then on she worked steadily, taking drink and food orders, serving plates of crisp fried chicken and steaming bowls piled high with mashed potatoes, and clearing tables quickly so they could be filled again.

At eight o'clock, Jon locked the door behind a middle-aged couple who clasped hands and smiled at each other as they stepped out the door. Bethany stacked their dishes on the cart and wiped the table quickly. Maybe if she hurried she could leave before Jon remembered wanting to talk.

"Bethany, no need to load those in the dishwasher. I can do that later. Go ahead and get yourself some dinner. I'm going to let Maisy out, and then we can talk."

Bethany trudged to the kitchen pushing the cart ahead of her. She didn't feel much like eating, but she didn't want to be sick again. She loaded a plate with some potatoes, a piece of chicken, a roll, and the last piece of cherry pie. Grabbing some silverware from the tray, she carried it into the dining room and took her favorite table, the one nestled by the bay window. Before she'd even spread butter on her roll, Jon flipped the sign in the window to closed, and pulled out a chair at her table.

He straddled it backward. Why did guys do that? It looked so uncomfortable.

"Let's talk while you're eating. I want you to get home before the trail gets dark."

Bethany glanced out at the sun sliding behind the giant maples that overhung the river. The days were getting shorter.

"So what's your plan?"

Did she have a plan? She shrugged her shoulders and nibbled on the roll. "I'm hoping to have enough credits to finish school in December."

"Have you talked to a counselor?"

She shook her head. "Not since last year."

There was a soft woof at the door. Jon walked over and let Maisy in. Her tail waved at Bethany, but Jon had trained her not to go in the dining room. She walked over to the rug by the stairs and sank down with a sigh.

When Jon sat back down his face was creased with a frown. "So, Bethany." He paused and she ate another forkful of potatoes. "Does anyone know you're pregnant? The father? Your mom?"

The potatoes hit her stomach with a thud. "No." She

whispered.

The creases in his forehead deepened and he leaned forward. "You have to tell them. Your mom first. I don't want the responsibility of a pregnant, underage employee without her mother's knowledge and permission."

Bethany used her napkin and pushed her half-eaten plate away. "I need to go. It's getting dark."

Jon nodded. "You discuss this with your mom and find out if it's okay to work. I don't mind taking you if your mom doesn't care."

Bethany carried her plate to the kitchen, lifted her bag from the hook, and trudged outside. She had no choice. She had to tell her mom the news that would crush her.

Chapter 23

BETHANY WHEELED HER bike into the garage and leaned it against the wall. Her mom's car was parked in its usual spot. She'd hoped all the way home that Mom would have chosen this night to go out with friends, or get some groceries, or even go to a bar. Anywhere but sitting in the family room, waiting for her, and available to talk.

Bethany dropped her bag on the kitchen counter. Mom was watching *The Voice*, and a young man in a plaid cowboy shirt was moaning into the microphone. She looked up and smiled. "How was your day?"

"Okay." Bethany sank into her favorite faded red and black chair with the high back and padded arms. She draped her legs over one arm and used first one foot, then the other to pry off her shoes. "I got an A minus on my essay."

"Good." The country singer finished and applause erupted on the TV. Her mom turned to watch.

"Mom, could we talk?"

"Just a minute, I want to see which coach he gets."

The TV continued to blare, and Bethany considered telling her mom that she changed her mind, she didn't need to talk. She could say it was nothing and just go to her room. But she was afraid Jon was serious about not letting her work without her mom's permission, and keeping her job might be more important than ever. Her mom switched off the sound on the TV. "What's up, honey?"

"I'm pregnant." Bethany blurted the words out, and suddenly, undeniably, she was.

Mom leaned forward. Her feet, which had been tucked up beside her on the couch, hit the floor. "What did you say?"

"I'm pregnant."

Mom switched off the muted TV. She raked her hands through her hair, then shook her head. Finally she looked at Bethany. "Do you know for sure?"

Bethany picked at some dried food on her jeans. "I took an early pregnancy test a few weeks ago. It was positive. And I have morning sickness. Only it lasts all day long."

Her mother squealed. "You've known for a few weeks and you haven't bothered to tell me?"

Bethany couldn't answer. If only she could turn back the clock and make sure this nightmare didn't happen. But it had.

Her mom went on with the questioning. "Who's the father?"

"Kyle. But he doesn't know." The tears Bethany had been struggling to hold back rolled down her cheeks.

Her mother's sigh held all the condemnation and disapproval Bethany had expected. "Why weren't you taking precautions? I tried to get you on birth control, you said you didn't need it. You said you weren't *sexually active*." The mocking words hurt as much as a physical slap.

"I wasn't. Just the once. We didn't plan for it to happen." She swiped at her face with the back of one hand.

"Once is all it takes." Her mother sighed again, looking as injured as if she herself were the pregnant one. "I'll make an appointment at a clinic in Kansas City."

Bethany sniffed and wiped at her nose with one sleeve. "Can't I just go see Dr. Nancy?"

"I don't think she does those procedures." Her mom's voice was brusque. She was a take-charge person, a solver of problems. She always said she had to be, as a single mom. "They have clinics in Kansas City that take care of things in one visit."

Bethany nodded. Then she slowly realized what her mom was talking about. "You mean—an abortion?" She whispered the word.

"Bethany, you have no other options. Your whole life is ahead of you. Finishing high school, college, a career. Does Kyle want to marry you?"

Bethany shook her head emphatically. She didn't need to think about that question. Kyle had big plans for his life, and they didn't include her.

Mom stood up. "You have no idea what it's like to raise a child on your own." She wasn't tall, maybe five-six, but tonight she seemed to tower over Bethany. "I'll call the clinic tomorrow." She walked down the hall and her bedroom door closed firmly behind her.

Chapter 24

THE ALARM JERKED Jon from a sleep that had taken him far away from Missouri bluff country.

He'd dreamed about Angie. They were riding bikes together on a trail, and she kept biking faster and faster, moving out of sight. His arm stretched out to the empty space beside him, but there was no reaching the empty place in his heart. And nothing to lessen the sharp ache of grief.

He swung his legs over the side of the bed, and Maisy was on her feet in an instant, brown eyes bright and tail wagging. He pulled on shorts and slipped into the flip-flops by the bed. Maisy led the way downstairs, her nails clicking on the wood floors.

A thunderstorm had rumbled through in the night, and clouds still scuttled across the sky.

Tiger waited on the deck. Maisy gave the cat's face a quick swipe with her tongue before bounding down the stairs and into the yard. Tiger gave a disgusted shake and meandered over to Jon.

"Ready for breakfast, Tiger? You aren't forgetting your part of the bargain, are you? You're supposed to be catching any rodents on the property."

Tiger gazed up at him and meowed, clearly letting him know he was tardy with the breakfast delivery service. Jon rubbed his stubbly chin and shivered. He needed a shave, a shirt, and coffee.

But not in that order. He'd start with the coffee. Using one foot to gently prod Tiger away from the door, he trudged to the kitchen.

His single-cup coffeemaker functioned well for early mornings and Sundays, leaving the large commercial pot for restaurant use.

He scooped up food for both animals and placed their dishes on the back deck. Maisy finished first and stood eyeing Tiger's dish. "That's Tiger's breakfast, girl. Ready for a run?"

Maisy whirled around him as he tied his running shoes and slipped into a tee shirt. They both needed to start the day by running—for Maisy to burn up excess energy, for him to handle stress. As they set out on the trail, he could see Tiger heading to the porch for a nap. Maisy trotted beside him except for occasional forays to the edge of the trail to sniff where other dogs or wild critters had been. Then she would race madly down the trail to catch up.

As he ran, Jon replayed last night's events in his head. He didn't want to lose Bethany. She was an excellent waitress, and they worked well together. He rarely had to tell her what to do. She just looked around and did the next thing that needed doing. But a pregnant teen-age employee presented all sorts of problems. Selfishly he hoped that no matter what she and her mom decided, Bethany would at least be able to work for him through the Maple Festival less than a month away.

He slowed to a walk, wiped his forehead on his shirt, and looked for Maisy. She was a few yards back, her nose buried in a clump of grass at the side of the trail. He turned around and called as he jogged, "Let's go, Maisy. Last one home is a rotten egg."

He laughed as she shot past him and into the yard. He could never beat her home.

Twenty minutes later, showered, shaved, and dressed, Jon sat at the computer and logged in to his bank account. His bills were set up to be deducted automatically, but the margin of money available was so slim he checked frequently to make sure he hadn't accidentally overdrawn the account.

River's Edge was making a profit, but after paying on the construction loan, the appliances, and employee salaries, he had little to nothing left over. He tried not to think what would happen if there was an emergency, some big, unexpected expense.

He sighed and leaned back in the chair, tipping his head up. That was when he saw it. A brown stain on the newly sheet-rocked ceiling. The roof was brand new. How could it develop a leak already? He pulled out his phone and punched in Paul's number. He got his voicemail and left a message to call him as soon as possible. Another headache.

Then he powered down the computer. Time to get ready for the lunch crowd.

～

Dr. Nancy called Margaret in the late afternoon on Wednesday, waking her from a nap in her chair, the mail unopened in her lap. As Margaret reached for the phone, the pile of advertisements slid to the floor.

"Hello?" She tried to sound alert.

"Margaret? This is Dr. Nancy."

She paused, and Margaret studied the ad showing a shapely woman in a bikini and the caption, *Are you ready for your swimsuit?*

"I hope you have good news for me," Margaret responded cheerfully.

Dr. Nancy's voice was guarded. "We're not ready to make

any diagnosis yet. Dr. Berkenbosch visited with you after the mammogram?"

"Yes, he's such a nice young man. He doesn't smile much, though."

"He told you about the needle biopsy. I scheduled it for Monday morning at eight."

"I work on Mondays," Margaret objected.

"We can't wait. We need to find out how to treat this."

Margaret reached down and picked up the pile of mail before answering. "All right. I'll let Jon know I won't be there."

"Dr. Alabsi will be the one performing the biopsy. I've ordered a prescription of Valium to calm you during the procedure. That's at the Medicap pharmacy. You can pick it up and take one before you go. Is there someone who can drive you?"

"Oh. I suppose." Margaret ran through potential drivers in her head. It seemed like asking a lot for someone to drive her to the hospital, wait while she had the surgery, and drive her home.

"The Valium will make you kind of loopy, so you shouldn't drive. No food or water after midnight the night before. No coffee in the morning – only water. Do you have any questions for me?"

So many questions. But even Dr. Nancy with all her degrees couldn't answer them. "No. I can't think of any."

After she hung up, she called Jon and told him she wouldn't be able to work on Monday. She'd make extra pies and put them in the freezer. All he'd have to do was pull them out and bake them.

Then she poured a cup of leftover coffee, warmed it in the microwave, and sat at the kitchen table. It wasn't breakfast time, but she needed a visit with her Lord. "Father, I just don't have time for this right now. Jon needs me at River's Edge." She nodded firmly, but her heart knew. Her schedules weren't hers, and whatever the doctors found was not in her control either.

"Be with Jon on Monday while I'm at the hospital. It's a lot for him to do by himself."

A tiny little sprout of fear wiggled into her mind. "God, you know that young man needs me. It's just not a good time to be sick. Let this turn out to be nothing – just Dr. Nancy being cautious."

She sipped her coffee. Then she bowed her head over the cup. "Not my will, Lord, but yours," she whispered.

Chapter 25

KIRSTEN SAT IN the hard plastic chair designed for a child and waited for the rest of the team to arrive.

The special education room seemed empty and sterile compared to other classrooms she'd passed by. They'd been full of chattering children, bright posters, and lopsided art projects. Josiah went to the special education classroom only for reading instruction. The rest of his day, he was mainstreamed with the help of an associate who explained assignments, helped him focus, and gave him needed breaks when he was over-stimulated.

Kirsten thought the plan was working well. She would find out in a few minutes at the meeting where the IEP— Individual Education Plan—would be reviewed and updated with new goals. The IEP was a legal document outlining modifications, goals and objectives, and an entire plan to make school successful for Josiah. Originally, today's meeting had been scheduled at the end of October. But for some reason they'd moved it up. And that made her nervous.

The tap, tap of high heels sounded in the hall. Kirsten sat up and put a smile on her face.

Mrs. Hardenbrook, Josiah's special education teacher, entered. "Good morning, Mrs. Danielson. I'm glad you could come in this morning. I know you're busy."

Didn't Josiah's teacher remember that Kirsten was a vet? She'd treated her kitten for diarrhea a few months ago. Kirsten jogged her memory. "Since there are two of us in the veterinary clinic, it gives us a little more flexibility. How's Molly doing?"

"Oh, Molly's fine. Growing like a weed and getting into everything. Now, since we're meeting today, we can call this our parent teacher conference if you wish. It will save you a meeting in a few weeks." Mrs. Hardenbrook sat in a comfortable, upholstered chair and spread a stack of papers on the table.

More voices sounded in the hall and five people entered. With a little shuffling and a few nods or smiles in her direction, they took their places around the table. Kirsten recognized Josiah's homeroom teacher, Miss Taylor, his special education associate, Gloria, and the principal, Mr. Patterson, but she was unsure who the other two were.

Mrs. Hardenbrook cleared her throat, and the small talk ceased. "Let's get started, shall we? I'm not sure everyone knows all our participants, so we'll have introductions first – just your name and your position. I'm Jane Hardenbrook, Josiah's special education teacher."

They went around the table. Kirsten learned the young man with the goatee was the school psychologist and behavioral specialist, and the older red-haired woman was the special education consultant. She tried to think positively, that it was wonderful to have all of these people committed to providing Josiah with the best education possible, but she wondered how many of them really knew *him*, not his diagnosis or test scores.

They started with general conversation, asking her how she felt sixth grade was going for Josiah. They reviewed his IEP goals and the progress he'd made. The next job would be to write the new goals for the coming year.

The man with the goatee—for some reason she couldn't remember his name—leaned forward. "Our mainstreaming plan is not working well. Since the beginning of the year, Josiah has had four episodes when I was called to assist Gloria. The entire social studies classroom had to relocate to the library three times while Josiah calmed down. We believe," he glanced at Jane as if to confirm with an ally, "we need to increase his time in the special education room."

Kirsten felt as if the world tilted and they slid back several years. Things she had fought for, things Josiah had accomplished, all swept away with one comment.

She swallowed and sat up straight. "No. We can't do that."

The man with the goatee smiled at her as if she were the student, not the mother. "We're just talking about one class. Social studies."

Kirsten took a breath before she responded. "But he makes good grades in social studies, and it's one of the best classes for interaction with peers." She glanced around the table. No one nodded in agreement, nor even looked friendly. "Why isn't Mrs. Gruss here?"

Jane answered. "Not everyone could be here. Mrs. Gruss has talked with both me and Miss Taylor. Sara, do you want to respond to this?"

Josiah's classroom teacher, who looked young enough to still be in high school, pulled out a sheet of paper. "As we said, Josiah has had four episodes when the rest of the class had to relocate."

Kirsten glared at her. "Are they using the stress balls? Is he allowed his breaks?" She turned and looked at Gloria. "What's going on, Gloria? Aren't you in this class?"

Gloria's eyes widened and her hands twisted in her lap. Her

brown eyes, large behind her dark-rimmed glasses, blinked several times. "Sometimes. If I wasn't able to take my lunch break, Jane said to take it at that time."

"So." Kirsten wondered if she resembled the Furry Friends Rottweiler patient who was fond of snarling at them. "He has no associate, he can't take breaks because there is no associate, and Josiah gets punished when he can't handle it."

Gloria looked at Jane. "I could eat while Josiah is at recess."

"That would leave us short a supervisor on the playground." Mr. Patterson's face morphed into a bulldog's dour visage.

What did the others at the table remind her of? She studied Mrs. Hardenbrook's features. Was she a poodle? A collie? She pulled herself back to the debate of how Gloria was to get her lunch and Josiah was to have an associate.

"What does the IEP say?" Kirsten asked, but already knew the answer. The legal document stated that Josiah was to have a one-on-one associate for the entire school day. There were periods of time when he could function well without assistance, but to not have one available was unacceptable.

The school psychologist leaned back and waved the pen he'd been using to make notes. He was definitely a rat terrier who wouldn't let go of his chew bone. "Due to the severity of the episodes Josiah has had in the classroom, we feel…" He paused and looked around the table. "The best option right now is to have him take social studies in the special education classroom."

Mrs. Hardenbrook, Jane, and Gloria all nodded in agreement. It didn't matter what she said. The decision had been made. She had no magic pill to prevent Josiah from having a meltdown. And she understood that an entire class should not be disrupted for one child. Even if that child were hers.

Kirsten sat up straight and leaned forward. "The middle

school transition has been a difficult one for him. He isn't used to traveling from class to class and having so many teachers. Can we write this as a temporary situation and review it, say, in a month?"

Mrs. Hardenbrook nodded, and her bushy hair shook like a collie ruff. "Five weeks takes us to the end of the quarter. How about reviewing it then?"

Kirsten nodded. "That would work. In the meantime—" She looked at the collie. "Could you make sure that he has his stress balls with him, that his associate is with him at all times in the regular classrooms, and that he is encouraged to take his scheduled breaks *before* he has a meltdown? These are things that have worked well in the past, and I want us moving toward full mainstreaming, not away from it. There are no problems with him handling the academics of the regular classroom, are there?"

Jane, a small, sleek whippet, slid a printed report across the table. "This is the skills assessment we took last week." One tapered finger pointed to the bar graph. "As you can see, Josiah scores at the fiftieth percentile or above in all categories. However, his grades don't reflect this. He doesn't always complete classroom work or projects."

Kirsten shifted on the little chair. "I always oversee his homework. He does it every night."

Jane opened a red grade book and used a finger to scan a column. "He's missing worksheet twelve that was to be done in class. The United States map, also done in class. And the oral report." She looked up at Kirsten. "All of the missing assignments were work that was to be completed in class."

Kirsten pressed one hand to her forehead where the beginnings of a new headache throbbed. She felt utterly defeated.

"Are we ready to set some goals for Josiah for the coming

year?" Mrs. Hardenbrook smiled brightly at the faces around table.

The talk swirled about her. Kirsten nodded or shook her head as the questions required, but she was most aware of the increasingly uncomfortable chair and the mounting pressure and pain of a headache.

They finally set goals, and she signed the forms. Chairs scraped, files snapped shut, and everyone stood. Kirsten felt like one of Furry Friends dogs for adoption, nose pressed against the cage door, waiting to be set free.

The collie smiled brightly at her. "Thanks for coming in today, Mrs. Danielson. I think this will be a positive move for Josiah."

Kirsten nodded, but didn't speak. How could moving backwards be construed as positive?

Chapter 26

FUZZY GRAY PRE-SUNRISE light filtered into Margaret's bedroom. For a moment she started to plan her day's baking. Then she remembered. The appointment at the hospital.

She swung her feet over the side of the bed and waited for a moment. At her age, it was never wise to stand too quickly. She padded to the bathroom without bothering with slippers.

Later, showered and hair dried, she sat down at the kitchen table. She remembered the doctor's orders not to eat anything, but she needed her meeting with Jesus more than ever. "God, I'd prefer not to do this." She read a few verses from the open Bible before her. "But your will be done. I'm trying real hard to trust you. It just isn't always easy." She shook out one pill from a prescription bottle into her palm, tipped it into her mouth, and swallowed it with a sip of water.

A few minutes later, Elizabeth's car pulled into the drive. She thought she'd done a great job convincing Elizabeth this was just a little test and no cause for concern.

The Valium was already making her groggy. Margaret pulled the door shut behind her and checked to make sure it was locked. Melanie had become much more cautious since moving to New York and regularly asked her mom if she remembered to lock her doors. Margaret didn't want to tell her daughter she didn't.

She slid into the passenger side seat. "Good morning, Elizabeth. Thanks for driving me. I don't know why Dr. Nancy insisted on it. It's such a little test."

Elizabeth gazed at her with her steady gray eyes. "It's not just a little test, is it? This is a biopsy to see if you have cancer somewhere, isn't it?"

Margaret sighed and looked out the window. Maybe it wasn't so easy to fool an old friend. She wished she could lie about it, but knew she couldn't. Not to Elizabeth. "Yes. I have a lump in my breast, and the mammogram indicated it was suspicious." She turned and looked at Elizabeth. "I would have told you eventually. I just didn't want it to be a big deal."

Elizabeth leaned over and wrapped her arms around Margaret. "But it is a big deal. And you shouldn't have to go through this alone. May I pray for you?"

Margaret nodded without moving her head from Elizabeth's shoulder. She didn't—couldn't—speak.

"God, take care of my friend. Please, let this lump be nothing. Let her be healthy and cancer-free. But if that is not your will, keep her safe in your arms. Give her peace. And give the doctors wisdom. Amen."

"Thanks." Margaret snuffled as she sat upright. "Now, drive me to the hospital before I decide not to go."

With a final pat on Margaret's arm, Elizabeth put the car in reverse.

When she pulled into the parking lot at Memorial Hospital, Margaret spoke. "You don't have to come in. Go get a cup of coffee or run errands, and I'll give you a call when it's over."

"Nonsense. I'm going in with you, and I'll stay until the procedure is over. I have a book to read while I'm waiting. Then, if you feel like it, we'll have an early lunch—either at the truck stop or out at River's Edge."

"Oh, I don't think I could eat at the truck stop. That's our competition."

"Okay. River's Edge it is. If you feel like it." They walked into the brick building together.

〜

Margaret blinked awake. The entire needle aspiration procedure had taken place in a dream-like sequence. She felt a little pinchy pain in her left breast, but otherwise, she might believe she'd drifted off and nothing had happened.

A young smiling female face peered down at her. "You're awake. Did you have a nice nap? How are you feeling?"

Margaret moistened her lips. "I'm okay. Is it over?"

"Yes. They got a good sample." The nurse was wrapping a blood pressure cuff around her right arm. "After I check your vitals, you'll be able to leave as soon as you feel up to it. Did someone come with you to drive you home?"

Margaret frowned. Had Elizabeth driven her, or had she dreamed that, too? She shook her head as if to clear it. "My friend is here. She's in the waiting room. Can I sit up?"

The nurse finished checking her blood pressure and recorded it on her chart. "Let me take your pulse." She held Margaret's wrist with a cool, gentle hand. Then she kept hold of her hand and pulled her to a sitting position.

The curtained area spun for a moment, and Margaret clutched the edge of the cot. The nurse reached out and laid a hand on her arm as if to steady her. "That Valium really knocked you out, didn't it? I want you to stay right here. Don't try to stand yet. I'm going to have your friend drive around to the door back to pick you up, and we'll walk you out to the car." She hurried toward the waiting room.

A few minutes later Margaret heard a heavy door opening and then she saw Elizabeth's smiling face in the doorway. "You do look a little woozy. Are you ready to go, or do you need to sit for a while longer?"

Margaret slid off the edge of the cot and stood. "Oh, I'm ready to go."

The nurse parted the curtain and stepped around Elizabeth. Margaret turned to her. "I suppose I have to wait for Dr. Nancy to call to find out the results."

"Yes, they'll send the sample to the lab for testing. And when your doctor gets the results, she'll call you."

"Okay." Margaret felt like she was finally waking up. She turned back to Elizabeth and smiled. "Let's go see if Jon has any of the broccoli-cheese soup left."

Chapter 27

JON CARRIED A wobbly stack of dirty plates and silverware to the kitchen. One thing he'd learned—never make a trip, either to or from the kitchen, without carrying something. The group polishing off the last of Margaret's cherry pie would probably be his final customers for lunch.

It had been hectic without Margaret's help. He realized her quiet and efficient assistance often went unnoticed and made a mental note to let her know he appreciated it.

She'd told him she had an appointment today. He hoped she wasn't ill. He depended on her, and not just for the pies. It was almost like she was a partner in this venture. He piled the dishes on the counter next to the dishwasher, then rinsed and wiped his hands. Then he wrote out the ticket for the pie group.

On his way back to their table, two women stepped up on the porch. He was tired and just wanted to clean up, but two more paying customers would be more cash in the register. And he needed that.

As they came inside, he realized it was Margaret and another woman her age who looked familiar.

"Did you save some broccoli-cheese soup for me? In a bread

bowl?" Margaret's perky smile made him sigh with relief. She looked fine.

"I think I could scrape together two bowls." He looked at Margaret's companion. "Is that what you'd like, too?"

"I'd better have some. Margaret's been raving about this soup for weeks. How's Maisy doing?"

That's why she looked familiar. She worked with Kirsten at Furry Friends. "She's good. Lying upstairs and snoozing after our morning run. I'll let her outside when you're finished eating. She always likes to coax Margaret into throwing one of her tennis balls."

"You've met Elizabeth, haven't you?" Margaret asked. "She's been here before."

"Sure, she took care of my Maisy at the clinic. What would you ladies like to drink?"

"Coffee." Margaret said.

"I'll have a glass of ice tea." Elizabeth unfolded her napkin and laid it in her lap.

Jon hurried to the kitchen to get drinks and then back again with soup in two golden-brown bread bowls. He placed Margaret's in front of her. "I hope everything went well at your appointment. I can't have my best baker getting ill."

An uncomfortable pause followed, and Jon reran his comment in his head. Had he said something offensive? Elizabeth reached across the table and touched Margaret's hand. Then Margaret looked up and smiled at him. "Yes. Everything's fine. I'll be back here to help tomorrow."

Jon returned to the kitchen. As he started loading the dishwasher, he replayed the conversation in his mind. Something about Margaret's answer and Elizabeth's gesture suggested there was more to the story. He brushed it away like crumbs from a tablecloth. He had too many real worries without imagining a problem with Margaret.

By the time Jon returned to the dining room with two pieces of pie, the women had finished their soup. "Lunch is on the house today." He placed the desserts in front of them and waved away their thanks.

Later, Jon stood behind the counter as Margaret and Elizabeth left. Margaret's hand was tucked in Elizabeth's arm, and she appeared much older than she did when bustling around the kitchen. Just looking more her age, Jon told himself. Maisy trotted up behind the women, but Margaret merely gave her a pat and continued to the car.

Jon's phone rang, and he glanced at the caller ID. "Hello, Paul."

"Well, now, I owe you an apology. I got the message to call you this mornin' but I been workin' on puttin' in a new window for an elderly lady. We needed to get that done. You say there's a water spot?"

"On the ceiling of my office upstairs. Should a new roof be leaking?"

"Probly just a vent that weren't sealed properly. We can fix that up in a jiffy. I'll drive out an' take a look at it. Okay to come now?"

Jon looked at the clock and tensed. "Sure, but I only have a little time between lunch and dinner." He dropped the phone in his pocket and hurried out to the kitchen to start preparations for supper.

Less than fifteen minutes later, Paul's Ford rattled into the parking lot. Maisy greeted him, her deep bark echoing off the bluff. Jon dried his hands and walked to the door. Maisy came in first, tail waving and feet prancing.

Upstairs, Jon showed Paul the stain. "I didn't think this would happen with a new roof."

Paul squinted up at it. "Hmm. Umm-hmm." He nodded. He seemed to be carrying on an entire conversation without words. "That there's where a vent is. Roofer didn't seal around it good enough. I got some tar in the truck. I'll get up there and fix that right up for you. May need to touch up the paint there on the ceiling." He reached in one deep overall pocket, pulled out a piece of taffy and popped it in his mouth. "You go on and get supper fixed for yer customers. Don'tcha worry 'bout this little spot."

Maisy followed Paul back outside and Jon returned to the kitchen. His frustration built as he mentally calculated more construction costs. When he dropped the first basket of chicken into the fryer, the hot oil spattered on his hand. He bit off an expletive when he heard the front door open. He ran cold water over the burn, wiped his hands, and stepped out in the dining room.

Paul stood on the rug by the counter. "Got your vent all tarred up. I'll come back later and cover that spot on your ceiling."

"Nothing has gone right on this place!" Jon's angry outburst must have surprised Paul. He stepped back as if he was afraid Jon might take a swing at him.

Paul's arm swept out at the dining room. "I think you got it lookin' right spiffy. A lil leak around a vent ain't nothin' to blow a gasket over. That's pretty common."

"It's not just the leak. I'm barely covering expenses, I've got problems with my staff, Maple Festival is coming up … I'd hoped this would be a less stressful place."

Paul patted his chest. "Maybe the stress is comin' from in here, not from River's Edge."

Jon huffed out his breath. "Yeah. The stress is inside all right. But this place," he took in the updated house and lawn beyond, "is the cause of it. What do I owe you for today?" He needed to get ready for the dinner crowd.

Paul waved his hand as if he was brushing away a pesky fly. "No charge for this. I just fixed up somethin' not done right to start with. I think, if you don't mind, I'll just sit out on the porch till you got some of that chicken fried up, and have me an early supper."

"Sure, Paul. But it'll be about forty-five minutes."

"No problem. I can enjoy the view God's put in your front yard." Paul settled himself in one of the wicker chairs facing the trail and river.

When Bethany arrived a little after four, Jon told her she could invite Paul in and seat him.

Later, as he greeted people in the packed dining room, he saw Paul at the corner table with a plate of half-eaten fried chicken. Jon walked over. "Your dinner is on the house. It's the least I can do."

"No need to. I'd be glad to pay for my supper." Paul wiped his chin with his napkin. "You make that chicken just like my momma did."

"Thanks. My wife's grandma taught me how to fry chicken." A memory surfaced. Angie and him frying chicken with her grandmother, laughing. Angie with a spot of flour on her nose, and he'd kissed it off. The pain sliced through him like a knife.

Paul pushed his plate back and leaned across the table. "Healin' don't come from a place, Jon. Only God can heal us. I been prayin' for you."

Jon nodded. How did he respond? Healing hadn't come from following Angie's dream, and he certainly wasn't counting on healing from a God who'd taken the love of his life from him.

"Hope you enjoyed your dinner." Jon turned to the next table.

Chapter 28

JON THUMPED DOWN the stairs with Maisy bouncing at his heels. She swooshed around him and stood at the back door. When he opened it, she shot out, chasing some invisible critter.

He made coffee and sipped it as he stood on the back deck. After a few moments he rubbed his bare arms. It wouldn't be long before he would need to dig out his sweatshirts and jackets.

Where was Maisy? She usually came back soon, ready for breakfast. Tiger meowed, and he bent to pet her. Still no sign of Maisy. He stepped inside and filled the cat's dish with food. He put it down on the deck and peered around the yard. Maybe she'd really seen something. Probably a squirrel she'd chased up a tree.

"Maisy! Maisy, you big yellow mutt, where are you?" His bare feet were getting cold. He stepped inside and went upstairs to dress for his run. When he came down, Maisy still hadn't returned.

A little seed of worry sprouted in his mind. Was she hurt? Did her collar catch on some brush? "Maisy," he called again. Just then, from far off in the brush on the bluff, he heard a sharp yelp.

He smelled her before he saw her. When Maisy emerged from the trees behind the house, she rolled on the grass. Then she pawed at her face. But no amount of rolling and pawing was going to eliminate the odor that preceded her. Maisy had met a skunk.

As Maisy caught sight of him and bounded across the yard, Jon retreated in the house and closed the door. He grabbed her bowl of dog food and, covering his nose, he shoved it out on the deck. As she ate, he changed into some old, paint-stained clothes. Then he grabbed a bottle of the strongest smelling shampoo he had and took it outside. Gagging, he used the hose, wet her down and poured on the shampoo. He held her collar with one hand and lathered her up with the other, working the soap down to her skin. Then he turned the nozzle of the hose and sprayed her thoroughly. But the scent of skunk remained. The bath hadn't even lessened it. He rinsed his hands with the hose and wiped them on the old towels he'd brought out.

What did he do now? He couldn't leave a smelly dog outside to greet people, and he couldn't let her in. The odor would drift down the stairs and drive away anyone who wanted to eat.

He pulled out his phone and scrolled until he found the number for Furry Friends. When someone answered, he asked, "Could I speak with Kirsten Danielson? Or if she is busy, could she call me back? Quickly? It's kind of an emergency with my dog."

The calm voice on the other end asked him to hold while she checked. And within a few moments he heard her cheerful voice, "This is Kirsten. How may I help you?"

"This is Jon out at River's Edge. I have a bit of a problem with Maisy. She found a skunk this morning, and the restaurant is due to open in less than three hours. Is there anything I can do to diminish the odor?"

He thought he heard Kirsten chuckle, but when she spoke

her voice was sympathetic. "You can use tomato juice, or baking soda, or vinegar. All those help. If you want to pay for it, you could bring her in here, and we'll bathe her for you."

Jon sighed with relief. "Oh, would you? I just don't have time to mess with it. And paying Furry Friends for a bath would be cheaper than closing the restaurant. I'll bring her right in."

Jon called Maisy who acted delighted to go for a ride in the truck. He laid down a towel to protect the seat from the wet, smelly dog, and shoed her into the back seat. As she danced from one window to the other, her feet pushed the towel to the floor. Jon pulled his tee shirt up over his nose and drove as fast as the speed limit would allow.

At Furry Friends, Kirsten met him outside. "Good morning. I thought it would be best to take her in the back."

Jon suddenly realized he was in the stained and faded clothes he'd put on to bathe Maisy. And he looked like he was the one who had gotten a bath with the hose. Why was he always a mess when he saw this woman?

Maisy, recognizing Kirsten, nearly pulled the leash out of his hand. They followed Kirsten around the corner of the building and into the back door.

"Thanks again," Jon said as he handed Kirsten the leash. "Can I pick her up after one? Will she be done?"

"Yes." Kirsten blinked her eyes. The smell must be getting to her, too. "Now, you understand there may be a lingering odor. We can't eliminate it completely. But at least you should be able to have her in the house with you."

"Great. That's all I need."

"Elizabeth, I have a nasty job for you," she called. Jon saw Margaret's friend come into the back room and immediately cover her nose. He backed out, closed the door behind him, and retreated to his truck.

At ten-thirty his phone rang. "River's Edge. This is Jon," he answered without looking at the caller ID.

"Jon, this is Kirsten. Maisy has had her bath and she smells much better. She's still a little wet, though, and I think she'll smell even better when she dries. Why don't you just leave her here, and I'll bring her out to you after Josiah is out of school? That way he has a chance to see her."

Jon held the phone with his shoulder as he chopped vegetables in a bowl. "You sure? I don't want to impose."

"I'm sure. We can take her for a walk on the trail, and then bring her in the back door and put her upstairs for you. Josiah would love it. Ever since we rode out on our bikes, Josiah has been begging to come out and see Maisy."

"Okay. We'll see you later then. How much is it for the bath? I'll have a check ready for you."

Kirsten named the amount, and he wrote it on the tablet by the register. Then he wrote a check and laid it under the piece of rose quartz he used for a paperweight.

When he returned to the kitchen, Margaret's cell phone was buzzing in her purse. "Do you need to answer that?" he asked.

"Oh, I hate that thing buzzing at me all the time." Margaret wiped her hands on a towel and pulled her phone out. "Hello."

"Today? ... I'm finished here about two."

"If you need to go earlier, it will be fine. I can manage without you." Jon couldn't help overhearing Margaret's part of the conversation, as she was standing right next to him. Margaret waved the towel at him.

"Okay, I'll be there by two-thirty." She fumbled with the button to turn off the phone and dropped it back in her purse. "I don't need to go early. My doctor just wants to go over the results of the test I had Monday. I'm sure she'll tell me I'm fine. I've been feeling much better."

Jon paused a moment, studying her face, before pulling a sheet of freshly baked rolls from the oven. She didn't seem to be concerned, so he wouldn't worry either. He placed the sheet on the rack to cool and put a second one in to bake.

The steady stream of lunch customers kept both Jon and Margaret busy until one-thirty. Two young women in biking gear left, and the dining room was empty. As Jon closed the cash register, Margaret sank into a chair and fanned herself with a towel.

Jon stopped by the table. "Can I bring you a bowl of soup?"

"Is there any ham and bean left?"

"Yeah. Most people think it's still not cold enough for soup. Just sit, and I'll bring it to you."

He filled a bowl with soup, made a roast beef sandwich for himself, and carried both out to the table.

"Thanks, Jon." Her silver head bowed briefly over the bowl, and he knew she was praying. He waited until she was finished before biting into his sandwich.

"Where's Maisy?"

They'd both been so busy he hadn't even told her about the morning escapade. When he finished the story, they were both laughing.

Margaret wiped tears from her eyes with a napkin. "Poor Elizabeth. I bet she wishes she'd taken today off instead of yesterday."

"I'm just grateful Kirsten offered to bring her home. I don't think I would get that kind of service from a vet in the cities."

"No, you wouldn't. There are advantages to living in Maple Grove. Of course, she may just want to see you." Margaret's eyes sparkled as she looked at him.

"Are you kidding? I'm a crusty old bachelor," Jon responded, but his heart wondered at her comment. Why would Kirsten be interested in someone so consumed with grief?

Jon swallowed the bite of sandwich he was chewing. "So, do I need to hire someone for the Maple Festival?"

Margaret's head jerked up. "Why? I'll be here."

"I'm counting on you. And Bethany can do both shifts on Saturday. But do I need to hire additional help?"

Margaret frowned. "I guess it wouldn't hurt to have someone extra. Do you have anyone in mind?"

"No. I was kind of hoping you knew someone."

She shook her head. "No. Not right off." She ate a spoonful of soup and then laid her spoon back in the bowl. "Wait a minute. Mary Beth Edwards shared in prayer group that her grandson just moved back to Maple Grove. He's looking for a job. I don't know a lot about him. I think he gave his parents some trouble, but you could say that about a lot of teenagers. His name is Carlton. He's staying with Mary Beth. Would you like me to ask her?"

"Sure. It would just be temporary for the Maple Festival, although if we get busier on the weekends, I could use a part time cook. But I don't want someone who's a troublemaker. If you think he's straightened his life out and that he would be an asset to River's Edge, have him stop by and I'll interview him."

"I'll call her as soon as I get home." Margaret looked at her watch. "Oh my. I better get going. And we haven't run the pots and pans through the dishwasher."

"I'll get the dishes. Just go."

He stacked the dishes, watching her as she stepped off the porch and crossed the yard. He hoped her doctor would have good news for her.

Chapter 29

"READY TO GO home?" Kirsten asked.

Maisy stood in the cage, her tail thumping against the wire. Kirsten opened the door and fastened the leash to her collar. Maisy stepped out, stretched and shook, then trotted down the hall as if she were in charge.

In the parking lot, Kirsten opened the back end of the Highlander, and Maisy leaped in the cargo area. When Kirsten pulled up to her dad's, Josiah waited outside. He hurtled toward the car, skidding to a stop just before hitting the side door.

"Can I ride in back with Maisy, please?" He opened the door and tossed in his backpack. Maisy leaned over the seat, her tongue aimed for his cheek.

"Not in the way back." Kirsten kept her voice even and hoped for compliance. "You have to wear a seatbelt."

"I'll just sit in the back seat, then." Josiah climbed in, and Maisy's tongue found its target. "Hello, girl." He ruffled the fur around her neck. "She smells funny, Mom."

Kirsten waited until she heard the click of his seatbelt before backing the car out. "She had a run-in with a skunk this morning. That's why she was at Furry Friends. We gave her a bath."

"She still smells." Josiah's left arm was around Maisy's neck, holding her close to him.

"Yeah, well, I guess you smell sometimes after you've been biking and haven't taken a shower." Kirsten teased, watching in the mirror to see Josiah's reaction. His tendency to take everything literally made joking risky.

But today he grinned. "I do, don't I? How long do we get to stay at River's Edge? Can we eat there?"

"We won't stay long. You have homework, and I need to do laundry. We can take Maisy for a walk down the trail, then we'll put her inside and go. I have stuff for tacos at home."

"Aww, Mom." Josiah whined, but when Maisy poked her nose at his arm, he quieted and scratched her ears. "Do you think she smells bad to herself? A dog's sense of smell is over 10,000 times better than ours, you know."

"No, I did not know that." Kirsten smiled, relishing her son's good mood and the conversation.

The lot at River's Edge was already half-full. Kirsten parked, and Josiah jumped out and opened the back end. He grabbed Maisy's leash. "Come on," he shouted. The Lab needed no encouragement. She bounded out and raced toward the trail, Josiah close behind. Kirsten followed at a more leisurely pace, counting on Maisy's need to stop and smell everything to keep them from getting too far ahead.

The lingering warmth of the afternoon sun still wrapped the trail. Fall wildflowers, spikey goldenrod and bright purple asters, embroidered the ditches. Colored leaves drifted to the trail and lay like floral offerings to a performer. Kirsten closed her eyes for a moment and breathed in the fragrance of Missouri's final fling before cold weather.

She opened them when she heard her son's giggle. He was

flying along at the end of the leash. When Maisy skidded to a stop and buried her nose in a large clump of grass, Josiah almost flew past, but at the last moment, caught himself and plunked down beside Maisy, laughing the whole time.

Kirsten jogged up to them. "What do you think Maisy smells?"

Josiah sniffed the air. "I don't know. Her sense of smell is 10,000 times more powerful than mine, remember?" He patted the broad yellow back, and Maisy's tail wagged. Then he scrambled to his feet and tugged on the leash. "Come on, girl, let's go."

"Stop at the bridge." She called to Josiah. They streaked off down the trail. and Kirsten followed more slowly, feeling the pressures of the day slipping away from her shoulders, just as surely as if she'd tossed them into Cadence River and the current carried them away.

At the bridge Josiah tossed sticks in the water on one side, then he and Maisy dashed to watch them come out the other. Josiah looked up and grinned. "Look, Mom, Maisy's playing Pooh Sticks with me. Only I have to throw her stick in for her."

Kirsten leaned against the iron railing and watched. She wished they didn't need to turn back and she could just hold on to this afternoon. An everyday moment with her son. A time that he was just happy. A flock of geese flew overhead, honking steadily as they moved south.

Kirsten sighed. "We need to turn back, son. I bet Maisy's getting hungry."

"Just one more stick?"

"One more set of sticks. I'll throw Maisy's for her." They stood pressed against the railing and counted, "One, two, three." Then they dropped the sticks and hurried to the other side to watch them bob down the river. Maisy's stick, the one Kirsten had thrown, was in the lead.

She used her best race announcer voice. "Here they come. And Maisy's stick is leading by a nose. Ooops. Here comes Josiah's stick, edging her out. And … it looks like Josiah is the winner."

Josiah leaped around the bridge shouting. "I'm the winner."

When Kirsten started back toward River's Edge, Josiah and Maisy followed, weaving from side to side, sometimes running ahead, sometimes lagging behind. But when they got to the path leading from the trail to the restaurant, Josiah walked next to his mom with Maisy close beside.

"Thanks, Mom, for bringing me out here." He actually made eye contact without her asking for it. His eyes shone.

"We'll ask Mr. Washington if we can do it again. We don't have to wait until Maisy gets skunked." Kirsten led them around to the back door. "Now remember, people are eating dinner here."

"I know." Josiah repeated what she'd already told him. "We go in quietly, put Maisy upstairs, and leave."

Upstairs, Josiah removed the leash, gave Maisy a last pat, and closed the gate. He didn't say a word, just followed Kirsten downstairs. If only his teachers could see him now. As they tiptoed back down the stairs, Jon stepped out from behind the cash register counter and met them in the hall.

He handed her the check made out to Furry Friends. "Thank you so much. I owe you big time. Can I treat you to dinner?"

"No dinner, Josiah has homework. And I got all the thanks I needed watching him and Maisy on the trail. But, keep her away from skunks, okay?"

Jon chuckled. "I've never had kids, but I think Maisy may be a little bit like one. She doesn't always do what I say. I hope she learned her lesson."

Another group walked in the door. "Gotta go." Jon's smile made her insides flip around in a way they hadn't for a long time. What was it about this man? She scolded herself as she shooed Josiah out the back door.

Kirsten waited until they were buckled in the car. "Thanks for doing exactly as you were told, Josiah. You were very responsible tonight. I think we'll order a pizza. We can have the tacos tomorrow night. Can you get your homework done while we wait for it?"

"Yes." Josiah's eyes stared out the window.

"What do you have to do?"

"Just spelling."

"Don't you need to work on your report for social studies?"

"I'm not doing a report. I'm back with the slow kids, and I don't have to do a report on Wisconsin, and all we have to do is listen to Ms. Hardenbrook read the book. That's all."

Kirsten's heart sank. Not only was he back in the special education room, he was getting watered-down curriculum and lowered expectations.

The joy of the afternoon ran smack into the realities of Asperger's, and her pain and frustration returned.

Chapter 30

THE PAINTING DREW Margaret into the scene. It must be a Thomas Kinkade, the "painter of light." A small chapel nestled among the pines. Mountains towered in the background. Just outside the chapel door, a sparkling stream flowed. Margaret could almost hear the water as it gurgled over the rocks. The windows of the church glowed with a warm, ethereal light. She imagined the strains of "Amazing Grace" floating out on the mountain air.

When the door of the small room opened and Dr. Nancy stepped in, Margaret let out a startled, "Oh."

"What, you were expecting Dr. Oz?" Dr. Nancy teased.

"No, I was just enjoying the painting. It's a Thomas Kinkade, isn't it?"

"Yes. I picked it up at an auction last summer for a fraction of what it's worth. I thought it would be perfect for this room."

Margaret sighed. "It is. I'd like to be there." She pointed at the chapel. "I just know they're singing 'Amazing Grace' inside."

Dr. Nancy gazed at the painting for a moment. "I bet they are." A small frown worked its way across her forehead as she sat on the stainless-steel stool by the exam table. "I wish I had better news for you, Margaret."

Margaret clutched her hands together in her lap. "I trust you. And more important, I trust God."

"The results of your biopsy show the lump that you felt in your left breast is cancer."

"Oh." Margaret's hand touched her breast briefly as if it could somehow verify the news.

"I've scheduled a CAT scan for Monday morning. We need to see what we are dealing with as soon as possible. We'll scan your head, chest, abdomen—checking for metastatic disease—to see if the cancer has spread to any other areas of your body. That information will guide us in making a treatment plan for you."

Margaret felt the walls of the small room closing in. She nodded at Doctor Nancy and forced herself to focus and listen as she went on.

"We don't want to delay treatment." She handed Margaret a piece of paper. "This is the name of a surgical oncologist. I want you to call this afternoon and make an appointment with him. He'll probably want to schedule a surgery to remove the lump, or maybe even the entire breast." She paused and cleared her throat. "This is a lot to take in, isn't it?"

"Oh." Margaret said again. She couldn't think clearly.

Dr. Nancy's eyes were warm and compassionate. "What questions do you have?"

Margaret rubbed her forehead. "I just thought—I thought it was nothing. Just a little lump. Are you sure?"

"I'm sure." Dr. Nancy's voice was almost stern.

"I guess I'd better have that scan, then. Monday morning you say?"

Dr. Nancy rattled off a list of instructions. Margaret's brain, still fuzzy from the news, didn't register most of it. But she knew she'd get a detailed written list. Dr. Nancy was thorough. How could she work pie-baking into her weekend, since she'd be at the hospital early Monday morning?

"And I want you here Tuesday afternoon so we can go over the results and plan your treatment."

Margaret tuned in for the final statement. A treatment plan. A few rounds of chemotherapy, maybe even losing her hair, not feeling well for a couple weeks, and then she'd be back to normal.

⁓⁓

Jon heard Maisy's greeting bark and glanced at the kitchen clock, a cutesy little design with a teapot that Margaret had brought to River's Edge the first week. It was too early yet for any of the dinner customers. He rinsed off his hands and dried them on his apron.

A young man stepped out of a rusty Jeep and walked up to the porch. He wore baggy shorts and a black tee shirt with *Metallica* across the front. Jon opened the door to tell him that they weren't open until four-thirty, when the man stuck out an arm so covered with tattoos that it looked like he was wearing a strangely-patterned long-sleeved shirt.

"I'm Carlton Edwards. Came to apply for the job."

It took a few seconds before Jon remembered that was the name of Margaret's friend's grandson. "Come on in. I'm getting ready for lunch, but you can fill out an application."

Jon liked to think he was open-minded, but a tattooed fan of hard rock was not who he had in mind for a second cook.

"Ever done any cooking?" Jon asked as he stepped behind the counter.

"Yep. I worked two years at a restaurant in Branson. The Lucky Duck. I cooked almost everything—breakfasts, fancy dinners. I ran the grill, too."

Jon pulled out an application form and a pen and handed them to Carlton. It didn't sound like he could just say, "Sorry, you don't have the experience." As a matter of fact, that was exactly the kind of experience that would be helpful here at River's Edge.

"This would be part time. I need someone during the Maple Festival. After that, it really depends on how busy we are." A young man would want a full-time job, wouldn't he?

"That would be great. In January, I'll be starting classes at the community college. First time in college. I went to work right after high school. So, I'm looking for something I can schedule around classes. And I don't need a full-time job. I don't have a lot of expenses. I'm living with my grandma, so that helps."

Jon looked for another reason to not hire the man. "Why did you leave your job in Branson?"

Carlton's gaze was level and direct. "My grandma needed help. I didn't trust my mom to look after her. Mom's an alcoholic. When she's been drinking, she doesn't always do what she says she'll do."

Jon nodded thoughtfully. "I need to get back to the kitchen. Just holler at me when you've finished filling that out." He backed through the swinging doors. He did the prep work for salads, but his mind was racing. What if Carlton was the only one who applied? What would Margaret say if he told her that her friend's grandson applied and he didn't hire him?

One side of the door swung inward. "Mr. Washington? I'm finished."

Jon couldn't fault Carlton's manners. He scanned the neatly written application, complete with detailed work history and references. "Thanks, Carlton. I'll be in touch. I put an ad in the

Maple Courier, and I want to give it a few days before I make a decision."

Carlton moved backward as Jon stepped through the door and went to the counter to file the application. Then he just stood, looking like a small boy who had expected candy and gotten a pencil. "Uh, Mr. Washington. I know I look like a hoodlum." He held out his arms. "I got all tatted when I first left home. I can clean up and wear long-sleeved shirts and look respectable. I'm a hard worker…" his voice trailed off.

"I appreciate knowing that, Carlton. I'll let you know."

When Carlton stepped outside, Maisy bounded up to him, her tail wagging frantically. He dropped to one knee and ruffled the fur on her neck. She leaned into him, obviously relishing the attention.

Jon sighed. Even his dog loved Carlton. Maybe he could work with a tattooed cook.

Chapter 31

BETHANY ROLLED OVER and looked at her alarm clock. Seventen. The one morning she could sleep in, and she was wide awake.

Light filtered in behind the lime green and purple curtains she'd bought with her own money. When she'd started middle school, she'd begged her mom to replace the Strawberry Shortcake bedroom theme. Her mom kept putting it off, so Bethany went shopping by herself and bought a comforter and curtains with Christmas money from Aunt Marie and Uncle Pete.

She pushed back the curtain and watched the morning sun light up the red maple in the front yard. Heavy dew sparkled like a field of precious gems. She flopped back to her pillow. Her mom had gone out with friends last night and wouldn't be up for hours.

She laid a hand on her midsection, thinking of what was happening inside. A baby, growing. Two weeks from Monday she had an appointment at the clinic. She would no longer be pregnant. No more throwing up. No more keeping secrets. No more worrying about college, or supporting a child, or being tied down. Since the baby would be gone, she wouldn't even need to tell Kyle anything—ever.

She slipped out from under her comforter, pulled a sweatshirt over her head, and padded out to the kitchen. She grabbed a Sprite from the fridge and opened it. She'd read an article on the internet that said caffeine wasn't good for babies, so she'd switched from her favorite drink, Mountain Dew.

She pushed open the back door and stepped outside. The temperature had dropped over night, and even though the sun's rays were warm, her toes curled in the chilly grass. Somewhere, church bells chimed, the melody floating overhead. She knew the tune, "Amazing Grace". She'd learned it in fourth grade when she went with a friend to Awana. It almost seemed like the bells were calling to her.

She turned and nearly skipped into the house. She used her phone to check on the times of the worship services at Maple Grove Fellowship, the church where she'd attended as a child. Her jeans didn't button all the way up, but they were clean, and the pink top she put on would cover the gap. She wrote a note to her mom and left it on the kitchen table.

When she pedaled her bike into the parking lot, she saw an old rack by the building, but it looked like she was the only one who rode a bike to church. Maybe this wasn't such a good idea. Maybe these people didn't want a pregnant teen-age girl here. Maybe she was supposed to wear a dress to church.

An old blue Buick slowly swiveled into a parking spot. Margaret, the baker from River's Edge, waved and smiled at her. She couldn't leave now. She slipped her bike in between the bars.

The door of the Buick opened and Margaret stepped out. "Bethany, welcome to Fellowship. Did you bike here?" She reached out and drew Bethany in for a warm hug. "Come on, you can sit with me."

Bethany followed Margaret into the large brick complex. People clustered in small groups, talking and laughing. She saw a few friends from school and waved a tentative hand in response to their greetings. A man with a nametag handed her a folded paper.

"Hello, Josh. How's the family?" Margaret beamed at the man before leading the way into the auditorium.

As they settled in comfortable theatre-type seats, Bethany's stomach fluttered. She tried on a few excuses for leaving, but none seemed to fit. And Margaret was sitting in the aisle seat and greeting everyone who walked by.

Margaret turned to her. "So, have you come here before, or is this your first time?"

"I went to Awana when I was a kid. And my mom and I came on Sundays for a while. But that was a few years ago. I usually sleep in on Sunday mornings, but I woke up early today. I really don't know why I'm here."

Margaret nodded. Her eyes looked wise behind the thick lenses of her glasses. It was as if she was privy to some information that Bethany wasn't. "I think you'll enjoy the service. We have a lot of young people." She chuckled. "People your age outnumber the people my age. And maybe you'll find the answer to why you're here."

A group of musicians filed onto the stage and began to play and sing. Bethany's foot tapped to the rhythm. Not the dreary hymns she remembered. She stood with the congregation and joined in the song.

When the pastor stood up to preach, Bethany looked around the auditorium and planned to zone out, the way she sometimes did in one of her classes. A scripture verse flashed up on the screen behind him, one she vaguely remembered memorizing in

Awana, Jeremiah 29:11. *For I know the plans I have for you, plans to give you a hope and a future.*

Bethany leaned forward. Suddenly the words had meaning. Did God have a purpose and a plan for *her* life? The pastor paced across the stage, using more verses and illustrations, showing again and again how God had a purpose and plan for everyone. As she listened, Bethany's hand rested once more on her midsection.

Did that mean God had a plan and purpose for the baby? But if it was aborted…

When the congregation stood for the last song, Bethany remained seated, fighting to keep the tears filling her eyes from spilling over.

Then, as she rose to her feet, she was filled with a sense of urgency. She needed to get home, she had to tell her mom the appointment must be cancelled.

"Thanks for sitting with me." Bethany squeezed past Margaret and wove her way through the thicket of people to the door. When she reached her bicycle, she pedaled home without stopping.

Her mom sat at the kitchen table in her pajamas, her long fingers wrapped around a cup of coffee. She raised her eyes, still hooded with sleep. "You went to church? What brought that on?"

"It was such a pretty morning. I heard church bells playing. And I just went." Bethany sat in the chair opposite her mom and reached for a Cutie. She peeled it slowly, spiraling around the fruit so the peel fell off in a single piece. She separated one segment and popped it in her mouth.

Bethany took a deep breath. "I decided I'm not going to that appointment in Kansas City."

Her mom frowned. "You decided not to go? What are you talking about? We don't have very long to get this taken care of."

Bethany's eyes filled with tears. "The pastor was talking—how God has plans for us—What if he has plans for this baby? Maybe she—or he—will discover a cure for cancer." The words tumbled out around the sobs.

Her mother's face hardened. "It's not really a baby yet, not till it's born. Focus on you, Bethany. Your plans. You're not ready to be a mom. And you're not going to throw your life away. Not if I have anything to say about it. You will go to that appointment—if I have to drag you there." Her last words were punctuated with a pointing index finger. Then she marched into her bedroom, slamming the door behind her.

Chapter 32

THE MONDAY MORNING before Maple Festival, Jon still had only one application for the part-time cooking job. Reluctantly, he called the number Carlton had written on his application.

"Carlton? This is Jon Washington at River's Edge. If you're still interested in the position, could you come in today for some on-the-job training? … Great. How about 11:00 until we close about 9:00?" Jon ended the call and began sketching out a work schedule for the next week, trying to estimate peak times.

Margaret had phoned early this morning to tell him she was having "a small procedure" at the hospital and might be a little late. "I have the pies all made, though," she assured him. He liked the sound of a small procedure. Something that could easily be fixed.

He pulled out vegetables and began to prepare salads.

The front door opened. "Margaret?" When there was no answer, he pushed through the swinging doors into the dining room. Margaret sat in one of the chairs close to the door. She'd let Maisy in. The Lab sat as close to her as she could possibly get. Margaret's arms were wrapped around the dog and her cheek lay against the golden fur on her head. Jon felt as if he'd stumbled into the middle of an intimate moment. Maisy looked at him, but she didn't twitch a muscle to move in his direction.

After a few moments, Margaret sat up and wiped a hand across one cheek. "Oh, hi, Jon. I didn't hear you come in. I was just giving Maisy here a little loving. She says you've been neglecting her."

Jon grimaced. "It's either neglect her or neglect my customers. And my customers pay the bills."

Margaret leaned on the table as she rose to her feet. She looked pale and drawn.

"If you need to go home and rest after your, umm, appointment this morning, you go ahead. I can handle things okay." Jon looked around. "You did bring pies, though, didn't you?"

Margaret chuckled softly. "You think I would come without them? I thought maybe you'd get them out of the car and carry them in. It's unlocked."

"Sure." Jon hurried out to the Buick. He stacked and balanced containers on top of each other and managed to carry all of them in one trip.

Margaret seemed to perk up a bit when she got into the kitchen. She and Jon swung into their familiar routine of lunch preparation.

"I hired Carlton." Jon stirred the potato soup simmering in the big pot on the stove.

"Mary Beth's grandson? Great. That's an answer to prayer." Margaret exclaimed.

Jon stifled a snort. How could anyone think that hiring Carlton to help at Maple Festival was somehow God's doing? God didn't care what happened to him or Carlton. And he wasn't sure the tattooed man could be an answer to anything.

Maisy barked a greeting and the front door squeaked open.

Carlton had arrived. He was dressed in black pants and a long-sleeved, white, button-down shirt. He looked as if he were ready to serve at a formal banquet. Jon's khakis and polo shirt suddenly seemed casual.

Carlton eased the door shut behind him. "Hope this is okay." He indicated his shirt and pants. "I don't have a lot of clothes. I got these when I waited tables at The Lucky Duck."

"It will work. Come on back to the kitchen and I'll let your grandma's friend, Margaret, show you the ropes."

Carlton followed Jon to the kitchen where Margaret was shelving the pie she'd just cut. She put down the pie cutter, wiped her hands on the flowered apron, and gave Carlton a quick hug. "Carlton, look at you. You grew up when I wasn't looking. I bet everyone is glad to have you back in Maple Grove."

He ducked his head, and a fine red color spread up his neck. "Hi, Mrs. Hanson. Yeah. At least Grandma's glad I'm here."

The buzzer on the front door sounded. "Margaret, would you show Carlton how we do sandwiches? We'll let him get his feet wet right away." Then he stepped through the swinging doors into the dining room to greet the first lunch customers.

After the lunch rush was over and Margaret left, Jon continued to give Carlton a crash orientation. Although his main duties would be cooking, Jon wanted him to know how to run the cash register, wait tables, and even take Maisy out if necessary. He didn't have the luxury of hiring people for single duties. Carlton, polite and respectful, listened as Jon explained things. Then he did whatever was asked. Jon began to feel more comfortable with his new hire.

When Bethany arrived, she hung up her bag and glanced at Carlton chopping vegetables.

Jon turned from the sink. "Bethany, this is Carlton. And

Carlton, meet Bethany, the best waitress in Maple Grove."

Bethany nodded and her ponytail bounced. "You went to school here didn't you? You were a couple years ahead of me, I think. What year did you graduate?"

Carlton concentrated on the vegetables he was chopping. "I didn't. I got my GED last month." He shot a look at Jon. "I took off just a few months before graduation."

Bethany washed her hands and began rolling silverware into the napkins. "At least you got your GED. That's good."

"Yep. And I'm starting classes at the community college in January. I'm taking hospitality-business. Maybe someday I'll have my own restaurant like Jon."

Jon left them and went out to the counter in the dining room. The two of them appeared to get along okay. He didn't want to worry about personnel issues during the busy weekend. He opened the door and escorted Maisy upstairs. She was used to their routine and never protested being gated. But once the last customer left, she'd poke her nose under the gate and whine softly.

Because of the influx of additional diners during the Maple Festival, Jon anticipated having even less time to spend with her. Maybe he'd call Kirsten and ask her if Josiah wanted to come out and take Maisy for a walk. And maybe she'd stay and have dinner.

As he came back down the stairs, he heard car tires crunching on the rock in the parking lot. Bethany stepped into the dining room. Her order pad was tucked into the pocket of her apron.

"Ready to go?" Jon asked.

She grinned at him. "I better be, right?"

"Right." Jon stepped back in the kitchen. Carlton had pre-made several salads and was checking on the roast in the oven.

This just might work. Jon got the meat slicer out to show him how he wanted the beef cut. And to warn him about the dangers associated with using one.

At a little before 9:00, Jon thanked Carlton for a great first night before the new cook drove away in the battered Jeep.

Jon turned to Bethany. "You better be going, too. Maybe after tonight you could get a ride with Carlton."

"I don't think so, Mr. Washington." She pulled down her bag and slipped her arms in so she could wear it like a backpack. "And unless he's changed, you'd better watch Carlton around the cash register. He wasn't known around town as being the most honest person in the world."

"What?" Jon blurted, but Bethany was already outside wheeling her bike toward the trail.

❧

Tuesday afternoon, Margaret waited again in the small room with the Thomas Kincaide print. She tried to imagine the strains of "Amazing Grace," but today it seemed something sinister lurked in the forest behind the church in the picture. She shivered and pulled her jacket around her shoulders.

A soft knock sounded on the door, and Dr. Nancy entered. When Margaret saw her friend's face, tears filled her eyes. She had to stop denying the facts. "It's not good, is it?"

Dr. Nancy shook her head and sat down in the empty chair. "I don't want you to give up hope. The treatment of cancer has made great advances in recent years. There's a lot we can do. We can fight this. That's the good news. The MRI did show a small tumor in your brain. That indicates that cancer has spread from your breast to other areas. It makes it more difficult, but not unbeatable."

Margaret struggled to keep her tears in check. "Do I need to call Melanie?"

"Yes." Dr. Nancy didn't hesitate. "You're probably going to need some help during treatment. I know the church will be good to help out, but if she can take some time off to be with you, your daughter may be more of a comfort to you. In any event, she needs to know what's going on."

"River's Edge?" Margaret couldn't keep the quiver out of her voice.

"You need to tell Mr. Washington to hire someone else. You're not going to feel like baking pies and waiting tables. And we want your energy focused on healing."

Margaret bit her lip, watching her hands in her lap as if they belonged to someone else. "I want to work through the Maple Festival. That's just a few days. Can I do that?"

"When is your appointment with Dr. Gulling?"

Margaret's brain froze. She never forgot dates or appointments. "I have it written down on my calendar at home. I can't remember for some reason. I think it's next week. Before Maple Festival."

"If you feel up to it, go ahead. But I don't want you to be exhausted going into surgery, either. After the surgery we'll use radiation..."

Margaret tried to listen to Dr. Nancy's detailed plan to attack the cancer, but she couldn't seem to focus on the words. The fog continued as she drove home, blinking back tears.

When she reached the comfort of her little home, she dropped her purse and jacket on the kitchen chair. In the living room, she sat, tucked her legs up into her blue upholstered rocker, and pulled the afghan around her. Then she let the tears come. She might never see her daughter married, or hold a grandchild in her arms, or know if Jon found the healing he sought and if he met the Healer of all. She cried as a child does, noisy wails that drifted at last into hiccupy sobs. And then she slept a little.

She woke with a start, remembered, and tucked the anguish somewhere deep inside. She washed her face in the bathroom, peered at her reddened, swollen eyes and prayed, "Give me the strength to make this the last time I cry over being sick. Lord, I trust you to walk me through this."

Then she walked out in the kitchen and found her phone. She would call Melanie.

Chapter 33

BETHANY DROPPED HER backpack on the floor and flopped down on her bed. She had algebra to finish. She needed to get ready for work. And all she wanted to do was close her eyes and sleep. She tried to get to bed early, but she still felt tired. Maybe it would be a quiet night at River's Edge, and she could leave a little early.

She stood up and went to the bathroom. She shook out her ponytail, combed her hair, and washed her face. As she was drying on the striped towel, she thought she heard the doorbell chime. With a glance in the mirror, she hurried out to the family room and peered through the glass. Kyle stood on the front step.

She fumbled with the lock and opened the wooden door. Then she spoke through the screen of the storm door. "What are you doing here?"

Kyle took a step back, his eyebrows raised. "Hey. I came to see you. It's Maple Festival weekend, so I took off a day early."

"You're skipping your Friday classes?"

Kyle smiled, showing the dimple that always made her heart lurch. "Yeah, you can do that in college and not get in trouble."

He cocked his head. "Are you going to ask me in or leave me standing here on the step all day?"

Bethany opened the door, hoping she wasn't opening her heart again. "I only have about fifteen minutes before I go to work."

Kyle stepped inside, and as he brushed past her, she could smell the musky odor of his cologne. She took a deep breath and tried to calm her racing heart.

Kyle sat on the couch, stretching his long legs out in front of him. "Where are you working?"

"River's Edge. Remember that big old house on the bike trail? It's been turned into a restaurant." She shrugged and picked at a thread on the chair. "I'm just a waitress, but I like Jon. He's the guy that owns it. Do you know Carlton Edwards? I think he was in the class before you. He works there as a cook."

"Carlton? How is he?"

"Okay, I guess." Bethany watched Kyle. He looked comfortable in their slightly shabby family room. Maybe she'd misjudged him. Maybe he was part of The Plan. "Kyle?"

He shifted his legs, leaned forward, and smiled at her. "I've missed you, Bethany. I'm sorry I didn't text or call much. College is a big adjustment. Come sit beside me." He patted the place next to him on the couch.

Warning bells sounded in Bethany's mind. She shook her head. "I really do have to go to work. I can't be late. But, I have to tell you something."

His smile diminished. The house roared with the silence as he waited. She had to tell him. Maybe he would be supportive. Maybe he would help her convince her mom not to go through with the abortion.

"I'm pregnant." She whispered the words and they hovered

like storm clouds on the ceiling.

"Pregnant? Are you sure?"

She nodded, not trusting her voice.

Kyle leaned forward, his legs folding under him, like a collapsible chair. "It's not—it's not mine, is it?"

Bethany nodded again. Her head was bowed and her hair hung down, hiding her face from him.

"How can you be sure?"

"I took a test, an early pregnancy test. They're pretty accurate and—"

"I mean, how can you be sure it's mine?" Kyle's hands pushed on the front of the couch like he was going to stand, but he didn't.

Bethany's head flew up. "Kyle, I've never had sex with anyone but you."

His handsome features creased in a frown. "How long have you known? Why didn't you tell me?"

"What was I supposed to do? Text you? Some things you need to say in person."

Kyle rubbed his head with both hands. "So what are you going to do?"

Bethany glanced at the clock. She needed to leave. She needed to eat a snack so she didn't get sick. Would Jon fire her if she was late?

She stared down at her feet, she couldn't look at him. "Mom wants me to have an abortion."

Kyle leaned back and his legs unfolded again. "Great. That would be the best solution. You don't want to screw up your life."

But what about the baby's life? Wouldn't an abortion screw it up? She shook her head, trying to clear her thoughts, and stood.

"I'm going to be late for work if I don't get going."

Kyle bounced to his feet. "Can I drop you off?"

"Thanks for offering. I ride my bike, though."

"Do you want to hang out this weekend? Maybe we could go to Benson for dinner one night?"

For a moment, she was tempted. It would be fun to act like a regular teenager without The Problem. She sighed. "No, I don't think that's a good idea, Kyle. And I'm going to be working most of the weekend out at River's Edge, anyway. Maple Festival will bring in lots of customers, and I'm the only waitress at dinnertime."

Kyle opened the screen door, stepped outside, then turned back to look at her. "Hey. Let me know when you have that—when you—you know, take care of that."

"Yeah, I will." Bethany closed door after him. After leaning her head against it for a minute, she gathered up her hair in a ponytail, twisted the tie around it, and hurried out to the kitchen to grab something she could eat while riding her bike.

Chapter 34

SATURDAY OF THE Maple Festival opened like a picture post card of autumn in Missouri.

Jon stood on the porch of River's Edge, watching the top of the bluffs light up, the leaves of the maples like flames among the green. The bike trail, winding through the canopy of trees, was covered with fallen leaves that gave a satisfying crunch when the bike tires passed. The river flowed by, shrouded with an early morning mist. The weatherman had forecast summer-like temperatures. Even before sunrise, a few bikers were pedaling toward Benson.

Two large pots of bright-colored mums stood on either side of the steps. Margaret had driven out with them Thursday morning. They would brighten up the yard and draw people in, she said. Maisy trotted up on the porch and stuck her snout deep into one pot.

"Come on, girl, leave the flowers alone. Hopefully, this place will be hopping in a few hours. Let's get some breakfast."

He fed Maisy and Tiger on the back deck, then stepped inside to fix himself a bowl of Cheerios. He stood outside to eat, keeping a close eye as Maisy wandered through the back yard. He didn't need her to get another skunking. Tiger nosed her small dish against the railing of the deck and it clinked softly. Jon dribbled the last of the milk from his cereal into her dish, and she lapped it up greedily. Maisy followed him in and flopped down on her rug in the hall as he went to the kitchen to start preparations. He wished he had an idea how many customers would leave the festivities in town to eat at River's Edge.

Margaret arrived early, probably just wanting to help. But when he looked up, something in her eyes made him pause, and he turned off the meat slicer. "Good morning, Margaret. Are you ready for Maple Festival? Think we'll have a line waiting on the porch?"

She smiled, but her expression didn't reassure him. "I think you'll have enough customers to make it the best Maple Festival you've ever had."

He laughed. "Yeah. It's my first."

"Jon, we need to talk." She set her containers down but continued to hold him in her gaze.

He resisted the urge to flee to the dining room, the back porch, anywhere away from the kind scrutiny of her gray eyes. "Okay. Do I need to sit down?" he asked, thinking he was making a joke.

"You might." Margaret marched through the swinging doors. When Jon stepped into the dining room, she was sitting in her favorite spot by the window, her hands folded on the table. She raised her eyes to meet Jon's. He thought he saw tears, but she blinked and her cheeks remained dry.

He pulled out a chair and sat down slowly. For a moment, neither of them spoke.

Then Margaret cleared her throat. "I haven't been entirely

honest with you. The procedure I had Monday was a full body scan to check for cancer." Her voice quavered and she stopped and swallowed. "I have stage four breast cancer, Jon. My doctor thinks I won't be able to continue working at River's Edge."

He couldn't breathe. For some reason, his brain flashed an image of the night he answered the door expecting to unload his wife's car of groceries, and found a state trooper on the steps. Tears came to his eyes.

"No, no, no," he whispered. The thought of losing Margaret, this woman he'd grown to love as his own mother, his partner in building the restaurant, was too much. "They're going to give you chemo, right? You'll be okay?"

She smiled, a sad, tender smile that tore at his heart. "Yes, I'm going to be okay. But not the way that you think. God may heal me, but he may take me home, too. I will keep on baking pies for you as long as I can. But once I start treatment, I might be too sick." She reached across and laid one soft hand over his. "You're a wonderful young man, Jon. Please don't add this to your list of grudges against God. He'll use my cancer for good."

Jon pulled his hand out from under hers with a disgusted snort. "I'm so sorry, Margaret. But how could cancer ever be used for good?" He used his freed hand to brush across his eyes. "Don't worry about pies. I'll figure something out. Do you need to go home now?"

Margaret stood up and pushed the chair back to the table. "Absolutely not. We have a Maple Festival crowd to serve. I feel fine today."

Jon pushed his chair in, too, but stood for a moment looking out across the lawn, littered with falling leaves. After he'd gotten his emotions under control, he followed Margaret back to the kitchen.

At ten, Jon put Maisy upstairs for the day. Before hurrying back downstairs, he sat for a moment, petting her golden back and calming his soul. He didn't have a lot of time to spend with Maisy, but sometimes she seemed like the only reason he had to keep going.

Carlton arrived on time and immediately pitched in. When the chimes on the front door signaled the first customer, they were ready. Jon went through the motions. He pasted a bright smile on his face, greeted all the diners, served meals, and rang up bills, but it almost felt like he was watching himself do it. Every time he passed Margaret in the kitchen or watched her clear a table, a pang of sorrow stabbed through the numbness. As the crowd thinned, he cleared two tables and carried the dishes to the kitchen.

"We're through the rush. Go on home now and rest," he told her.

Margaret pushed back a strand of gray hair from her forehead. She looked weary. "You'll be okay through the dinner hour?"

"Carlton's here, and Bethany is coming. We're good. You go on, now." Jon made a little shooing motion.

Margaret picked up her purse and started toward the back door. "I'll bring pies on Monday."

"Not necessary," Jon called out as she opened the door. "You just take care of yourself. I'll provide desserts from now on."

"Thank you." Margaret slipped out and closed the door behind her.

Jon pushed through the swinging doors into the dining room to greet customers.

≈

Kirsten slipped the headphones over her son's head. They would deaden sounds and make it possible for him to watch the parade.

Although they'd moved to Maple Grove more than two years ago, this was the first Maple Festival they'd attended. Crowds, loud noises, and junk food set up an impossible situation for controlling Josiah. This year he'd begged to go. Kirsten agreed only as long as he wore the headphones and worked hard at listening to her.

They set up chairs on the lawn in front of Grandpa's house. She hoped her dad's presence would be calming as well. The parade began downtown, then looped through a residential area, down the street past her dad's house, and back where it started. This was an ideal spot. If Josiah couldn't handle it, they could go inside and watch through a window.

The sirens on the fire trucks and police cars announced the parade's approach. Kirsten watched Josiah. He sat upright in the lawn chair, his hands lying limply in his lap. Every so often his right hand would flutter slightly then drop again to rest beside the left. His eyes were focused on the end of the street where the parade would appear at any moment. Her dad sat on the other side of Josiah, visiting with the neighbors sitting to his left.

When the police car leading the parade turned the corner, Josiah stood up, glanced at his mom, and sat back down, both hands fluttering now. He was talking, but she was pretty sure he wasn't making conversation. Probably quoting statistics on dogs or repeating some National Geographic show verbatim.

The police car rolled slowly by and thankfully kept its sirens quiet. Kirsten stood as the flag bearers, members of the local VFW, passed. She touched Josiah's shoulder. He flinched, but looked up at her and when she nodded her head toward the flag, he stood too. Several fire trucks followed, some of them sounding their sirens in short blasts. Josiah jumped every time, but now watched with fascination as one of the firemen stuck his hand out the window and let loose a handful of candy. Children scattered along the edge of the street, scooping up bubble gum, butterscotch drops and cellophane-wrapped packages of Smarties. Josiah glanced over at his mom and Kirsten lifted one corner of the headphones.

"You may pick up candy, but only along the curb. Don't go out into the street where the vehicles are moving." Just as Kirsten finished talking, an ambulance driver aimed a handful of hard candies at Josiah's feet. He scurried around, stuffing the treats into his pockets.

Kirsten smiled at his obvious delight, although she was already dreading the battle of limiting the amount of candy he could eat when they got home.

Next came antique cars, but most of them were not tossing candy. Josiah unwrapped a package of Smarties and popped a few into his mouth. Several pickups moved by filled with soccer and Little League baseball teams. Some of the players had paper sacks with candy.

"Hey, Sarah! Catch this, Aaron!" They searched the crowd for people they knew and aimed candy missiles at them. No one shouted, "Hey, Josiah," even though Josiah had removed his headphones and was jumping up and down and waving his arms. They looked in the opposite direction, as if Josiah were invisible.

Next, tractors rumbled by pulling decorated floats. Most of them had some kind of tissue paper and cardboard version of the town's famous maples, a message or advertisement, and a few smiling and waving people. Josiah waved back to an elderly couple on the Fellowship Church float. They stood under a live maple tree in a huge pot. Letters on the side of the float proclaimed:

"Blessed is the man who does not walk in the counsel of the wicked,
He is like a tree planted by streams of water."
Psalm 1:1 and 3

Last summer, someone had asked if she and Josiah would like to ride on this year's float. She'd declined, not knowing how her son would react in that situation.

When several horses clopped into view, Kirsten knew the parade was almost over. A crew with scoop shovels and garbage cans on wheels brought up the rear.

Josiah had moved the headphones down so they circled his neck. "Can we go downtown, Mom? Can we play some games? Can we eat lunch there?"

Kirsten weighed the possibilities. So far, Josiah had listened to her and maintained self-control. Could she trust him to continue for several hours more?

"We'll go for a while," she decided. "But when I say it's time to go, you have to listen."

"Do I have to wear these stupid headphones?"

"There may be more sirens or loud noise." She warned him.

"I'm okay." His hand fluttered slightly.

Kirsten turned to her dad. "Want to come with us?"

He shook his head. "You go ahead and take the boy. I'd just slow you down. My hip's been flaring up again." He rubbed his side. "Maybe I'll go downtown tonight. I'm going inside and fix me a sandwich. Then maybe I'll take a nap." He stretched out his hand towards Josiah, and then, as if remembering, dropped it to his side. He reached in his pocket and pulled out a five dollar bill. "This is for you to spend on what you want. Eat a corndog for me, okay?"

Josiah stuffed the bill into his pocket and danced around his mom. "Thanks! Let's go, Mom. Grandpa wants me to eat a corndog."

"Or anything else you want." Her dad folded up his chair. "Go on, now; I'll put your chairs up by the house."

Josiah charged down the sidewalk and Kirsten jogged after him. "Josiah, wait for me."

He circled back. "Hurry up, Mom."

The summer bike rides and basketball had built up muscles in his long legs. His face had lost some of the little-boy roundness. He was changing so rapidly. Kirsten stifled her worry over his future. The parade had gone well, she needed to focus on having a good time with her son.

Chapter 35

A YOUNG MAN in a florescent green biking jersey handed Jon his bill for a sandwich and drink.

Jon slid the man's card through the reader. "On your way to Benson, or heading home?"

"Actually, we're visiting from Iowa, staying with my uncle in Maple Grove. I'm training for a ride this fall. I need to get in about thirty more miles today. So, I'll go out on the highway from here."

As Jon handed him the receipt to sign along with his card, the bell on the door sounded, and he looked up with his "hello to customers" smile.

Kirsten and Josiah stepped in. Kirsten wore blue jeans with a teal top that made her green eyes sparkle. She smiled in his direction and he caught his breath. Why had he never noticed how attractive she was? Immediately, guilt flooded over him, almost like he'd cheated on Angie somehow.

"Hello, Josiah and Josiah's mom. Left the excitement in town for River's Edge, huh?"

Kirsten brushed a stray wisp of curly brown hair off her forehead. "Hello, Jon. Yes, we opted for a quieter venue. Josiah's played every game, looked in every booth, and watched every show. He's done really well." She glanced at Josiah, unmistakably proud. "Dinner here is a reward for holding it together the entire day."

Josiah fidgeted behind his mom. "Where's Maisy?" His eyes were on the gate at the top of the stairs.

Jon took a ticket and a wad of bills an older man handed him. At least ten adults and children pushed back from the tables and moved toward the door. "Thanks. Just a minute and I'll get your change."

Turning back to Josiah, he answered his question. "Maisy's upstairs. Probably lying on my bed. She's got her own bed, but somehow she thinks when the restaurant is open, she can get up on mine. You can go say hi, if your mom doesn't mind. Just leave her upstairs when you come back down. She can't be in here when we're open."

Josiah looked at his mom, his dark eyes pleading. "Can I, Mom?"

"Go ahead." Kirsten nodded as Bethany arrived with two menus tucked under one arm. Kirsten followed her to a table by the window, while Josiah raced up the stairs. Jon turned back to the cash register and the customer waiting to pay his bill.

After counting change and watching the large family exit, Jon glanced over at Kirsten. She gazed out the window, the early evening sunlight lighting her hair and making it appear golden instead of brown. Her shoulders drooped slightly, as if the burdens that rested on them weighted her down. Jon shook off an impulse to go and sit at her table for a minute, as he often did with customers he knew. Instead, he took the back way into the kitchen to check on Carlton.

His new cook was busy. Carlton stacked two plates filled

with chicken, a large bowl of mashed potatoes, and a smaller bowl of coleslaw on a tray just as Bethany bustled in. She took the tray without a word and left for the dining room. Carlton loaded the fryer basket with chicken, lowered it into the fryer and set the timer. "We're running a little low on rolls, Jon. Are there more in the freezer? I looked once, but didn't see any."

Jon frowned. "I think so. Why don't you run the cash register? I'll check for those rolls and finish up this chicken. Did you use the seasoning?"

"Yes, sir." Carlton nodded, then stepped into the dining room.

Jon walked through the cooler and into the freezer, the cold air chilling and drying the perspiration that had beaded on his forehead. He found the packages of frozen rolls behind a box of meat and mentally noted the need for some reorganizing. Back in the kitchen, he separated the chunks of dough and put the pan on the rack to defrost and rise, hoping they'd be done before they needed them. The timer on the fryer buzzed, and he dumped the crisp, golden pieces of chicken onto a platter to drain before placing them in the warming oven. Bethany brought in another ticket and clipped it above the counter. Carlton could handle this. He wiped his hand on a paper towel, tossed it in the garbage, and stepped through the swinging doors.

When Jon stepped behind the counter Carlton appeared startled, as if he'd been daydreaming. "You can take over in the kitchen again. I put the rolls in the rack to rise. Bethany brought in one ticket. Those meals should be up next."

"Sure thing, Mr. Washington." Carlton stepped behind Jon and down the hall to the kitchen.

At the table by the window, Kirsten chatted away while Josiah stared out at the river. He didn't appear to be listening to his mother at all, but Jon had learned Josiah took in a great deal, even when he never acknowledged the speaker. They had drinks, but no meals, so the ticket in the kitchen must have been theirs.

Several more tables were occupied, and Bethany stood at one, taking orders. Jon weaved his way through the dining room, greeting the customers and getting drinks or refills. He stopped at Kirsten and Josiah's table. "Your meals should be out soon. May I get you a refill on your drinks while you wait?"

Kirsten smiled up at him. Once again, feelings he'd thought were long buried stirred within. "We're fine," she responded.

Josiah scowled. "I think Maisy's lonely up there."

"Sorry, buddy. It's state law. A dog can't be in a restaurant unless she's a service dog. And Maisy doesn't qualify."

"A service dog? Like helps blind people?"

"Yep. They help people with all kinds of disabilities." Jon stepped back and helped Bethany fold out the tray holder and set down the tray with the plates.

"Careful, the food is hot," Bethany cautioned as she handed out the plates piled high with chicken. Then she added a basket of rolls and bowls of crisp coleslaw, chilled applesauce, and steaming mashed potatoes.

Josiah held his hands clasped tightly in his lap. Jon wondered for a moment if it was another of his rituals. Then he bowed his head and squeezed his eyes shut. He was waiting to pray. Jon stepped over to another table.

Out of the corner of his eye, he saw Kirsten bow her head and her lips move. When she raised her head, she flashed another breath-taking smile and reached for the basket of rolls.

Much later, Jon flipped the sign in the window to *Closed* and locked the front door. The day had left him exhausted, but elated. The record-breaking crowds would help with the finances.

Bethany shrugged her bag over her shoulder. "Anything else, Mr. Washington?"

Jon looked outside at the shadowed front lawn. Darkness had swallowed the bike trail beyond.

"My bike light works really well. It lights up the whole path. I'll be okay." She must have read his mind.

"You get on home, then. Thanks for all your work, Bethany. Maple Festival was a test for all of us, but I think we passed with an A plus." Bethany hurried out the door as Jon picked up a towel someone had left on a table.

The dishwasher hummed and swished as it turned on. In the kitchen, Carlton was running the last load.

Jon glanced over the shining stainless-steel surfaces. "Thanks, Carlton. You did a good job today."

Carlton shook his head. "We were crazy-busy." He took a final swipe at the counter with the disinfecting wipe. "When did you say we get paid? I'm running a little short."

"I usually make out checks the first of the month. But maybe I could figure up hours and get your first check to you next week. Would that help?"

Carlton frowned. "Yeah, that'd help. I'll take off now." He wrote the time on his card and stuck it back in the slot. "See ya Monday."

There was a rattle from the top of the stairs. Maisy's nose poked through the gate. Jon went upstairs and unlatched it. Maisy bounded down the stairs and skittered along the hall. She waited for him at the back door, her tongue hanging out and a playful gleam in her eyes. Jon stepped outside with her, and the chill in the evening air prickled his arms.

Maisy rooted in the long, unmown grass where the bluff rose steeply. Her tail circled like a helicopter propeller.

"Just hurry up and pee," he called. "It's cold out here."

Maisy looked up and gave him a tail wave before she squatted in the weeds, then galloped back. He opened the door and followed her in.

The thought of putting off balancing the cash register until morning tempted him, but that would mean working on his only free day. So, as Maisy cruised the hallway looking for crumbs, Jon sorted the credit receipts, cash, and checks. An hour later, he'd added everything three times, checked under and around the register, but the drawer was still twenty dollars short. Either there was an error he couldn't find, or someone had taken money out.

An image of Carlton's startled face at the cash register surfaced at the same time as Jon recalled his comment, "I'm a little short."

Jon walked into the kitchen for a Pepsi. Did he have an employee he couldn't trust?

Chapter 36

SUNDAY MORNING, JON woke to a cold wet nose nudging his arm. Maisy hadn't done that since she was a puppy.

He rolled over and looked at his phone. Nine o'clock. He hadn't slept this late in a long time, either. He slipped into sweats and padded downstairs in his bare feet. He let Maisy out the back door before going to the kitchen for coffee. Grateful for the one cup machine that only took minutes, he pulled out his favorite stained and chipped mug, set it to brew, and waited.

After a few sips, he stepped out on the back porch. Both pets pranced around him. Tiger tried to stay out from under Maisy's feet yet be in a position to gaze imploringly up at Jon, voicing her pleas with loud yowls.

"I know. Sleeping in just doesn't fit on your schedules, does it?" Jon stepped into the pantry and returned with their food. He fed Tiger first, and she sniffed delicately before taking a small bite. Maisy finished hers in three gulps, looked up, and wagged. "No, you're not getting seconds." Jon laughed at the dog's sad expression. He went inside, and after one last look at the yard and the woods beyond, Maisy followed.

Jon dropped an English muffin in the toaster. When it

popped up, he spread it with cream cheese and topped it with a slice of leftover ham. He opened the front door to catch the river breeze, sat at the table by the window, and considered what to do with his day. He'd worked so hard building up to Maple Festival, he wanted to enjoy his day off. He could ride his bike to Benson, but that would mean leaving Maisy alone.

He glanced at the cash register and wondered again where the missing twenty dollars had gone. And why Bethany had warned him about Carlton. He seemed polite and well-mannered, but maybe that was a front. She'd gone to school with him, so she ought to know him better than he did. He wished he could talk it over with Margaret, but even if he did have the chance to visit with her, he wouldn't burden her with his problems. She had enough of her own.

The muted sound of distant church bells drifted through the open door, and a memory surfaced. He was sitting in a church pew listening to Angie and the rest of the team belt out praise songs. Peace had washed over him, calming him from the stress of his job. He longed to recapture that moment--and have both Angie and peace.

He finished the English muffin and washed it down with the rest of his coffee. "How about a walk, Maisy?" She was on her feet in an instant, tail wagging. Jon put on a shirt and shoes, and in a short time they were scuffing through leaves on the trail.

Maisy wandered from one side to the other, poking her nose in every clump of grass and shrub. Jon didn't have to worry about her jumping in the river, though. Although Labs are known for their love of water, she couldn't be coaxed near the river. She would plant her feet and hunker back. That was fine with Jon. He didn't need a wet dog to mop up after every day.

When they reached the bench, Jon recalled his lengthy to-do

list. "Time to head back, girl." Maisy's tail waved but she buried her nose deeper into the particularly fascinating section of brush she was inspecting. "Let's go." Jon's voice took on a sterner note, but there was still no response from the dog.

Jon waded through the foliage, took hold of her collar, and pulled her back to the trail, wishing he had more time to train her. She walked sedately beside him for a few minutes before racing ahead to chase a cardinal back to its tree.

When they approached River's Edge, Maisy lifted her head, sniffed the air and barked. Then she ran through the opening in the trees. Fearing another skunk incident, Jon sprinted after her. He leaped over the ditch shouting, "Maisy! Come back here."

Maisy stood in the parking lot beside Carlton. He'd laid his mountain bike down in the gravel and was on his knees ruffling her fur and rubbing her ears. A lit cigarette dangled from his mouth. He stood, took one last, long draw on the cigarette, threw it to the ground and ground it out on the gravel.

Jon dropped to a walk, but his hands fisted at his side. When he reached the parking lot he said, "Carlton, I thought I told you during our orientation that there was to be no smoking at River's Edge."

Carlton's smile faded. "I'm sorry, Mr. Washington. I thought you meant during business hours. It won't happen again. I'm trying to quit smoking. It's one more bad thing I picked up in Branson."

Jon frowned. "I don't have a check for you yet. I said 'next week' meaning Monday at the earliest."

"Oh, I'm not here for a check. I think I left my cell phone here. You know how you want us to turn them off and leave them behind the counter except at breaks? I got home last night and it wasn't in my pocket, so I figured I'd left it here."

Jon, still winded after his sprint after Maisy, bent at the waist, hands on his ankles. "Give me a minute, and we'll go look." He certainly wasn't going to tell Carlton to go on in and provide him with another opportunity to steal from the cash register. He put his arms behind his head, stretched, then headed to the house, Carlton following. Maisy trotted around back, probably checking to see if Tiger had left any of her breakfast.

Carlton rummaged around on the shelf behind the counter. "Here it is." He held it up high as if it were a sports trophy. "Thanks, Mr. Washington."

"You're welcome," Jon answered, still feeling a little cross.

Carlton immediately turned the phone on. As he rode away on his bike, he appeared to be reading texts.

Jon stood watching until the bike disappeared behind the trees. Then he closed the door, locked it, and went upstairs to shower.

Chapter 37

THE SUNDAY MORNING a week after Maple Fest, Bethany sat at the kitchen table and stirred her cereal. She'd been thinking, and the flakes were all mushy. She took a bite and gagged. After dumping the contents of the bowl in the garbage disposal, she grabbed a strawberry Pop-Tart and stepped onto the patio. Clouds blocked the sunrise, and a cool breeze stirred the leaves clustered under the lawn chairs. Bethany shivered as she sat on the cold, damp seat and nibbled her breakfast.

Mom was still sleeping, and that was okay with Bethany. They'd spoken very little during the week. Last night, her mom had reminded her, "You have an appointment on Monday." Her voice softened slightly as she added, "I know it isn't easy, but it's the right choice for everyone. You'll see."

But how could it be the right choice for the little baby inside of her? To never even have a chance at life? Her eyes filled with tears. There had to be another answer. A few raindrops spattered on the brick. She stuffed the rest of the Pop-Tart in her mouth and went inside.

Mom still wasn't awake, so Bethany dressed quietly, put on a rain jacket, and slipped out of the house. She rolled her bike from the garage, wondering if you could ride a bike all through a pregnancy. Although she had her driver's license, they only had one car. And her mom usually needed it.

When Bethany entered the church, the man with the bulletins handed her one and greeted her with a hearty, "Good morning."

Just then a small dark-skinned boy with curly hair streaked across the foyer and slid to a stop, winding his arm around one of the man's legs. He reached out with a small brown hand and chirruped, "Good morning."

Bethany smiled and shook the boy's hand. She looked around for the River's Edge baker, but didn't see her.

Then, Courtney Phillips, a classmate, entered with her parents. "Hey, Bethany. I saw you here last week but didn't get a chance to speak to you. You sat with Mrs. Hanson. Is she a relative?"

Bethany giggled. "No, I just work with her at River's Edge. I wouldn't mind if she was my grandma or an aunt or something, though. She's pretty cool."

"Are you by yourself today? Want some company?"

"Sure." Bethany followed Courtney into the sanctuary and they sat near her parents but not in the same row.

"Did you see Josh Peterson's little boy handing out bulletins? Isn't he cute?" Courtney asked.

"The little dark-haired boy? Umm-hmm. Is that his dad? He doesn't look like him."

"He's adopted. From somewhere in Africa. I don't think his parents could have children. So they adopted Navad. Isn't that cool?"

"Yeah." The music started, and Bethany stood for the song. But her mind was on the little boy with his dad, an unwanted child who now had a loving family.

When the service concluded with one more rousing song of praise, Bethany had no more answers than she had when she entered. But somehow, she felt she'd been dipped in a warm bath of peace.

At home, her mother had laid out chicken breasts to thaw and was standing at the counter chopping vegetables. She must be in one of her rare cooking moods. "Where have you been so early in the morning?"

"I went to church again." Bethany leaned against the kitchen table. As with most of their arguments, after a few frosty days, they resumed talking as if there had never been anything wrong.

"How about grilled chicken for dinner?"

"Sounds great. Let me wash my hands and I'll help." Bethany headed for the bathroom to wash her hands. She wouldn't say anything now that would ruin Mom's pleasant mood. But she was not going to that appointment tomorrow morning.

Margaret hated missing church. She knew she could worship God anywhere, but she missed her church family, the uplifting music, and the messages that always spoke God's words to her heart. But Melanie's plane from New York arrived in Kansas City at noon. That meant she had to set her alarm and be on the road by eight. Melanie had been concerned about her driving and wanted to rent a car to drive to Maple Grove, but Margaret wouldn't hear of it. With a good night's sleep and a cup of coffee in the holder, she was ready to go. Her conversation with God could be done in the car just as well as sitting at the kitchen table.

Her prayers today were for others: for Melanie's safe flight, and gratitude for her daughter's willingness to stay with her during the first week of chemotherapy; for Jon, Carlton, and sweet Bethany at River's Edge; and Harold from Fellowship Church whose wife had just been diagnosed with Alzheimer's.

Outside the car window the rolling woods around Maple Grove gave way to corn and soybean fields. Several huge combines rolled through them, gobbling plants, emptying the grain into a hopper, and spitting out chewed-up stalks. The picked fields looked clean and bare.

Farm houses nestled between the acres of fields, some with huge old wooden barns reminiscent of an earlier era. On one broad green yard, a yellow Lab ran and wrestled with two children. Margaret smiled and thought of Maisy, the energetic and playful dog who always made her laugh.

Closer to Kansas City, she turned on the radio and found a station broadcasting a church service. Not the same as being in her own church, but still inspiring. At the airport, she slowed, trying to read signs and figure out where she should go. A car swerved around her, honking.

"You need to be patient with an old lady," Margaret muttered. "I can't read signs as fast as I used to. There it is." The sign read *cell phone lot*. That was where Melanie had told her to wait. Melanie would call, then Margaret would drive to the front of the airport, and Melanie would be outside waiting.

She was glad she'd brought a book to read. The clock showed she had forty-five minutes before the plane was due. When the phone did ring, it startled her for a moment. Francine Rivers's novel had transported her to another time and place.

"Hello, dear. I'm here in the cell lot. Has your plane landed?"

"Hi, Mom. Yes, we landed, and I'm waiting for my bags. Just stay there about ten minutes, and then pull up in front of the baggage claim area."

"All right, honey." It would be so good to have her daughter home. Margaret wished it was for other reasons, but she would take a visit from Melanie however she could get it. She put her book and phone in her bag, hefted it into the back seat and fidgeted, watching the minutes tick down on the dashboard clock. When exactly ten minutes had passed, she started the car. After circling the airport, she pulled into the lane closest to the front. The doors under the sign that read *baggage claim* swished open and her daughter emerged. She wore dark grey pants, a silky hot pink top, and a scarf in muted pastel tones. Margaret thought she'd never seen anyone more beautiful.

Melanie opened the trunk and lifted three bags in. Then she slid into the passenger seat. Margaret held out her arms, and they hugged. How good it felt to hold her only child in her arms again.

Melanie put her purse in the back and settled in her seat. "Mom, you'd better move out. If you go ahead a little, you can pull to the curb and I'll drive. I'd like to stop and get something to eat before we go back to Maple Grove."

"Okay, I'm going." Clutching the steering wheel, Margaret eased the car back into the stream of traffic. Melanie hadn't changed. Ever since she was little, she liked to take charge. That was probably what made her so successful in New York City.

As soon as Margaret got onto the main airport road, she pulled to the right, put on her flashers, and put the car into park. Like a car full of teenagers playing "fire drill" at a red light, they switched positions.

Margaret sank into the passenger seat with a sigh and a chuckle. "I haven't done that since your dad and I used to switch on vacations."

Melanie pulled the car back into traffic. Her face was sweet and dreamy. "Remember the trips we used to take to the lake?

Those were good times."

"Some of my favorite memories." Margaret watched out the window. "There's a Wendy's just off the interstate about fifteen miles from here. They have free frosties for seniors."

"Not many options for those of us that eat vegan, though."

Margaret couldn't keep up with her daughter. One week she wasn't eating bread, then she wasn't eating desserts, now it was animal products and meat. "I'm sorry, honey, I didn't remember."

Melanie changed lanes, then glanced at Margaret. "How are you feeling?"

"Oh, I'm not in any pain. I just don't have the energy I used to. And occasionally my vision gets a little fuzzy."

"The tumor is causing that?"

"Yes, that's what Doctor … oh, I can't remember his name. I have so many doctors now, I can't keep them straight. There's my surgeon and the oncologist and I don't know who all."

Melanie pursed her lips. "I'll help you with that. I'll go with you to any appointments. You won't have surgery until after chemo?"

"That's right. Doctor Helms, that's the surgeon's name. He thought with the type of cancer I have, we should start radiation and chemo first."

Melanie pulled into the parking lot of a convenience store. "Do you mind if we stop here? I need a water, and I was in such a hurry to get my suitcases and find you, I didn't stop to use the restroom. While we're here, we can use the GPS app on my phone and find a place to eat."

"Sounds good to me. I could use a restroom break, too." Margaret picked up her purse off the floor. It would be nice to have someone else making the decisions. At least for a week.

Chapter 38

Jon stood and stretched. The day had slipped away from him. His early morning walk with Maisy was the only thing he'd done that wasn't connected with the running of River's Edge. He'd paid bills, balanced the checking account, checked his supply of frozen pies, inventoried the pantry and done some reorganizing, and put in an order for meat to be delivered.

Maisy leaped up from her spot on the carpet. She waggled around him. When she didn't get much of a response, she caught the edge of his jeans leg in her teeth and tugged.

"Maisy. Cut that out!" Jon scolded. Then he laughed. "Okay, what do you want? Another walk?"

Maisy's feet clattered down the steps and hall, then she bounced around in the entryway like an over-grown beach ball with fur. Jon opened the door, and she raced out. When he followed her, she ran around in huge circles, her hindquarters tucked under her, her tongue hanging out in a kind of doggy laugh.

The trail had more bike traffic than during their morning walk. Jon kept a close eye out and called Maisy off to the side when bikers sped by. He jogged some and Maisy even followed at his heels for a short stretch. They passed the bench. Maisy sidetracked to sniff around it, her tail wagging. Then she galloped down the trail.

Jon's rumbling stomach reminded him he hadn't eaten much lunch. He'd been working at the computer and had barely taken time to fix a sandwich to eat upstairs. "Hey, Maisy. It's suppertime. Let's turn around here."

Maisy glanced over her shoulder at him, considering. Then her nose went up, and with one short "woof!" she took off down the trail towards the bridge.

Jon called her two or three times, but she continued. When he got closer, he thought she'd found some trash on the bridge, but then he realized it was a person, sitting on the edge, legs dangling and body bent over. He jogged onto the bridge, and then he realized why Maisy was so exuberant.

Bethany lifted a tear-stained face to look at him. "Hi, Mr. Washington."

With three quick strides he was beside her. "Bethany, you weren't thinking ..."

She scrambled to her feet. "Oh, no. I wasn't going to jump. I don't know what to do, but I wouldn't do that."

Maisy nudged her hand, and Bethany stroked her head.

A bicycle approached, and Jon flattened himself against the bridge railing as it passed. He wished he could take Maisy and just run back down the trail the way he'd come. Bethany always cried when he was around. He couldn't deal with his own emotions, so he definitely couldn't handle a teenager's tears.

"Is there something I can do to help?" Jon asked, hoping she'd say "no."

To his consternation, her blue eyes filled with tears, and then they started running down her cheeks. Should he pat her back or something? She gave a little hiccupy sob and sniffed. He didn't even have a handkerchief like his dad used to carry and hand to his mom at times like this.

"My mom wants me to have an abortion."

Now he really was out of his comfort zone. "Ummm. What do you think?" he stammered.

"I think it's a baby that God has plans for. I think it would be wrong to just get rid of it. But I can't change my mom's mind. What should I do, Mr. Washington?"

Jon took a deep breath and puffed it out through his lips. He had no answers, no wisdom. He'd never been a parent. He didn't know the right thing to do for his life, let alone advise a teenager. "Isn't there someone who could talk to both of you?"

Suddenly he had an idea. Margaret was a wealth of wisdom. She'd know what to do. "Why don't we call Margaret? I bet she'd have some ideas."

Bethany's face wrinkled into a puzzled frown. "Margaret? You mean your baker?"

Jon scrolled through his phone contacts. "Here's the number. Shall I call her?"

Bethany still looked unsure. "I guess."

Jon pushed send and the phone rang. Several rings. Then an unfamiliar female voice answered. For a moment, Jon wondered if he'd gotten a wrong number somehow. "Is—Margaret there?"

"Sure, just a minute."

When Margaret's warm voice came over the line, Jon felt relief wash over him. "This is Jon."

"Do you need pies? I don't think I can do them tomorrow, but—"

"No pies, this time. Bethany is here with me. She's got a problem, and I thought maybe you would talk with her."

There was a slight pause, and Jon wondered if Margaret had heard him. Then she said, "Bless her heart, does she *want* to talk to me?"

"I think so." Jon glanced at Bethany who appeared to be ignoring his conversation and having her own chit-chat with Maisy. "It's getting late. How about I put her bike in the back of the pickup and bring her to your house? Are you up to this, are you feeling okay?" Jon was suddenly overwhelmed with guilt. Maybe Margaret just needed to rest.

"Oh, I'm fine. My daughter, Melanie, arrived today, and she's fussing over me like an old biddy hen. Just bring Bethany over."

"Okay. We'll be there in a few minutes." Jon dropped the phone in his pocket. "Margaret is expecting you. We'll save time and daylight if I take you to her house in the truck. We can just put your bike in the back."

Bethany opened her mouth.

"Come on, I have to go in to town anyway. I'm getting supper at P.J.'s Pizza."

Her mouth closed. "All right." She followed him down the trail, pushing her bike. Maisy trotted beside her.

Fifteen minutes later, they parked in front of a cute gray house with flowers everywhere. Bethany stood beside the truck and watched as Jon lifted her bike over the tailgate. "Thanks, Mr. Washington," she mumbled.

"No problem." He climbed back in the truck, backed out, and gave her a little half-wave as he headed down the street toward P.J.'s. On the street, a light pattering of raindrops had begun.

Chapter 39

BETHANY DEBATED. SHE could get on her bike and head home, or she could swallow her fear and knock on the door. She wasn't crazy about spilling her guts to Margaret, even if she was a nice lady. But she had no solution herself.

Just then the front door opened and Margaret stood in the doorway, the entryway light illuminating her gray curls so they glowed around her face like a halo. "Come on in out of the rain, dear. I put on some water for tea. Do you like tea?"

"Yes, I do. Thanks." Bethany dropped her bike at the edge of the lawn and traipsed up the sidewalk. The faint fragrance of blooming mums floated past as she stepped into the house.

"This is my daughter, Melanie."

A tall, attractive woman in designer jeans smiled briefly at Bethany. "Nice to meet you."

"She lives in New York." The pride in Margaret's voice was unmistakable, and Bethany felt the knife prick of guilt. There wasn't any way now she could make her mom proud.

Margaret bubbled on. "Bethany works with me at River's Edge. Well, not with me most of the time, because she comes in after school and I'm gone. But Jon thinks she's the best little waitress ever. Although I hope you don't always want to be a waitress. Do you plan on going to college?"

Bethany crumpled. The tears began again and she frantically swiped at them with one hand. Then her nose ran. She needed a tissue.

"Oh, my. Here, you sit on the couch." A box of tissues appeared from somewhere, and Margaret sat beside her, one arm circling her shoulders. Bethany leaned over and sobbed, feeling like a very little girl crying on her mom's shoulder. Only trouble was, Margaret wasn't her mom, she wasn't a little girl, and a good cry wasn't going to make this any better.

When the storm of tears abated, she sat up and pulled several tissues from the box. She blew her nose and spoke without looking at Margaret. "I'm sorry. I'm not usually such a mess."

"You're pregnant, aren't you?"

Bethany nodded, wondering if she'd guessed or if Jon had told her.

"Sometimes the hormones can do that to you. Especially when you have big decisions to make."

Bethany fought against a second round of tears. Afraid to speak, she just nodded again. Much to her relief, Melanie had left the room the first time she let loose. Unloading to Margaret was one thing; falling apart in front of her smartly dressed, successful daughter was another.

"I'm pregnant. And my mom—my mom made an appointment for me at this clinic—for—" Bethany couldn't go on. Her mouth just didn't seem to be able to form the word *abortion*.

"To terminate the pregnancy?" Margaret's voice was soft, with no trace of condemnation.

Bethany's head bobbed, and she sniffed again.

"What do *you* want, honey?"

"I don't know." Her words came out in a wail. "I want to go to college. But—but—when Pastor Allen talked about God having a plan for your life, I thought maybe He has a plan for my baby's life, and—" Her voice trailed off as a fresh burst of tears cascaded down her cheeks.

Margaret waited without speaking, her head bowed, her wrinkled, veined hands clasped in her lap. It wasn't until much later that Bethany wondered if she was praying.

After Bethany mopped her face with another tissue, Margaret leaned forward and took one of Bethany's hands in hers. "This is a big decision. I don't want to step between you and your mother. But I do believe God has a plan for every life He creates. Would your mom listen to Pastor Allen? Could we call your mom and arrange a meeting with him?"

Bethany shrugged. "I'm not sure. She doesn't go to church." She gave a short laugh. "Neither did I, until two weeks ago. I tried to tell my mom I didn't want to go to that clinic, but she thinks I will ruin my life if I don't."

"Do you want me to call and ask her if she would meet with us?"

Bethany heard a small noise in the hallway, and a moment later, Melanie cruised into the room. She'd changed clothes and wore what might be pajamas, but they weren't flannel pants like Bethany wore to bed. These were some silky fabric and her bare toes poking out from underneath the pantlegs were polished pale blue. She laid a hand on her mom's shoulder. Her fingernails were the same shade of blue as her toes. "Mom, we need to get you to bed soon. We have to be at the clinic early tomorrow for your treatment."

Margaret reached up and patted her daughter's hand. "Don't worry about me, Melanie. You go on to bed. I'm going to stay here with Bethany."

Embarrassed, Bethany dropped the phone she'd fished out of her pocket. "I'll just go on home."

Margaret bent over and scooped up the pink phone. She held Bethany with a level gaze. "If you go home now, will anything change? When is your appointment?"

"Tomorrow," Bethany whispered.

"Well, we don't have a lot of time, do we? Let's call your mom. What's the number?"

Bethany took her phone back, scrolled through her contacts and pushed her mom's number. Then she handed the phone to Margaret, knowing her mom's reaction. She would be sweet and pleasant, but wouldn't change her mind.

"Hello, Mrs. Alcanter? This is Margaret Hanson… Bethany is here visiting, and we didn't notice it had started raining. I don't think she should be riding her bike home on the slick streets at night. She didn't want me to call and bother you, but…"

Bethany thought she saw a twinkle in Margaret's gray eyes as she looked up at her.

"That's great. No hurry." She rattled off her address before she ended the call and handed the phone back to Bethany. Then she grabbed hers off the table. "Now for the next participant." She glanced at Bethany. "I hope you don't mind my not being entirely honest with your mom. I think it's really important that she be here to talk this over with you."

She dialed a number. "Pastor Allen. This is Margaret. I have kind of an emergency. I know it's late, and Sunday night, too, but could you come over?…No, I don't need an ambulance, just your wisdom…Thanks, we'll see you in a few minutes." Margaret placed the phone back on the end table. Her grin was undeniably conspiratorial.

Bethany squirmed, suddenly aware she was sweating. "What are we going to tell them? Mom's going to freak out when she realizes we brought Pastor Allen to talk to her. Maybe I should just get my bike and go with her when she gets here."

"Is that what you want?"

"No." What a mess her life was in.

"Before everyone gets here, can we pray?"

Pray, like in church? Bethany nodded. "I guess."

Margaret reached for her hand. "Heavenly Father, we ask for your wisdom. Give Bethany the strength to stand up for what she knows is right. Open her mom's ears to hear. Help all of us to be united and supportive of Bethany and the little life inside. Amen."

Bethany swiped at her eyes with the back of one hand. "Thanks," she whispered.

The doorbell rang, and Margaret and Bethany looked at each other. Was it her mom or the pastor?

Chapter 40

BETHANY SAT FROZEN on the couch as Margaret used her arms to push to a standing position and limped to the door. Pastor Allen stood on the other side.

Margaret opened the door wide. "Come in, Pastor. You know Bethany Alcanter?" She gestured at the couch where Bethany still sat, wishing she could disappear into the cushions.

Pastor Allen walked across the room and took her hand. "Not sure we've been introduced. You're a friend of Courtney Phillips, is that right?"

"We go to school together," Bethany mumbled.

Margaret closed the door and sat in her blue flowered chair. "I'm going to give you a very quick synopsis. Bethany came to talk to me this afternoon. She's pregnant. Her mother, who'll be here any minute, has scheduled an abortion for her tomorrow in Kansas City. Bethany doesn't want to go through with it, but can't reason with her mom. We were hoping you could facilitate a conversation with her."

Pastor Allen stood in the middle of the room looking from Bethany to Margaret. He ran his fingers through his hair. Finally he turned to Bethany, "Does your mom want me to talk with her and you?"

Bethany shook her head. "She doesn't know you're here. She just thinks she's coming to pick me up 'cause it's raining."

Pastor Allen gave Margaret a look that clearly said *what did you get me into?*

Outside, a horn honked. Bethany jumped up from the couch. "That's Mom." For a moment, no one moved. Then Bethany trudged to the door.

"Let's see if she is even open to talking with us." Pastor Allen followed Bethany outside.

Mom waited in the dingy green Ford Explorer. The back gaped open, waiting for her bike. The driver side window was open and her elbow hung out.

"Mom." Bethany stood in front of the open window, aware of Pastor Allen behind her. "This is Pastor Allen from Fellowship Church. He wants to talk to us."

Her mom frowned. "Are you in some kind of trouble?" When Bethany shook her head, Mom asked, "This isn't about tomorrow, is it?"

Pastor Allen stepped forward. "I know this is really awkward, Mrs. Alcanter. But please, come inside and give Bethany just a few minutes."

Mom's jaw tightened and her eyes narrowed. "I don't need help talking to my daughter. We've always communicated well. And just because she's gone to church a couple of times, I'm not letting some pastor talk her into doing something that will ruin her life."

It was no use. Her mom wasn't going to listen to Pastor Allen, or Margaret, or even her. This whole afternoon was a mistake. Bethany started for her bike to put it in the back. But soft as the fragrance of the mums came the thought, *Is there no one who will fight for this baby?*

Her hands tightened into fists, and she stood up straight. "No, Mom. We haven't always communicated. I need to let you know how I feel. Please come into Margaret's house and talk to me."

For a few moments, her mom sat, clutching the steering wheel, and staring straight ahead. Then she opened the car door and stepped out. "Okay. But let's make it snappy. We have to get up early tomorrow."

Inside, Bethany made introductions. Margaret greeted her mom warmly and led her to the couch. "Can I get you something to drink? Water? Tea?"

"No, I'm fine." Her mom sat down, looking so uncomfortable Bethany felt sorry for her. She must feel like she was being ganged up on.

Margaret lowered herself into her chair, Bethany took the spot beside her mom, and Pastor Allen chose a straight-backed chair. After a long moment of silence, Pastor Allen cleared his throat. "Bethany, this is about you. Why don't you tell your mom what you've been thinking?"

Bethany didn't say a word, but tears began to run down her cheeks again. She grabbed a tissue from the box and wiped at them. She couldn't look at her mom, or any of them, so she studied a stain on the carpet. "Mom, I'm sorry. But I can't go to the appointment tomorrow. I just can't do it."

Her mom leaned forward and her voice had the edge it always had when she was about ready to explode at someone. "Who talked you out of it?"

Margaret shifted in her chair. She cleared her throat, and then she spoke. "Bethany came here this afternoon to talk. She just wanted to put her thoughts out to a third party. I don't think anyone has done anything but listen to her."

Pastor Allen's voice that boomed through the church on Sunday morning was quiet and gentle tonight. "Bethany, can you tell your mom why you don't want to have an abortion?"

Bethany talked around her sobs. "Because the little baby didn't do anything wrong...he doesn't deserve to die...I want to give him a chance...maybe God has a plan for his life..."

Her mom's arms folded across her chest and she scowled. "It's not really a baby, yet, Bethany. Not really."

Bethany's muffled sobs were the only sound in the room.

Then, Pastor Allen's soft voice. "Do you agree with your mom?"

"No...I don't think so...I don't know." Bethany wailed and reached for another tissue.

"So," her mom glared at Margaret and Pastor Allen, "if we don't take care of this pregnancy, can either of you tell my daughter what her life will be like? No? Well, I can. I was married when I had Bethany, and I was counting on Andrew coming back from Iraq, finding a good job, and supporting me while I went to school. I had the grades to go to college, and I was motivated. But Andrew didn't come back. So I had to support myself and Bethany. I lost my chance to go to school. I don't want Bethany to lose hers."

After another long pause in the tension-filled room, Margaret spoke up. "I'm sorry, Allison. What happened to you doesn't seem fair. But Bethany isn't you. She has options. Just because she chooses to give birth to the baby doesn't mean she has to raise it. She could choose adoption."

"She could choose to go with me tomorrow morning and then go on with her life as planned."

Margaret nodded at Bethany's mom. "She could. But she's

decided that is wrong for her. I think you need to respect that." Margaret's reprimand sounded as soft and gentle as a spring rain.

Bethany took a sideways glance at her mom, who seemed a tiny bit less angry. Maybe even thoughtful. "Mom, I'm grateful for all the sacrifices you've made for me. You've always been there, and I've never wanted for anything. I'm so sorry that—this happened. That I—did this." She wanted to wrap her arms around her mom, and be held and told everything was going to be okay.

Her mom's eyes softened a bit more, but her arms remained crossed in front of her, and there was no smile on her face. "Okay. I'll cancel the appointment for tomorrow." She scowled at Bethany. "You realize that a few weeks more, and it will be too late to change your mind."

"I know. I won't change my mind."

Her mom stood up. She glared at Pastor Allen and Margaret again. "I hope you two meddlers are happy. I only hope you're as happy to meddle when there's a crying baby and nobody to take care of it." She stomped to the door and let herself out. The door banged behind her.

Bethany followed, but she stopped when she reached the door. "I'm sorry for dragging you guys into this."

Margaret folded her into her arms. "Don't be a bit sorry, honey. We were glad to be here. Not sure we helped out a lot, but you know now that you don't have to have an abortion. And I think that makes God smile."

Pastor Allen gave her an awkward pat on the shoulder. "You just call the church if you need anything, Bethany. We'll be glad to help or to connect you with the proper resources."

"I will. Thanks, Pastor Allen." Bethany hurried out to the car. Her mom had already stuffed her bicycle into the trunk. The lid stood open, and her back wheel hung out part way. Bethany climbed into the passenger seat. Her mom did not speak to her all the way home.

Chapter 41

Jon slid the tub of salad greens into the cooler where it would be easy to grab at lunchtime. He glanced at the clock. Ten-thirty. About the time he'd usually hear Margaret's car and her cheerful greeting to Maisy. But she and her daughter were probably already at the cancer center in Lutheran Hospital for her first chemo treatment. If only there were something he could do to let her know he was thinking of her.

He glanced out the window. Thunderstorms had rolled through all night, but the sun peeped out now. It looked like another beautiful day.

The bell chimed. Carlton must be here. Jon used his shoulder to prop open the swinging door.

"Good morning,"

Carlton looked up, a surprised look on his face. Why was he always so jumpy?

"Morning." Carlton hung his backpack on the back porch and filled in his time card on the counter. After washing his hands, he checked the menu and meal preparation lists that Jon posted.

"Think we'll be busy today?" Carlton laid out sandwich ingredients.

"No, I expect it will be rather quiet. It seemed the entire town ate here for Maple Festival, so I don't look for many people to drive out today. But I could be surprised."

They fell silent as they continued preparations. Carlton had never shared much about his personal life, and after the missing twenty, Jon didn't encourage any small talk.

By noon, the dining room held an average crowd, mostly sandwich and salad orders. Jon seated customers, waited tables and took payments, leaving Carlton in the kitchen. When Jon's cell phone rang, he wiped his hands on his apron, pulled the phone from his pocket, and answered.

Kirsten sounded frantic. "Have you seen Josiah? He took off on his bike about an hour ago."

"From school?"

"No school today. Professional day for teachers. He was at my dad's and got mad—something about a video game—and he took off. I've driven all over town and can't find him. I thought he might have come to see Maisy."

Jon glanced up the stairs. Maisy lay on the other side of the gate, her head on her paws, watching. "Maisy's inside, and I haven't seen Josiah."

He heard her sharp intake of breath.

"Don't panic. I'll go down the trail and look for him."

"Thanks, Jon." Her voice had calmed a tiny bit. "Call me if you find him. We're going to check the library and stores downtown."

Jon looked around the dining room. Only four tables full. Carlton could handle it. But that meant allowing him to use the cash register. Jon thought about Josiah, how naïve he was, alone on the bike trail. Then he strode back to the kitchen.

"I have an emergency. A friend's son is missing. He likes to visit Maisy, so she thought he might be headed out here. There are only four tables occupied. Can you handle the front and back?"

"Sure, Mr. Washington. Go on, look for the kid. I'll take care of things here."

"Thanks." Jon hurried out of the kitchen. He made sure the bell was on the counter, so if a customer decided to pay while Carlton was in the kitchen, they could summon him. Then just before he went out the door, he thought of something. Taking the stairs two at a time, he unlatched the gate and called Maisy. "Come on, girl. Maybe you can help me find Josiah."

Maisy trotted behind Jon out the back door, and both of them ran toward the trail. Josiah wouldn't pass right by River's Edge without stopping to see his favorite dog, so Jon turned east on the trail toward Maple Grove. They jogged along together, Maisy's tail waving with delight at the unexpected treat of a run with Jon in the middle of the day.

Every once in a while, Jon stopped and called. "Josiah! Josiah!" Then he froze and listened. He wasn't sure if Josiah would even answer if he heard him. His stomach knotted and churned. Kidnapped? Hit by a car on the crossroad? Lost in the timber on the bluff? He shook his head, trying to clear the imagined scenarios.

Farther along the trail, he stopped to catch his breath. "Maisy," he panted, "we're looking for Josiah. Find Josiah."

Maisy cocked her head and studied his face. Jon wished she could understand. If only he could take her to Josiah's grandfather's house, and she could follow the boy's scent to wherever he was. But she wasn't a bloodhound, she was just a slightly goofy yellow Lab.

When he neared the bridge, Jon stopped, bent over and

gasped for air. He was certainly not in shape to run the full length of this trail.

He could hear the river as it flowed under the bridge. The old iron structure rose above the trail, creaking in the wind. Suddenly Maisy's head went up. Her nose lifted, sniffing the air.

"No, girl, we're not chasing any critters." Jon lunged for her collar. But just as he grabbed, she started down the steep bank toward the river. "Maisy, get back here!" What on earth was wrong with that dog? She'd never gone to the river. Rough shrubbery covered most of the steep incline, but a faint trail – probably used by deer on their way to get a drink – wove through the brush. Keeping a wary eye out for poison ivy, Jon started after his dog.

Then he spotted the bike. The chrome handlebars were just visible above the undergrowth. He sped up, stumbling through the tangle of saplings, vines and grasses. He couldn't see Maisy, but he could hear her, far ahead of him, crashing her way through. And then he heard her bark. It was a bark he'd never heard before, not the one she used when she treed a possum or greeted someone in the driveway or wanted breakfast. This was a one-note command. He plunged through the last of the brush and hit the muddy bank. His feet shot out from under him, and he almost slid into the swiftly flowing river, full from the previous night's storms.

Maisy stood chest deep in the water. Josiah had his arms wrapped around her, holding on as if his life depended on it. Jon scrambled to his feet and waded into the river. He held out his hand. "Take my hand, Josiah, let's get you out of the water."

Josiah looked up at Jon, his eyes wide and fearful. He shook his head and his hands tightened on Maisy's fur. "I can't."

"Yes, you can. Just grab hold of me."

The current swirled around them, and Josiah staggered and cried out. Maisy paddled for a moment before regaining her footing.

"Josiah, the water's rising. You need to take my hand."

"My foot's stuck in something."

Should he call for help? He didn't know how long Josiah had been trapped, but they didn't have time to waste. He took a deep breath and ducked beneath the muddy swirling waters. He couldn't see anything, but he grabbed Josiah's leg and felt his way down. He could hear Josiah hollering, probably more because Jon held his leg, rather than fear from the dangerous situation.

Josiah's foot was wedged between two metal bridge supports. Jon gave a tug, but the foot didn't budge. He popped out of the water to get a breath.

"Josiah, what shoes are you wearing?"

Josiah sniffled. "My green hightops."

"Do they tie?" Jon asked.

Josiah nodded.

"Okay, buddy. We'll get you out of here. I'm going underwater again and I'm going to untie your shoe. Then I want you to wiggle your foot out of your shoe."

"Nooo," Josiah wailed. "I can't leave my shoe."

Jon wiped water off his face with his hand. "Here's the deal. In order to get you out of the river, we need to leave your shoe. But I promise you a new pair. How about that?"

"Will they be green?"

"Absolutely."

Josiah still looked tearful, but he nodded. "Okay."

Once more, Jon ducked beneath the surface of the murky waters. His fingers felt around the trapped shoe for the laces. Then tugging and pulling, he untied them. Nearly bursting with the need for oxygen, he popped up again.

"Now, Josiah. Wiggle your foot out." Not caring how Josiah felt about being touched, Jon grasped him around chest, supporting him as he worked his foot out.

Then suddenly, Josiah reached for him and his arms went around his neck. Jon lifted him out of the water and carried him up the bank, struggling through mud that sucked his feet down. When he reached firm ground, Jon collapsed. Josiah's arms still clung to his neck, the rest of him spilled over his lap.

For a few minutes no one spoke: Jon catching his breath, Maisy panting hard, and Josiah whimpering. Jon cradled Josiah, filled with relief that he was safe, and the realization of how much he loved this boy.

Josiah slid off Jon's lap and stared at his wet sock. "How am I going to ride my bike without my shoe?"

"We'll call your mom and let her know you're okay. She can pick you up." Jon reached for his phone. With a sinking feeling, he realized he'd dived into the water with his cell phone in his pocket.

"Well, I can't use my cell phone because it's wet. Let's climb up the bank. We'll call your mom from River's Edge."

"I don't have a shoe." Josiah's voice trailed off into loud wails.

Jon sighed and ran his fingers through his wet hair. He pointed at his dog, wagging her tail and watching Josiah. "Look at Maisy. She doesn't have shoes either. Here, grab her collar, and she'll help you get up."

Still wailing, Josiah did as Jon directed. Clutching the sturdy shrubbery, Jon pulled himself up the bank. When he reached Josiah's bike, he grasped the handlebars and pulled it up with him. Maisy followed behind with Josiah holding tightly to her collar. Once on the trail, Jon dropped the bike and slipped out of his wet shoes and socks.

"I'll go barefoot, too. See, the trail's paved. We can walk back to River's Edge barefoot."

Jon led the way, carrying his socks and shoes in one hand and guiding the bike with the other. Josiah never loosened his grip on Maisy's collar. He limped along in one wet shoe and one sock foot, but his wails gradually diminished to an occasional sniffle.

When they reached the path, Jon asked Josiah, "Do you want me to lift you over the ditch, or do you want to walk?"

"I can walk."

Maisy, who usually bounded over the ditch and hit the yard running, slowed to Josiah's hobbling pace and walked with him into the yard. Not until they reached the steps leading to the porch did he finally let go of her collar. He sat on the step and rubbed at the mud and scratches on his legs.

There were no cars left in the parking lot except Carlton's dented red Jeep. "I'm going inside to call your mom." Jon wished he could make Josiah look at him so he was sure he understood. "Stay right here on the step and don't go anywhere."

"I will." Josiah peeled off his ruined sock.

Jon hurried inside and dialed Kirsten's number.

She answered immediately. "Yes?"

"He's here at River's Edge. He's safe, just a little wet and muddy and a few scratches."

"I'll be there in ten minutes."

Carlton emerged from the kitchen. "Did you find the kid?"

"Yes. I just need to wash him up a little before his mom picks him up."

Carlton shuffled his feet. "The kitchen's all cleaned. Want me to start anything for dinner?"

Dinner. Jon couldn't even remember what was on the menu, although he'd looked at it this morning. "Yeah. Go ahead and start the potatoes. I'll be back there in a little bit."

Carlton gave him a nod. "Okay."

Jon hurried back outside. "Would you like to get squirted with the hose to clean the mud off your legs? That's how I clean up Maisy."

Josiah looked skeptical, but he followed Jon around the corner of the house. Jon hooked up the hose. Maisy trotted over and cocked her head.

"Come on girl, let's show Josiah how we do this."

Maisy moved closer and Jon sprayed her legs and underbelly. She sidestepped and bit at the water. When Jon twisted the nozzle to pause the flow, she looked up and barked once as if to say, "More, please."

"Nope, it's Josiah's turn." Jon turned to the boy who stood with his back against the house, watching with wide eyes. "Maisy likes to play with it. It's like a waterpark to her."

"I don't like water slides."

"This won't be like a slide at all. Here, you hold the hose," Jon held it out to Josiah who took it as gingerly as if Jon were handing him a live snake. "You control the water with this. You can have a hard spray like Maisy had, or a gentle shower, or a fine spray." Jon showed him how to turn the nozzle.

Josiah tried it, finally choosing a spray that was almost a mist. He sprayed one leg, watching the water wash the mud in a dirty streak down his leg. Then he turned it on the other leg. When he giggled, Jon had to laugh, too.

"Do you want me to squirt you and Maisy?" Jon asked.

Josiah paused the spray. He looked at Maisy, wet coat dripping. "Okay." He handed the hose to Jon.

Using the fine mist spray that Josiah had chosen, and keeping it low, Jon squirted first Maisy, then Josiah. Maisy chased the water, running around Josiah, biting the water and barking. Josiah spun in the center laughing as the water hit his legs and splashed around him. When Jon spotted a car turning into the driveway, he twisted the nozzle shut. "I think your mom is here, Josiah."

Maisy shook, spattering water everywhere. Josiah giggled again. When he turned to look at his mom's car he said, "I don't want to go home yet."

Jon gave his shoulder a quick pat. "I think your mom would like to get you home and dried off." Josiah trudged behind Jon to the parking lot.

Kirsten parked the car, jumped out, and ran toward them. When she reached Josiah, she threw her arms around him. He stood as still as a plastic figurine, his arms at his sides. "Oh, Josiah, where were you?" She stepped back, but held his shoulders. "I was so worried. You mustn't ever do that again."

Josiah looked away from her. "Grandpa wouldn't let me play Minecraft."

Kirsten looked at his feet. "Where's your shoe? Why are you all wet?" Then she looked up at Jon. "What happened? Where did you find him?" Tears trickled down her cheeks, and suddenly all he wanted was to take her in his arms, hold her as he'd held her son, and wipe the tears away.

He stepped to her side. "He was in the river."

Kirsten gasped. "The river!"

"Just at the edge, but his foot became wedged in one of the old bridge supports. That's why he only has one shoe on."

Josiah's head swiveled back to his mom. "Jon's going to buy me new green Nikes, Mom. He promised."

"You pulled him out?" Kirsten looked from Josiah to Jon,

eying his wet hair and clothes and his bare feet.

"Maisy got to him first. I just helped get his foot out."

Kirsten bent to pet Maisy's head. "Good girl. You have turned out to be an amazing dog." She straightened and turned to Josiah. "Let's get you home and cleaned up. You know we will discuss consequences for this at home."

"Jon will buy me new shoes." Josiah's voice was insistent.

"That's very kind of him, but losing a shoe is not the issue. Leaving Grandpa's place without permission is." Kirsten turned back to Jon, her green eyes still sparkling with tears. "I don't know how I can ever thank you. This is twice you've rescued my son."

Jon felt warmth rising on his neck and he shrugged. "I just did what anybody would have done. I'd have called you at the river to tell you he was okay, but like a fool, I jumped in with my phone in my pocket."

"Oh, no. I can replace your phone."

Jon shrugged "They're tough. It may work fine once it dries out."

"Don't feel like you need to buy him new shoes, either."

"I do. I promised him."

Suddenly, Kirsten's arms circled him. He reached out to draw her into the hug, but his arms only grazed her back as she quickly stepped away.

"Thanks, Jon," she called over her shoulder as she hurried to her car, Josiah mincing along behind in his bare feet.

Jon stood watching, his arms strangely empty and his heart aching with loneliness.

Chapter 42

MARGARET WOKE TO the tantalizing smell of coffee. She hadn't had the pleasure of waking to coffee since Nathaniel passed away. She closed her eyes for a few minutes, relishing the warmth and comfort of her bed. Then she swung her feet out and into her slippers. Her robe lay across the end of her bed, and she slipped into it, made a stop in the bathroom, and then shuffled into the kitchen.

"Morning, Mom." Melanie's cheerful voice sang out. "I made breakfast, but we need to get groceries today. Do you still shop at Maple Grove Foods?"

"Thank you for doing this, dear. I thought I would be up early enough to make breakfast for you." Margaret looked at the table set for two. "Yes, I still shop at Maple Grove Foods. There's a new store in town, but I know where everything is at the old one. Why?"

Melanie stirred some vegetables sautéing in a skillet. "I don't suppose they carry organic foods. Do they have a gluten-free section?"

Margaret frowned. "I'm not sure. We'll have to look."

"Sit down, Mom. I'll pour you a cup of coffee."

Margaret sank to her chair, feeling a little displaced. She couldn't remember the last time someone had served her. She took the cup Melanie handed her. "Honey, this is just wonderful. But you can't do this every morning."

Melanie smiled as she slid a perfectly cooked omelet onto a plate and handed it to her. Margaret took the folded napkin by her plate and laid it in her lap.

As Melanie stepped back to the stove, she said, "Go ahead and eat, Mom. Don't wait for me, or yours will get cold."

"I thought we would pray."

"Sure." Melanie paused with the spoon she'd been using still in the air. "Go ahead, I'm listening."

"Heavenly Father, thank you for my daughter. Thank you for the blessing of having her here and her willingness to come and take care of me. And thank you for this delicious breakfast. Amen."

Melanie jostled the omelet in the skillet. "Now, eat your breakfast."

Margaret cut off a piece of the omelet with her fork and popped it in her mouth. Why did food taste so much better when someone else prepared it for you? "Ummm, delicious."

Melanie slid into the chair across from her and set down a plate with her omelet on it.

Margaret took a sip of her coffee. "You know you don't need to stay with me during the chemo. You could go shopping or out for a walk."

"I'll take my iPad and check emails. And I have a whole list of books on it that I haven't read. I'll be fine."

"I just think it's kind of depressing to sit in a hospital."

"Not at all. It will give us a chance to visit."

Margaret smiled at her daughter and scooped up the last of her omelet. "Okay, then. We'll just pretend it's a girls' outing." She reached for her Bible. Melanie had moved it from the table and laid it on the extra chair. "I've been reading in Joshua. Would you like me to read out loud?"

Melanie glanced at the clock. "Mom, you need to be at the hospital at eight. I don't think you have time."

"It doesn't take me that long to get dressed, and I took my shower last night. I have time." Margaret opened her Bible to where her bookmark held her place and began reading. Melanie stacked her plate on her mother's, carried the dishes to the counter, and ran water in the sink. She didn't appear to be listening, but Margaret read out loud anyway. She needed to hear those ringing commands, "Be strong and courageous … the Lord your God will be with you wherever you go."

She closed the Bible and bowed her head, praying silently for the daughter who seemed to be pushing away the only One able to comfort her.

When Margaret raised her head, the kitchen sparkled and the shower ran in the bathroom.

In the bedroom she opened her closet and peered in. What does the fashionable sixty-five-year-old wear to a chemotherapy treatment? She snorted softly and pulled out a comfy knit shirt and pair of jeans.

After dressing and a quick comb-through of her silver curls, she was ready. She put her Bible and a book by Anne Graham Lotz in her oversized bag. If she was forced to lie in a recliner, she might as well have some good reading material handy.

Melanie stepped from the guest bedroom in a peasant skirt and top. Her blonde hair was swept back and held with an over-sized barrette. Her small leather purse sported a little gold manufacturer's tag that raised the price exponentially. "Ready?"

"As ready as I'll ever be. This is not how I'd choose to spend the morning with you."

Melanie took her arm and gave it a gentle squeeze. "I'm glad I could come home to be here for you, Mom."

Margaret stretched up to place a kiss on Melanie's cheek. "Oh, I am too, dear."

At the hospital they were ushered into a room with several alcoves, each containing a recliner. As they passed, Margaret could see two of them were occupied. One held a bald, elderly man who slept with his head back and his mouth gaping open. A young dark-haired woman leafed through a magazine in another chair. Did she still have her own hair, or was she wearing an expensive wig? Her hand went to her head, touching the thick curls. What would it be like to have a head that was slick and shiny?

"Is this chair okay?"

Margaret realized the nurse was speaking to her. "Oh, yes, it's fine."

Within a short time, they'd started the IV, and the nurse hung the bag of medicine on a pole. Melanie chatted for a while about her job and the different fashion shows she had traveled to recently.

When she fell silent, Margaret did too. She was just thinking of asking Melanie if she would read some of Anne Graham Lotz's book to her when Melanie stood up. "I need to stretch my legs. Can I bring you anything, Mom? A drink? A snack?"

"No, I'm okay. Drinking something would just make me have to go the bathroom." Margaret looked at the IV pole. "And in this get-up, it's a hassle."

"I'll be right back, then."

Margaret watched as Melanie left. The man to her right had begun to snore softly. The younger woman was on her phone. A nurse was hooking another woman to an IV two chairs to her left. She looked fearful, and Margaret gave her what she hoped was an encouraging smile.

An hour later, a young nurse with a pony tail that reminded her of Bethany gave them the post-chemo instructions. Despite her best efforts, Margaret's mind wandered. She was glad Melanie seemed to listen intently, nodding her head and asking questions.

At home, Melanie held her arm as they walked into the house. Margaret wanted to tell her it wasn't necessary, she wasn't elderly, but her daughter's touch comforted her.

"I think I'll lie down for a few minutes," Margaret announced.

"It's almost lunch time, Mom. You sure you don't want to eat first?"

"No, I'm just going to rest my eyes a few minutes and then I'll come out and help you fix lunch."

Melanie fluffed her pillow while Margaret removed her shoes. She leaned back and closed her eyes and barely heard Melanie's footsteps leaving the room.

"Mom. Are you hungry?" Melanie stood in the doorway.

Margaret felt foggy and disorientated. "What time is it?"

"Two-o'clock. You've been asleep for over two hours."

Margaret sat up and slipped into her shoes. "I hope you didn't wait for me to eat lunch. I really didn't mean to go to sleep for more than a few minutes. Why didn't you wake me sooner?"

"I thought you needed your sleep. I made a quinoa salad. Want to try it?"

The salad was delicious, but Margaret could barely force down a few forkfuls. Where had her hearty appetite gone?

"That's all?" Melanie asked as Margaret rinsed her plate and put it in the dishwasher. "You need to eat to keep up your strength."

"I'll eat a good supper." Margaret patted her daughter's arm. "Maybe we'll go out to River's Edge. I'd like you to meet Jon."

In the afternoon, Melanie went grocery shopping. Elizabeth stopped by while she was gone to see how Margaret's first day of chemo had gone. She brought her famous chicken and noodles, so when Melanie returned, they decided to eat that instead of going to River's Edge.

Despite her long nap, Margaret found herself yawning over her book long before the evening news. "I didn't sleep well last night. I think I'll go ahead and tuck myself in." She leaned over to give Melanie a kiss on the cheek. "Don't you dare get out of that chair. You've been fussing too much over this old lady."

Melanie smiled up at her. "Night, Mom."

Hours later, Margaret woke with an uneasy, nauseated feeling. She turned to one side, then the other. She rearranged the covers and flipped her pillow around, but still felt ill. Finally she knew she couldn't avoid it, she was going to be sick. In the bathroom she gripped the rim of the toilet as she emptied the contents of her stomach. Then, continuing to heave, she sank to the floor. The hall light switched on and Melanie, hair tousled like a little girl's, stood in the doorway.

She grabbed a washcloth, wet it, and handed it to her mom. Margaret wiped her face and tried to smile. "I did this with you a few times."

"More than a few, I'm sure." Melanie reached a hand down and helped her mom to her feet. "Feel better now?"

"Just tired. I'm so sorry I woke you. I hope we can both get back to sleep."

"It won't be a problem for me." Melanie watched from the hallway as Margaret lay back on her pillow and pulled the blanket up.

"Night, dear." Margaret called as her daughter's footsteps faded down the hall.

Who would take care of her when Melanie went back to New York?

God, you've always provided. Please don't let me be a burden to anyone.

Chapter 43

J ON STEPPED OFF the trail onto the path toward the yard. "Come on, Maisy, time to get the food ready for the hungry hordes." She leaped over the ditch and trotted after him into the restaurant.

As the days shortened and temperatures dropped, runs became harder to squeeze in, but they always cleared his mind and helped him focus on the day. And he needed to focus this morning. His thoughts tumbled like vegetables in the food processor, the blades dissecting his needs, motives, and plans.

He couldn't stop thinking about yesterday. Was Kirsten's hug simply a grateful gesture to a friend? Or something more?

Not only could he not sort out her intentions, he couldn't sort out his own feelings. He missed Angie every day, every minute almost. He couldn't imagine himself with another woman, but he wasn't sure he wanted to spend his life alone, either. He found himself drawn to Kirsten—she was an attractive woman—and he felt guilty. But were his feelings just compassion for her situation, raising Josiah alone?

Mechanically, he pulled out ingredients for the day's lunches. When Carlton arrived, he acknowledged him with a nod and "good morning," and continued preparations. Last night, he had meticulously tallied the register. It balanced perfectly, to the penny. Other than the comments Bethany had made, and the one evening when the register came up twenty dollars short, he had no reason to mistrust Carlton. But he did.

He and Carlton worked side by side, chopping the vegetables for salads, heating up soups, baking frozen pies, and laying out ingredients to make sandwiches.

Carlton expertly sliced a red onion. "Is Margaret coming back?"

Jon set the peach pie he'd pulled out of the oven onto the counter. "She'd like to. But chemo really wears a person out. I told her to wait a few weeks and see how she feels."

"No offense. But those frozen pies don't taste like hers."

Jon used the pie slicer to cut eight equal portions and set the pan on the rack. "I know. But it's what we have for now. This is a small operation, and our time is limited."

Carlton shrugged as he opened a jar of pickles. "Well, I'm just saying, those don't taste like Margaret's pies."

The lunch crowd kept them busy. Then, as the dining room began to empty, Paul and two of his men came. When Jon approached the table, Paul grinned up at him. "Well, howdy-do. How's the restaurant business a-goin'?"

"Not too bad. How's building?" Jon handed each of the men a menu and took drink orders.

"We can't complain. Good Lord keeps givin' us work."

When Jon returned with two sweet teas and a Mountain Dew, Paul still squinted at the menu. "Don't have any of your fried chicken for lunch, huh?"

"No, sorry, but come back at dinner time tomorrow night and you can indulge."

Paul shook his head. "Guess I'll have some soup. What kind

you got?"

"Chicken noodle, vegetable, and tomato basil."

"I'll take a bowl of chicken noodle." Paul handed him back the menu. The two men with him ordered sandwich plates. One of them pulled his phone from a back pocket and scrolled through messages.

"I'll be back soon with your meals." Jon hurried through the swinging doors. He handed Carlton the order and made sure everything was on track in the kitchen. No problems.

Carlton sliced open a sandwich bun. "I'll take these orders out when they're ready."

Jon wandered back to the dining room and sat on the stool behind the counter. He watched as Carlton brought out the tray with the meals for Paul's table.

When Paul and his two men were finished, Paul came up to the counter and the other two went out to the porch. Paul must be treating.

"Was your soup okay?" Jon took the receipt and the cash Paul handed him.

"Yep. Soup was great. It tasted just like my Gramaw used to make. But I miss Margaret's pies. Those you're servin' just ain't the same."

Jon felt a prick of anger, and he calmed himself before he spoke. "I'm sorry. Margaret can't make pies for us right now. I'm hoping she'll be back before too long." He glanced down at the slip, punched the charges in the cash register, and handed Paul his change.

Paul's characteristic grin was gone, and his face was creased with sorrow. "You do know, she might not be able to come back. She might just be a goin' home."

For a minute, Jon couldn't figure out what Paul was talking

about. Then it was as if something exploded in him. He gripped the counter, leaned forward, and nearly shouted in Paul's face.

"I thought you were a church-going man. Where's your faith? Margaret doesn't need someone telling everyone in town she's going to...to..." He couldn't bring himself to say the word *die*. "She's a strong woman. She'll beat this cancer."

Paul folded the bills and pushed them deep in the pocket of his dusty jeans. "Sorry, Jon. I sure didn't mean to upset you. I talked to Margaret on Sunday, and she told me she's leavin' it in the Lord's hands, but whether he heals her or takes her home, it's okay with her. Those were her words. She's trustin' God to take care of her."

Jon spit out the words. "She'd better trust her doctors."

Paul gazed back at him, steady and unflinching. "My friend, healing don't come from a doctor any more than it does from a place. I pray for you every day, that you can find healing. You see, Margaret's already got it."

Jon didn't respond. He respected Paul, and didn't want to damage their friendship. The anger subsided, sinking deep within. Paul turned, joined his men, and walked across the lawn to his truck. Jon cleared the table, carried the dirty dishes out to the kitchen, then trudged upstairs and opened the gate to let Maisy out.

Outside, he threw a tennis ball for Maisy to chase, still thinking about his conversation with Paul. He felt guilty for losing his temper, and with a friend and a customer no less. But the anger still simmered, like a pot of chicken soup that might boil over any minute. He threw the tennis ball and it disappeared in the shrubbery lining the trail. Undaunted, Maisy crashed after it, bouncing out minutes later with a vine trailing from her broad nose, but the ball firmly tucked in her cheek. She dropped the ball at his feet and looked up at him, one leaf covering her eye. In spite of his foul mood, Jon laughed and pulled the vine from her head. "Maisy, you're crazy. But you make me smile. Let's go peel some potatoes." He dropped the ball into his pocket, and Maisy trotted after him.

Chapter 44

BETHANY PULLED AND tugged at the jeans. No matter how hard she tried, they wouldn't fasten.

She peeled them off and looked in her closet. Her choices were gym shorts, sweat pants or pajama bottoms—none of which she thought would be appropriate for waitressing at River's Edge. She didn't dare ask her mom to buy her some clothes.

After the night at Margaret's, they'd settled into a polite but icy silence. Her mom had not brought up the appointment, and Bethany assumed she'd canceled it. But now she had so many other questions. And no one to ask for answers. She was trying to trust God, like Pastor Allen said she should, but she'd still like a flesh-and-bone person to talk to.

Bethany pushed open her mom's bedroom door. Clothes were piled everywhere. Although her mom insisted on the rest of the house being kept neat and tidy, her own bedroom was a messy extension of her closet. Bethany pulled a pair of jeans from the bottom of a pile that looked clean. Her mom was big enough so the jeans fit around her expanding midsection. With her favorite purple top over it, she was pretty sure no one would know she was wearing her mother's jeans.

She wheeled her bike out of the garage and pushed on her front tire with her thumb. It felt low again. She used the tire pump to add air until it felt firm. How long before she had to buy new tires?

A stiff breeze chilled her and made pedaling difficult. How would she manage being nine months pregnant, balancing on a bike, and pedaling through snow on the trail?

She rode slowly through the residential area, watching for cars, but once on the trail, she sped up. It wouldn't be good to be late to work. She needed her job now more than ever.

~

Margaret stared listlessly out the window. Melanie had served her a lovely breakfast—scrambled eggs, whole-wheat toast, fruit, and yogurt.

She pushed the food around the plate while Melanie ate, but now that she'd left the room to shower and dress, she didn't have to pretend. Her appetite was gone. And she'd developed sores in her mouth, so it hurt to eat. She took a small sip of water, then pushed the plate away. Melanie would probably scold her for not eating, but she needed the Bread of Life more than eggs and toast.

She picked up her Bible and began to read, pausing every now and then to pray.

"And whatever it takes, help Jon realize his need for you, Lord."

"Be with Bethany. She's such a sweet young girl and she's got some tough circumstances. Oh, I know, she's suffering consequences of her own actions, but if there's any way I can help, make that clear to me."

Melanie's footsteps sounded in the hallway. "Who are you talking to?"

"I'm just praying."

Melanie had a towel wrapped turban-style around her hair. She reached for Margaret's plate. Her voice reflected her disappointment. "Mom, you didn't eat."

Margaret sighed. "I don't have any appetite. I tried, honey, I really did." She used the table to lean on as she stood. "Do you need help cleaning up?"

Melanie waved her away. "I think I can start the dishwasher."

"I'm tired. I'll go sit in my chair for a while." Margaret started toward the living room and one knee buckled. She grabbed at the table.

Suddenly Melanie's arms were around her waist, supporting her. "Lean on me."

They made their way to Margaret's chair, and she sank into it. "Thanks, dear." Her eyelids fluttered and she was aware of Melanie lifting her glasses off her face. "I'll just close my eyes a bit before I get dressed."

She heard Melanie's footsteps going toward the kitchen before she faded into sleep.

Later, when her eyes opened, Melanie's hair had been blown dry and styled. She sat on the couch by the window. Sun slanted through the windows and pooled in warm patches on the carpet by her feet. Her iPad was on her lap, and one manicured finger swiped across the screen.

Margaret shifted in her chair. "What time is it?"

Melanie looked up and smiled. "It's almost noon."

"And here I am still in my pajamas." Margaret fumbled for her glasses.

"We need to talk." Melanie laid her iPad on the couch beside her and leaned forward.

Where were her glasses? Her fingers felt the rims. She pulled them from behind the lamp and slipped them on. "I'll start to feel better and I'll eat more. You'll see." She patted her hips. "I have plenty of reserve here."

Melanie's brow creased. "Mom, it's more than that. The chemo makes you ill. You're tired and you've lost strength. I'd stay here and take care of you, but I have a job in New York, and eventually I have to go back. Who's going to take care of you when I leave?"

"Elizabeth will help out. She takes me to appointments."

"Elizabeth has a job at Furry Friends. And didn't you say she takes care of her grandchildren after school? You can't expect her to be around all the time."

Margaret set her mouth and tilted her chin. "I can do it. I can take care of myself. I'll be fine." Inside she quivered. She'd asked herself the same questions.

Melanie laid her hands on her knees. "I want you to move back to New York with me. My apartment has two bedrooms. We can have your records transferred to Mt. Sinai hospital, you can get your treatments there, and I will be home in the evenings to take care of you. You can take a cab anywhere you want to go. We can get a—"

"No." Margaret used the chair arms to hoist herself up. "I appreciate your concern, but I can't leave Maple Grove. Or my home. If need be, I have enough money I could hire help when I need it."

The crease in Melanie's forehead deepened. "Who would you hire? Maple Grove's not teeming with health care professionals looking for jobs. The best thing would be for you to come to New York. It wouldn't have to be permanent. When you're better, then you can come back."

"And what if I don't get better?" Margaret asked.

"Mom. You know how I feel about negative thoughts."

Margaret put her hands on her hips and faced Melanie. "I was healed the day I accepted Christ as my Savior. Someday, whether from this cancer or something else, my body's going to wear out. But praise God, I'll have a new one, an eternal one. That's about as positive a thought as I can think."

Melanie remained silent as Margaret shuffled down the hall to her bedroom to get dressed.

Chapter 45

THE TEXT CAME during last period study hall. Bethany heard the small vibration in her backpack lying at her feet. The temptation was great to pull it out and read it, but the fear of consequences if caught with a phone was greater. She'd wait.

When the bell rang, she dropped her algebra book and papers into her backpack, slung it over her shoulder, and hurried outside. She jerked out her phone and looked at it. Kyle.

Home for the weekend. Want to hang out? Drive to Benson?

His invitation sounded wonderful. She never had time to enjoy being a teen. Working nights at River's Edge cut down on her social life, and she didn't fit in so well anymore, either. Her friends were shopping and planning for prom. She was planning for a baby. She texted back:

Sure. Want to pick me up @ 9 @ River's Edge?

Then she crossed the parking lot and slid into the back seat of her friend, Cassandra's, car. Cassy and Bryce were in the front giggling over something on Bryce's phone. Cassy swiveled to look at her. "Hey, Beth. Need to go home? Bryce and I are going to P.J.'s."

"Sounds fun, but, yeah, I do need to get home. I have to work tonight. Kyle's home and we're going out after work."

Bryce cocked his head at her. "Kyle Davis? Are you two still an item?"

Bethany shook her head. "Not really an item. We're just good friends." And parents. The thought came like a dousing of ice water.

When Cassy pulled into her driveway, Bethany said a quick "thanks," and stepped out of the car. Inside, she took the time to apply eye makeup and change her top. Should she choose something flattering, modest, or standard work-wear? She took out a long sweater in a shade of blue that matched her eyes. It fit loosely and hid her expanding middle. She pulled it on and took a moment to appraise her looks in the mirror. Did she look like a teenager on a date or an expectant mother?

Later, as she pedaled her way to River's Edge, she carried on imaginary conversations with Kyle in her head.

"I'll support you, Bethany, in every way." "We're in this together." "I'll take care of you and the baby."

By the time she reached the restaurant, she was almost giddy with excitement for her date. Time dragged as she waited tables. She must have glanced at the clock a thousand times before Jon finally said, "I can wait the last two tables if you want to leave early."

She felt a twinge of guilt. Had he seen her staring at the clock? "Someone is picking me up. Is it okay to leave my bike here until tomorrow?"

"Sure. Why don't you put it around by the deck in back?" Jon picked up the pies she'd set out and returned to the dining room.

Bethany filled out her time card, grabbed her jacket, and hurried out the front door. Kyle's green Honda Civic sat in the parking lot with the motor running. She waved and breathed in deeply, hoping to still her wildly beating heart.

When she slid into the passenger seat, Kyle leaned over, pulled her close, and kissed her. His lips were sweet and gentle, and she wished the kiss would never end.

Kyle shifted the car in reverse. "Mark Brewbaker's having a party at his girlfriend's house in Benson. Want to go hang out there for awhile?" He maneuvered the car out of the parking lot and sped up.

Bethany felt a twinge of disappointment. "Umm, okay. I can't drink, though."

"Can't drink? Why? I'm driving."

She took a deep breath. This wasn't how she'd planned on telling him. "I'm still pregnant, Kyle. I didn't have the abortion."

Kyle stopped the car so suddenly the books and trash on the back seat tumbled to the floor. "What? You're still pregnant?"

Bethany didn't look at him as she adjusted her seat belt. "Yes."

Kyle's voice rocked the small car. "That's the stupidest thing I ever heard. Are you planning on keeping it?"

"Please don't holler at me." Her arm wrapped protectively around her middle. "It's not an it, this is our baby. I don't know if I'm keeping him—or her. I just couldn't end his life. He deserves a chance."

Kyle's fist hit the steering wheel. "This is great. Just great." He turned to look at her, his face contorted with rage. "You can screw up your own life with a kid, but you're not screwing up mine."

Bethany bit her lip, holding back the tears. What happened to the happy conversations she envisioned just a few hours ago? "I won't screw your life up, Kyle. I'll stay completely out of your life, if that's what you want. Starting right now. Take me home, please."

Kyle stomped on the accelerator and the car fishtailed, spraying gravel as it shot down the road.

Chapter 46

KIRSTEN SLIPPED OUT of her white lab coat and hung it over her arm. After the incident with the West Highland White Terrier, the coat needed laundered. She took one last loop around the cages of the animals boarded and those available for adoption. There was a new occupant, a little stray beagle someone had brought in this morning.

As she drew near, the beagle put his paws up on the cage. His long ears drooped on either side of his legs and his brown eyes pleaded with her. Kirsten ran her hand on the underside of his paws, feeling the rough pads scrape her fingers. "Ahh, little fella, I don't think you'll have to be here for too long. Someone's going to fall in love with those brown eyes."

For a moment, she pictured Josiah running around the back yard with the flop-eared dog following. But beagles were avid hunters, and what if he took off? Josiah would take off after him, and she'd have another situation like the night Jon plucked him out of the river. She shivered again with the thought of what could have happened.

She flipped out the lights and then closed and locked the

clinic doors behind her.

When she pulled up in front of her dad's house, Josiah sat on the porch steps wearing his jacket and backpack. Her dad stood behind the glass storm door. As soon as the car came to a stop, Josiah marched out to the car, climbed in, and slammed the door behind him. The scowl on his face deepened, and he tucked his chin to his chest and refused to look at her.

Kirsten knew better than to greet him cheerfully or to ask for any kind of conversation. But she needed to find out what was going on.

"I can see your day hasn't been the best." She watched him in the rearview mirror. "We can talk about it at home. You must get your seatbelt fastened before we go. I need to ask Grandpa a quick question. Wait here, please."

Kirsten slipped out of the car and hurried up to the house. Her dad stepped out on the porch. His face was creased with a frown as deep as Josiah's, but filled with concern, too.

"He's mad at me. There was something about a football game at the school, and he said he had to go. You hadn't said anything about it, and I didn't think I could walk that far. My knees are acting up again." He reached down and rubbed his leg. "I worried he would take off like last time, but he just sat on the porch, so I stood behind the door and watched him. I'm not sure I can keep doing this. I love Josiah, but I'm afraid I won't be able to prevent him from doing something dangerous."

Panic gripped Kirsten's heart. It was difficult raising Josiah on her own, but if she didn't have her dad's support, what would she do?

"Please, Dad, can we talk about this? I'll figure something out."

Her dad patted her arm. "I know it isn't easy, honey. And I'm helping all I can. But I'm just getting too old for that boy's shenanigans." He turned and hobbled back into his house.

Kirsten walked back to the car. She glanced in the back seat. Josiah still wore a scowl, but he'd buckled his seat belt. She started the car and drove home without talking.

As she went through Josiah's backpack, Kirsten discovered the root of the controversy. A flyer announced that students would be admitted free to Friday night's football game if they brought something to donate to the local food pantry. As usual, Josiah had only assimilated part of the information.

She showed him the flyer and the calendar. "This game is not until Friday, Josiah. And not until seven o'clock. Grandpa was just keeping you safe. And you were rude to him."

Josiah studied the flyer. "The Rottweiler breed makes the best guard dogs, keeping both home and family safe."

Kirsten sighed and handed Josiah his homework folder. "It's time to write your spelling words. And then I want you to write an apology to Grandpa. Tell him, 'I'm sorry I didn't obey you.' I'll get supper going."

Josiah sat at the counter without protesting and Kirsten could hear the soft scratch of his pencil on the paper as she cut the vegetables for the salad. Pushing the problem of her dad and Josiah to the back of her mind was like forcing an unwilling St Bernard into a cage, but she managed it. She'd deal with tonight's challenges and think about the rest later.

Margaret wasn't asleep, but she was deep in thought in her blue chair. Melanie checked emails on her iPad, and Margaret's mind drifted to the conversation this morning. She didn't want to be a burden to anyone, but right now, she had to admit, she needed assistance. Melanie's visit had been a blessing, but the idea of living in an apartment in New York City filled her with dread. She would be alone for long days while her daughter worked. And here, in her own home, she was never alone. Nathaniel's presence was as real and comforting as the cushions of her blue chair.

Margaret didn't hear the knock. So when Melanie hopped up to answer the door, it startled her, and she let out a little, "Oh."

Bethany, wearing an oversized sweatshirt and a pair of baggy jeans, stood on the doorstep. Margaret leaned forward and spoke from her chair, "Why, Bethany, what a treat, come on in."

Bethany scuffed the toe of her shoe against the cement landing. "I don't want to bother you. Are you feeling okay, Margaret?"

Melanie swung the door wider. "Come on in, Bethany. Mom would love to visit with you for a few minutes." Maybe Melanie felt badly about the chilly reception she'd given Bethany the first time she visited.

Bethany took a seat on the couch and asked again, "How are you?"

Margaret smiled. "I'm okay. I'm not up to running on the bike trail, but I can still make it out of bed in the morning. I don't know what I would do without Melanie. She takes good care of this old lady. Enough about me. How are things at River's Edge?"

Bethany shrugged. "It's okay. We've really been busy. Carlton is doing more of the cooking at night, and I think that's helped Jon. He can concentrate on greeting the people and just keeping things going."

"How is Carlton?"

Bethany's eyes narrowed a little. "He's good. He isn't any more talkative, if that's what you mean. But he hasn't gotten in trouble with Jon yet. I think maybe he's changed since high school."

Margaret nodded. "That's good. His grandma prays for him."

Bethany gave a little wry smile. "That's what I need. A grandma to pray for me."

Margaret leaned over the arm of her chair, reached out, and patted Bethany's arm. "I'm not your grandma, but I pray for you."

Bethany looked surprised and a bit teary. "Thanks."

"Is Carlton helping out during lunch?"

"Yeah. He does a split shift most of the time. Then he can work on his classes in the afternoon."

"Good for him."

Bethany twisted a strand of hair around her finger. "I came to ask you something."

Margaret's mind flashed through possible requests. Money? Advice concerning her pregnancy? "Ask away."

"Would you teach me how to make pies?"

Margaret laughed. "I thought you were going to ask something difficult. Of course I will. Do you want pies for a special occasion?"

"There've been lots of comments from the customers on how they miss your pies. I know Jon can't give me more hours right now, but I thought if I could make some pies at home and bring them in, he'd pay me extra. I'll need more money this spring. Especially if I have to get my own apartment. Not that I could make pies as good as yours, but they'd be better than those frozen ones. Everybody complains."

"Oh, Bethany, I could teach you to make wonderful pies. And I'm sure Jon would pay for them. When shall we start?"

"How about Sunday? In the afternoon, after church, of course. Would that work?"

"That would work fine for me."

Bethany stood and walked to the door. "I better get going." She looked at Melanie. "Sorry to take your time with your mom."

Melanie looked up from the iPad and smiled. "Oh, no problem. Mom loves to have visitors."

Bethany stepped out and pulled the door shut behind her. Both Margaret and Melanie watched as she got on her bike and pedaled down the street.

"Mom." Melanie hissed. "What are you thinking? It takes all your strength just to recover from the chemo treatments. You can't be taking on something like teaching a teenager how to make pies."

Margaret hoisted herself out of the blue chair. "What I'm thinking is that God is still pointing out some things for me to do here on earth. There's no way I'm going to refuse that!"

Chapter 47

JON LEANED OVER the counter as four middle-aged women, giggly as a group of teenagers, left the restaurant.

He should feel great. The restaurant books were inching toward being in the black. He'd thought things might slow down after Maple Festival, but the clientele continued to grow. Carlton had stepped up and proved able to turn out meals as well as Jon. And Bethany bustled around and charmed the diners with her smile and sweet manners.

If business remained steady, the restaurant would soon be making a profit. There was the construction and start-up loan to pay back, but Jon lived simply and could make the payments on those.

He stepped out on the porch and looked at the black sky lit with stars as bright as fireworks. *I made your dream a reality, Angie. So where's my feeling of accomplishment?*

He felt as dried up and empty as he had seven months ago when he'd first laid eyes on the house. The knife edge of grief had dulled, but the gaping wound had not begun to heal.

He remembered Paul's words, *healing don't come from a place.* So where could he find healing?

A bitter taste rose in his mouth. He shot a wad of spit into the darkness, turned and strode back to the kitchen.

Carlton lifted a basket of French fries from the fryer. He blinked with his usual startled look of guilt. "Hi, Mr. Washington. I made myself some fries because I didn't take much of a dinner break earlier."

"That's fine, Carlton. We were busy tonight. Why don't you sit down and eat, and I'll finish cleaning up?"

"I think I'll just take these with me. I drove tonight. Gotta get home and do some homework." Carlton dumped his fries into a Styrofoam container, sprinkled on a thick layer of salt, and liberally squirted ketchup over the top. Then he closed the lid, marked the time on his card and slipped out the back door.

Jon opened the cooler and slid the salad cart inside. When he stepped back into the kitchen, he picked up a cloth to clean the counters when he heard a bark from upstairs. He'd forgotten to let Maisy out. Tossing the cloth at the sink, he took a last look at the kitchen. Nothing that couldn't wait until morning. He trudged up the stairs.

"Sorry, Maisy. It's just been too crazy here tonight." He followed her down and let her out the back door. While he waited for her to do her nightly business, which included a great deal of sniffing around the yard, he went back inside to balance the cash register. It took longer than he expected, and he still hadn't heard Maisy's customary bark at the door. He stepped outside for the second time that night. Tiger wound between his legs, and he reached down to pet her.

He stood and shouted into the darkness. "Maisy, you better come in if you know what's good for you." Just then she trotted around the house carrying something in her mouth. A deer leg. Deer season had begun for bow hunters, and it looked like someone had bagged one close to River's Edge, field dressed it, and left parts for Maisy to find.

"Drop it," he commanded. Maisy's tail stopped its proud wag. She lowered her head and slowly let the leg drop to the deck floor. It fell with a soft clunk.

"Ewww. Really Maisy? Is that better than Iams?" He opened the door and shooed her inside. Then he picked up the leg and dropped it in the small dumpster out back.

He washed up thoroughly in the restaurant bathroom. Then he called Maisy and went upstairs, looking forward to watching the evening news and maybe a movie on Netflix before falling asleep.

Maisy's deep bark woke him. At first he thought he'd left her outside, but then he realized she was standing on the rug by the bed. Suddenly her front paws were on the mattress, and she was barking in his face.

Jon sat up. Then he smelled it.

Smoke!

He leaped out of bed, wrestled into a pair of sweats and a tee shirt and jammed his feet into flip-flops. Then he grabbed hold of Maisy by the collar and pulled her out into the hall.

The downstairs was thick with smoke. His phone. He grabbed it from the charger, slid it in his pocket and, still holding Maisy, felt his way downstairs through the smoke. He coughed, gagged, and pulled his shirt over his mouth and nose. Maisy tugged him forward. He followed, arm outstretched until he felt the front door. He threw it open and stepped out into the night. He dropped Maisy's collar. With trembling hands he punched 911.

It seemed an eternity before he heard the wail of the sirens.

The sound drew nearer until finally, fire trucks skidded into the parking lot. The firemen wasted no time. Fat hoses from the tanker truck were pulled out. One hose snaked in the back door and another in the front. Jon stood watching, helpless and shivering as his dream—Angie's dream—drifted into the night with the clouds of smoke.

One of the firefighters stomped by in his heavy boots and thick coat talking on a walky-talky he held in a soot-smeared hand. Jon caught words and phrases, but his mind couldn't sort through them.

How had this happened? What started a fire?

An image of Carlton smoking flashed in his memory. His gut tightened into a ball of anger. He pictured Carlton as he left, pulling a cigarette out, lighting it, then carelessly tossing it where it could catch the house on fire.

Cars pulled into the parking lot. Some of them must have held volunteer firemen, because they wore appropriate gear and raced to join others around the trucks. Others parked at the back, and the people inside sat and watched. What made people want to gawk at someone else's tragedy?

Streaks of pink showed in the sky over Maple Grove when a man with a badge identifying him as the chief approached Jon. "I'm sorry, Mr. Washington. This is really tough."

Jon nodded, too numb to respond.

"I'm pretty sure we got the fire out, but some of us will stick around for a while to make sure. We kept the fire contained in the kitchen and storage room, but there is smoke and water damage all through the downstairs. You should be able to rebuild, though."

Jon choked out the question. "Were you able to determine where the fire began?"

The fire chief tipped back his helmet. "Definitely started in the kitchen. I hate to say for sure before the state fire marshal takes a look, but my guess is the deep fat fryer. Mighta been a malfunction."

Jon couldn't breathe. He'd left the fryer on when he'd gone to let Maisy out. He was the one who'd set fire to his own dreams. Bile rose in his mouth.

The fire chief shrugged. "It happens all the time in restaurants. Someone forgets to turn the fryer off, the hot grease spatters, and—we get the call."

Jon looked over at River's Edge. A jagged hole with charred edges gaped where the back wall of the storage room had once been. Food, equipment, and supplies lay in blackened heaps, most of them burned beyond recognition. Smoke curled in lazy circles above the ruins.

Waves of nausea flooded over him, and Jon thought for a moment that he was going to be physically sick.

"You've got insurance don't you?" the fire chief asked.

Jon nodded and forced his lips to move. "Yeah, I've got insurance." *What would the minimal policy he'd purchased cover?*

"Why don't you get a motel room for the rest of the night? You can call your insurance agent in the morning."

Jon rubbed his hands over his face and hair, wishing he could clear his thoughts. Sleep? He didn't think so. He reached down for Maisy's collar.

Maisy? Where was she? His heart plummeted, and the nausea returned. He tried to remember. She'd pulled him down the stairs and outside, but he couldn't remember seeing her since then. Sirens. Cars coming and going. Fire trucks. She must be terrified. But if she couldn't run inside, where would she go?

"Maisy. Maisy." Jon called as he walked around the

restaurant, the gray house rising like a ghostly specter in the early morning light. After one lap, he stopped at the fire truck. The chief and several firefighters were loading hoses and equipment onto the truck.

"Have any of you seen my dog? She's a yellow Lab."

"Was she inside?" The fire chief's eyebrows knotted together in worry.

"No. She pulled me downstairs. I held onto her collar, and she pulled me to the front door. We came outside together, but then I let go of her."

The frown smoothed out. "I'm sure she's around somewhere. The sirens probably scared her off. Soon as we get loaded up and take off, she'll turn up."

One of the firemen was wrapping yellow tape around River's Edge. Bandaging an injury. But to Jon, the gaping hole, the charred remnants of the kitchen, looked like a mortal wound.

He turned away, stumbling across the yard and calling out Maisy's name.

When the sun poked bright rays over River's Edge, Jon collapsed on the front step. There was still no sign of Maisy, but Tiger paced back and forth in front of him, meowing loudly. She didn't know her breakfast had burned up. Jon limped to his truck and rummaged through the trash on the back floor. One stale granola bar was all he could find.

When he broke off a bite for Tiger, she sniffed at it in disgust and stalked away, her tail waving to show her displeasure.

The two firemen who had stayed behind to watch over the smoldering remains walked around the corner of the house.

Jon asked, "Could I go upstairs and get some clothes and things?"

The men looked at each other, then back at him. One of them

spoke, "I don't see why not. The fire was contained in the kitchen and storage area. I'll go with you, just in case." He held up the yellow tape and Jon ducked under.

Inside his home, the smell of smoke was overwhelming. Jon held his breath as he hurried upstairs. He grabbed a duffel bag from the closet and threw in jeans, T-shirts, underwear, and socks, then added some toiletries from the bathroom. On the way out he grabbed his keys and locked the front door. Then he let loose a disgusted snort. "If someone wanted to break in, they could just walk through the hole."

The fireman nodded his agreement. "You might call someone to board that up as soon as possible. Not that anyone here in Maple Grove would do that, but better to be safe than sorry." He gave Jon an awkward pat on the back. "Hey, I'm real sorry for this. But we did save the house. It can be repaired. And no lives lost. Your dog will be back."

Jon looked toward the restaurant. The sign in the front window said *Closed*. He turned back to the fireman. "Not sure I'll reopen it. Not sure it's worth it."

He strode toward his truck without looking back.

Chapter 48

JON RUBBED HIS eyes and looked at the clock on the nightstand. Almost noon.

After checking into the motel, he'd showered, changed clothes, and called his insurance agent. The agent lived in Maple Grove and had already heard about the fire. He gave the standard "I'm so sorry" speech and promised to get an adjuster out as soon as possible.

Within a few minutes he had a call from the adjuster, a Ms. Gallaher. She would meet him at River's Edge at three. At her suggestion, he called Paul, who agreed to meet with them.

Then he called Carlton and Bethany. Both spoke consoling words, but Jon knew part of their sorrow was the loss of a job they needed. He shrugged it off. He couldn't deal with anyone else's problems today.

When he'd collapsed on the bed, he had only meant to relax for a minute and then resume his search for Maisy. Now he'd slept for almost three hours.

He stepped to the sink and splashed water on his face. He rubbed his chin, considered shaving, and decided against it. Without customers to please, he had more important things to do than scrape off whiskers.

He stopped mid-stride on his way to the door. Margaret. Had the Maple Grove gossip line informed her of the fire? He pulled out his phone and punched in her number.

She answered before he even heard a ring. "Oh, Jon, I am so sorry. What can I do to help?"

Despite his anguish, he chuckled. "What happened to hello?"

"I have a smart phone. I could see that it was you. I didn't think you needed chit-chat this morning. How are you?" Margaret emphasized each syllable, and he knew there was genuine concern in the question.

Jon sank to the edge of the bed and stretched his legs out in front of him. He could be honest with Margaret. "I don't know. I meet with the adjuster this afternoon. I'll know more then. But Maisy's gone. She disappeared shortly after the fire started."

"She'll be back. She's just scared."

"I hope so."

"Keep me posted on what's going on, will you?"

"Sure."

"And Jon, you know I'm praying for Maisy's return, and for you."

After he said good-bye and dropped the phone in his pocket, he realized he hadn't even asked how she felt. He added more guilt to the load he was carrying and hurried out to his truck.

He stopped at Maple Grove Foods for pet food, some cheap plastic bowls, and a premade sandwich from the deli. When he got to River's Edge, Tiger trotted out to greet him and eagerly munched down the cat food he poured into the new bowl, not even minding eating on the front porch instead of the deck. He filled another bowl with water from the outside faucet. But there was still no sign of Maisy.

He walked down the trail in both directions, calling and

listening. Nothing. Feeling more lost than ever, he returned to River's Edge and waited for the adjuster and Paul.

Paul was the first to arrive. Jon braced himself for the condolences.

"Well, my friend." Paul sank to the step beside him. "Just a chance to prove what yer made of."

Jon frowned. "What I'm made of?"

"Not for sure, but it looks like God is givin' you a little test. We can build this back up right purty, like it was before, but I'm a thinkin' it's you God wants to build up."

Jon shook his head. How could he respond to that? He didn't even believe in God. What kind of God would take a man's wife and then burn down his house? Not one he wanted to believe in.

Thankfully, he spotted a car on the road. The adjuster pulled into the driveway in a sporty red Mazda RX3. Jon walked out to meet her. An attractive young woman with a blond ponytail stepped out and held out her hand.

"I'm Darcy Gallaher."

"Jon Washington." Jon shook her hand briefly.

Paul pulled a hand deep out of his jean pocket. He'd probably been searching for taffy. "I'm the contractor. Paul Donovan."

"Let's take a look, shall we?" Darcy led the way, circling the perimeter of the property, asking a few questions, but mostly just looking and making notes in a leather-bound portfolio. Paul had a small, worn spiral notebook. He jotted things down with a flat carpenter's pencil that he stuck behind his ear when he wasn't using it.

When they stepped inside, the smell of smoke almost choked Jon. Darcy coughed, pulled a tissue from her pocket, and held it to her nose. They stepped cautiously through the downstairs, but as they got to the kitchen, Darcy stopped. "I don't think it would be wise to walk on the floor here. Jon, can you give me a rundown of all the equipment you had?"

Jon tipped his head back, trying to clear his thoughts and remember. "Commercial grade six-burner Maytag gas stove with a convection oven…" In his mind he traveled through his kitchen, listing equipment and supplies.

Darcy looked up from the portfolio. "Do you have an inventory of the foods in the cooler and pantry?"

Jon handed her the print-out he'd made this morning in the motel's business room.

She took the paper and glanced over it. Then she went around to the swinging doors. Paul held one of the doors wide open, and Darcy spent a long time looking, asking questions and writing things down.

When they finally stepped back onto the porch, Darcy closed her portfolio. "I could drive back to Kansas City, but I know you're anxious to start rebuilding. If you don't mind, I'll get my computer out of the car and figure out the settlement."

Jon nodded. "Sure. Stay as long as you like. It's not like I have anything to do."

Darcy looked at Paul. "Can we put our heads together and compare costs of construction?"

"Sure thing."

Just then a yellow blur leaped from around the corner of the house and onto the porch. She had a smear of mud on her back and a string of burs down one leg.

"Maisy!" Jon dropped to his knees and threw his arms around the dog. Her long, wet tongue licked his face.

"Well, now. That's an answer to prayer." Paul patted Maisy's head, and she licked his fingers, which probably tasted like taffy.

Jon gently stroked his dog, picking the burs off and tossing them into the trash can. "Where have you been? Are you hungry?" Maisy followed Jon as he got the dog food out of the car and poured some in the plastic dish. She ate the entire bowlful and wagged up at him, hopeful for more. Then she emptied the water dish.

Meanwhile, Darcy got her laptop from the car and set up in the dining room, and Paul followed her inside. Through the open window, Jon could hear the muted murmur of their voices and the click of her fingers on the keys of her computer. He lowered himself to the porch swing, and Maisy sprawled at his feet, her head on her paws.

After a while, Paul stepped outside. "I think we're all done for now. I'll mosey on back to town. Let me know if there's anything else I can do. And let me know when you want to start on this." He waved his arm toward River's Edge.

"I'll be in touch. And Paul, thanks for helping."

"No problem. Here." He'd dug two pieces of taffy from his pocket and he tossed one to Jon. "Good medicine." Then he sauntered to his truck and drove off.

Jon settled back on the porch swing. He woke with a start when the front door opened.

Darcy stood in the doorway. "I've completed the figures, Mr. Washington, and I'm prepared to offer you a settlement."

Jon stumbled to his feet. Maisy raised her head but didn't stand. She must be exhausted, too. "Come on, girl, let's go inside." He followed Darcy, holding the door for Maisy. She headed for her rug at the top of the stairs.

Jon sat opposite Darcy. She slid a form across the table. "Based on your coverage package, this is what the payout will be."

Jon looked at the figures, then up at her in astonishment.

"But that's less than half of the rebuilding costs."

Darcy shook her head. "I'm sorry, Mr. Washington. You had minimal coverage on the restaurant. Perhaps you could do some of the rebuilding yourself? Buy second-hand equipment?"

Jon raked his fingers through his hair. It was worse than he'd thought. He still owed on the original loan, and there would be no income for months. He didn't even have a place to live, and now the cost of rebuilding was far more than the insurance would cover. He expelled his breath in a huff. "Do I have to accept this? Can I appeal or protest or something?"

Darcy slid the paper back toward her. "Sure you can. I can rework the figures. My supervisor will look at it. But in the end, I think you'll find it will be the same. And you'll only delay getting your check." She shrugged. "It's up to you."

Without a word, Jon took the pen she'd laid on the table and signed where she'd highlighted.

After the papers were returned to her, Darcy stood and slid her computer back into the case. "I am sorry, Mr. Washington. We'll get a check to you this week." She looked around the dining room. "This is a lovely place, and I hope you get it rebuilt soon."

Jon stood on the porch with Maisy and watched Darcy drive away. Then he pulled his phone out and punched in Paul's number.

"This is Paul."

"Hi, Paul. Jon Washington. Yeah, go ahead and put up the plywood to cover the hole so we can lock up the house. Insurance is only going to pay $50,000. That's only half the rebuilding costs. Not sure what I'm going to do. I'm thinking seriously about just cutting my losses and walking away. Maybe get my old job back in Minneapolis."

He could picture Paul swallowing his wad of taffy so he could talk more clearly. "Just don't be hasty. We can work something out. You know, I don't have to be paid up front. We could maybe work out somethin' with payments. You think on it for a day or so before makin' a decision that'll follow you the rest of your life."

Even though he knew Paul couldn't see him, he nodded. "Thanks, Paul." He dropped the phone back in his pocket. Maisy leaned against him, and he ran his fingers over her head.

What was he going to do with Maisy? The motel had a no-pets policy, but he couldn't leave her at River's Edge alone. Tiger would be fine, she was used to being outside by herself. He could come by every day to put out some food and water. But Maisy couldn't…

He reached for his phone again. When the receptionist answered, he asked, "Could I speak to Dr. Danielson, please? It's kind of an emergency."

There was a pause, then, "Name please."

"Jon Washington."

"Just a minute, Mr. Washington. I'll see if it's possible for her to come to the phone."

She put him on hold, and a commercial about some flea medication droned in his ear.

"Jon?" It was Kirsten's voice, and he suddenly felt like he'd just been allowed to sit and drink cool water after six rounds in a boxing ring.

"Kirsten, I'm sorry to bother you at work, but I didn't know who else to call. Did you hear about the fire?"

"I did. I'm so sorry. But you're okay? And Maisy and Tiger?"

"We're all okay. But I can't stay at River's Edge. They turned off the electricity. Maisy disappeared during the fire, but she came back this afternoon. I don't have a place to keep her. Could you and Josiah possibly take her for a few days? Just until I decide what I'm going to do?"

There was a tiny pause, long enough for a moment of dread, but then he could hear the smile in her voice. "We'd be glad to take care of her for you. Just bring her to the clinic, or after six to the house, if you want to see Josiah."

"I'll bring her now, if you don't mind."

"That would be great. I'm getting ready for surgery on a Great Dane, so just leave her with Yvonne, the receptionist."

Disappointment rose for a moment. "Okay. I'll leave her at the desk."

Jon slipped the phone in his pocket and called. "Come on, Maisy girl. You're going to see a couple of your favorite people. They'll take good care of you until I get things figured out."

After leaving Maisy at Furry Friends, Jon stopped by the motel. He picked up the sack of dirty clothes that still reeked of smoke. At the front desk, he paid cash for his room. He dropped the key on the counter and walked out to his truck.

At the stoplight, he turned onto the highway, leaving town.

Chapter 49

KIRSTEN OPENED THE door, and Maisy hopped in the back seat without hesitation. Jon had brought bowls and a small bag of food, and she stowed them in the back. He'd apologized for not having a leash, since it had burned up in the fire. She borrowed one from Furry Friends, so she was all set for her guest.

Josiah would be delighted with the opportunity to dog-sit. The only problem would be when Jon returned. It would break Josiah's heart to give Maisy back.

She drove the short distance to her dad's. He'd agreed to watch Josiah until she found someone else. She'd threatened to take away all of Josiah's video games if there were any more problems obeying his grandpa and, so far, things had gone well. She honked the horn to let him know she was there.

Within a few minutes, Josiah opened the door and stepped out. Her dad waved to her from the doorway. He was smiling, and she sighed with relief. Maybe he would reconsider and continue to watch his grandson.

Josiah was almost to the car before he spotted Maisy. He ran the rest of the way and threw open the door. Maisy sprang to her feet and waggled all over.

Kirsten shouted, "Don't let her out, Josiah. Get in and shut the door."

Josiah climbed in, put both arms around the dog's neck, and buried his face in her fur. "I'm so glad to see you, girl."

Kirsten couldn't help but smile at his greeting. She'd never gotten a welcome like that. "There was a fire last night at River's Edge, and Jon doesn't have a place to keep Maisy. He asked if we would keep her for a few days. Do you think you can help take care of her?"

Josiah's eyes met hers in the rearview mirror. "She's staying at our house?"

"Yep. For a few days."

"Where's Jon?"

"I'm not sure. He just can't stay out at River's Edge."

Josiah turned back to Maisy. "Did you hear that, girl? You get to stay at our house. And I'll feed you, a half-cup for every twenty pounds of body weight, and I'll get you fresh water, and I'll take you for a walk, and you can sleep in my room. Mom, Maisy can sleep in my room, can't she?"

"Maybe." Kirsten didn't like giving Josiah indefinite answers, as he functioned much better with black and whites. But this might work in her favor. "Let's see how the evening goes. We still have our regular routine, even if Maisy is here."

"Okay." Josiah continued his conversation with Maisy. As Kirsten listened to her son, she wondered if anyone who heard him chattering away to the dog would guess he had communication problems.

When they got home, Josiah held the leash while Kirsten got the food and bowls from the back. Maisy followed them inside like she'd lived there all of her life. Josiah removed her leash and filled up one dish with water. "Should I feed her now, Mom?"

"Why don't you wait until we eat? Jon said she had dog food

earlier this afternoon."

"Can I take her for a walk?"

Kirsten glanced at the clock and hesitated. She certainly didn't want to get Josiah out of his routine. "You know we need to do your homework first. If you want to walk Maisy during your video time, that's fine. But let's get homework out of the way first."

She heard a little whine of protest, and at the same time Maisy walked over and pressed against Josiah's legs. Kirsten opened the backpack Josiah had dropped on the floor and pulled out his folder. Two math sheets, spelling words to write, and a reading assignment. She laid them on the table with a pencil. Josiah slouched into his chair. Maisy followed and lay down, her head stretched across his feet.

Josiah reached down and gave her a pat. "Good girl, you're gonna help, aren't you?" Then he started on the homework.

Kirsten smiled as she pulled out vegetables for a salad. She'd put chicken and potatoes in the slow cooker this morning, and the warm, meaty smell filled the kitchen. After making the salads, she started a load of laundry and checked emails on her laptop.

Thirty minutes later, Josiah laid down the pencil. "Done. Now can we go?"

Kirsten braced herself. "Put your papers back in your folder. Then you may take Maisy for a walk, but if you do, it will be suppertime when you get back. There won't be time for video games tonight."

"That's okay. I don't need to play video games all the time." Josiah grabbed the leash from the counter and fastened it to Maisy's collar.

Kirsten stood in front of him and used their signal for him to make eye contact. "You may go around the double block, but no farther. Stay on the sidewalk. Please repeat the directions."

"We can go around the double block, but no farther. Stay on the sidewalk." Josiah parroted back. "Come on, Maisy, let's go. See you, Mom." He flashed one of his rare smiles at her before opening the door and following Maisy's waving tail outside. Kirsten watched out the window as they headed down the sidewalk. Maisy trotted out eagerly, but she kept by Josiah's side, not racing ahead or pulling on the leash.

Kirsten felt a stab of anxiety as she always did when Josiah was out of her sight, but the double block was familiar territory. The only street he had to cross was deep in the residential section and had little traffic.

She sat on the couch in the front room and picked up a magazine, but she didn't really read anything. When she heard Josiah returning, she stepped into the kitchen so he wouldn't know she'd been waiting for him. The door opened, and both dog and boy galloped in.

Kirsten started toward the dining table.

"Wait," Josiah cautioned. "Maisy gets fed first." He carefully measured food into her bowl and set it on the floor for her. Then, without being told, he washed his hands at the kitchen sink and joined her at the table.

"Would you like to say the prayer?" Kirsten asked. He rarely did. His communication problems seemed to include talking to God.

Josiah had already bowed his head. He looked up without making eye contact. "Okay." His head bowed again. "God thank you for this day. Thanks for Maisy staying with us. Thanks for dinner."

When he looked up again, Kirsten prompted. "Say amen."

"Amen. Pass the potatoes." Josiah reached for the bowl.

After all three of them had eaten their fill, Kirsten cleaned up the kitchen. Josiah found a tennis ball from somewhere in his room and rolled it down the hallway for Maisy to chase. Her toenails skittered on the wood floor as she scooped up the ball in her mouth and brought it back to him.

Later, Josiah took a shower without protest, although Kirsten did have to tell him that Maisy did not need to shower with him. When she went in his bedroom to pray and tell him goodnight, Maisy lay on the rug beside his bed. Josiah dangled one hand over the edge so he could touch her.

Kirsten said a brief prayer and kissed him on the forehead. Then she bent to give Maisy a pat. In her own bedroom, she tried to sort out her feelings. She'd never seen Josiah so calm and compliant. Did the dog really have that effect? What would Josiah do when Jon came back and wanted his dog? Would he handle it without a total meltdown? Maybe it was time to rethink her "no dogs" policy with Josiah. But would just any dog respond to him the way Maisy did?

She slipped into her pajamas, but before climbing into her bed, she knelt at the side. *God, I really need guidance. Can you help Josiah handle losing Maisy when she has to go back? And God, please be with Jon, he must be devastated by this fire.*

She'd almost drifted off to sleep before she added one more request.

And can you help me handle it if Jon doesn't come back?

Chapter 50

JON DROVE WITH no destination, no purpose in mind. He was running away, he knew that. But what was he running from? He just knew he would explode if he didn't go. Besides, there was nothing left for him in Maple Grove.

He headed out on Highway 51. The Cadence River was on his right, flowing steadily away from Maple Grove. And he drove in the same direction. His speedometer registered ten miles over the limit, but he didn't care.

The miles rolled by. He needed to stop to eat and use a restroom, but he just kept moving.

Almost a hundred miles down the road, the truck swerved toward the ditch. He jerked the steering wheel. It kept pulling to the right, toward the river. He pulled it back again. And then he heard it. Thump, thump, thump. He steered the truck onto the shoulder and braked to a stop. He hopped out of the truck, leaving the door standing open.

The right front tire was nearly flat.

He could no longer contain his mounting fury. He kicked the offending tire, slammed the driver's door so hard the glass rattled, and then punched the side of his truck with his fist. A round dent appeared even as a searing pain shot from his knuckles clear up to his shoulder. He screamed, a primal shout that echoed off the river bluffs and bounced back, mocking him. Leaving the roadway, he charged through the underbrush until he stood beside the river.

Large trees drooped over the water, shielding it from the road. Below his feet, the bank dropped off for several feet. The fall rains had swollen the waterway, and it thundered by, fast and full. The dark brown water held secrets. He could see no more than a few inches beneath the surface.

Jon teetered on the bank. Was there any reason not to end the pain? Just let go, sink below the surface, and let the cold water close over his head? Would anyone know—or care?

For what seemed like a very long time he stood there, the water's rush in his ears, his heart as cold as the river and hard as the rocks beneath the surface.

Then, as he wavered at the brink, the River's Edge family came to mind. Margaret, Bethany, Carlton. People who'd worked hard to restore the house. Paul and his crew. Customers. Others he'd come to care for. Kirsten, Josiah. Even Maisy and Tiger. It wouldn't be fair to them to have it end this way.

Jon stumbled back from the river's edge and sank down in the weeds and mud. He heard Paul's words again, "Healing don't come from a place."

That was true. River's Edge hadn't brought healing. Only more pain. He knew what Paul thought he needed.

And as if he had poked a sore and tender spot in his heart, he thought of Angie. His beloved wife. Did he honor her by sitting here in the mud with thoughts of throwing himself into the river? He knew what Angie would say he needed, too.

"Oh, God." He screamed. But the river seemed to snatch his words and sweep them downstream. His head sank to his hands.

"God, if you are real, show me You love me. Show me that You are able to heal."

There was no answer, only the roar of the river.

Jon rose to his feet and trudged back to the truck. He slid beneath it, unfastened the spare tire's bolt and maneuvered it out. He pulled the jack from the back seat. He jacked up the front end, loosened the lug nuts from the flat tire, and pulled it off. Then he fastened the spare tire on. He threw the flat tire in the bed of the truck and returned the jack to the back seat.

Spare tires are not designed to drive on for long distances. And he was over a hundred miles from Maple Grove, deep in the Ozark hills. Small towns popped up along the highway every twenty miles or so, but most were only a collection of weathered homes and maybe a convenience store. He wasn't likely to find a place to fix a flat tire before morning. But maybe he could at least find a place for supper. He drove on down the highway, keeping the truck at a more moderate speed.

Chapter 51

BETHANY ROLLED OUT of bed and stood in front of her closet. She had only one pair of jeans she could wear—the pair she'd taken from her mom—and not very many tops either.

Jon's call Wednesday morning had put her in a black mood. She felt like she was carrying around a huge bundle of problems with each day adding a new one. Since the restaurant fire, she had no job, nor any chance of supplementing her job by making pies. Her dreams of college were crumbling. She didn't even know how she would support herself, let alone a baby.

She pulled on the jeans and slipped into a clean sweatshirt. In the kitchen, she opened the refrigerator. No Sprite. She pulled a bottle of Mountain Dew out of the fridge, opened it, and hesitated. Caffeine wasn't good for babies, was it? She sighed, put the top back on the bottle and put it away. Maybe she could buy some juice, but she didn't have time this morning. Feeling the need to talk to someone, she'd made an appointment with the school guidance counselor.

She put a frozen waffle in the toaster. When it popped up, she spread peanut butter on it and ate while she checked to make sure everything was in her backpack. Then she walked out the back door, locking it behind her.

At school, she stopped in her first period homeroom. Mr. Johnson looked up from the newspaper. "Good morning, Bethany. You're either here early, or I didn't hear the bell."

She smiled. Mr. Johnson was one of her favorite teachers. She had him for homeroom and Algebra II. "I have a pass to go see Mrs. Beasley." She dug in the front pocket of her backpack for the pink slip.

"I believe you. Don't worry about finding the pass. Backpacks are notorious for eating them."

Bethany giggled. "Thanks, Mr. Johnson. See you in Algebra. And yes, I have my homework done."

The bell rang, and students lounging around lockers suddenly moved with a purpose. They knew they had only five minutes to make it to their homerooms. Bethany ducked into the guidance office and told the secretary she had a meeting. Within a few minutes, the door opened and Mrs. Beasley, a plump, middle-aged woman who smiled too much, beckoned her in.

After Bethany sat, Mrs. Beasley folded her hands on the desk before her, leaned forward and smiled some more. "What can we do for you this morning, Bethany?"

"I need help." Bethany sighed. Then she opened the bag of worries and spilled them out.

Mrs. Beasley listened well. Bethany left the office with a handful of pamphlets listing resources and help for pregnant teenagers—from healthcare, to baby supplies, to government assistance.

Mrs. Beasley had checked her credits and reassured Bethany that she was on track to graduate in January. But she still had no job, and no way to support herself or a baby.

That night, when her mom walked in the house after work, Bethany sat at the kitchen table working on homework. Her mom dropped her purse on the table and sank in a chair. "You're not working tonight?"

Bethany laid down her pencil. "You didn't hear about the fire?"

Her mom frowned and shook her head. "What fire?"

"There was a fire at River's Edge. It burned the whole kitchen and pantry. I won't be working there for a long time."

Her mom's frown deepened. "That's just great. No job and a kid on the way. Now you see why I didn't think you should keep it?"

Bethany blinked away tears, trying to focus on the paper in front of her.

"I'll graduate in January. When do you want me to move out?"

"Just be out before the kid comes. I've done my stint. I don't want to raise another one. And if you lived here, I know who would get stuck with it. Just like that spotted dog you brought home and promised me you'd take care of."

"I was nine years old," Bethany protested. But her mom had gone into the front room and turned on the TV. Bethany closed her algebra book and let the tears run down her cheeks. The huge load of worries was back, heavier than ever.

Margaret stood at the window and waved as Melanie pulled out of the driveway. She'd worked hard to convince her daughter to call her high school friend and meet her for dinner in Benson. Before she left, Melanie fixed a kale salad for Margaret's supper and put it in the refrigerator. She wondered if Melanie would find out if she ordered a pizza from P.J.'s instead.

She shuffled back to the living room and found her phone

underneath the pile of mail she'd been sorting. Then she scrolled down until she found Bethany's number. She punched it in and sat down.

"Bethany, this is Margaret. I happen to have the evening free. Would you like to come over for your first pie lesson?"

For a minute the phone was silent. Bethany's voice was cautious. "You do know about the fire?"

"Oh, yes, honey. But we can still make pies. As a matter of fact, I talked to Paul Donovan today..." Margaret filled Bethany in on her plans. But not the big plan. That needed to wait until she was here in person. "So what do you think? Do you have time to make some pies tonight?"

"I can be there in fifteen minutes. I'll ask my mom if I can drive the car."

On impulse, Margaret asked, "Have you had supper?"

"No."

"Well, if you drive, why don't you stop by Pete's and get a pizza? Whatever kind you like best. I'll pay you for it, I just can't drive to pick it up."

"Sure." Bethany actually sounded excited.

Margaret stood, went out to the kitchen and began to pull out her pie-baking supplies.

Chapter 52

BETHANY COULDN'T HELP but smile when she saw the pies lined up on her kitchen counter. She cut a tiny slice from the apple one and popped it into her mouth. Then she hurried to the garage, wheeled her bike out, and rode down the street.

She stopped at the edge of a street cluttered with orange maple leaves. As her feet dropped from the pedals into the leaves, it sounded like her first bite into the crisp skin of a piece of Jon's fried chicken.

Margaret had given her the address of the white two-story house with a wooden swing set in the backyard. Just the kind she'd always begged for, but her mom said, "Costs way more than we have." A little playhouse perched above a sand box, the slide spilling out from an opening in the side and multiple swings hanging from the cross beam.

Bethany took a deep breath and walked her bike up the sloping driveway. She couldn't back out now.

She laid her bike against the garage and went to the side door. Anxiety knotted her stomach, and she held one hand over it. She tapped softly on the door.

Bethany heard footsteps before she saw him. A tall man with

sandy blond hair and a muscular build opened the door.

She stepped forward and held out a hand. "Hi. My name's Bethany Alcanter."

He grasped her hand firmly. "Hi, Bethany. I'm Josh Peterson. I've seen you at church, haven't I?"

She nodded. "Umm-hmm. I've been going for a few months." She shifted from one foot to the other. "I wondered – could I talk to you about adoption?"

Josh's eyes drifted to her belly. She added quickly, "I just had some questions. Someone told me your son was adopted."

He held the door wider. "Sure. We can talk. Come on in." He used his foot to scoot a pile of mostly little boy's shoes off the mat.

She entered a sunny kitchen. A half-built Lego creation rose from a pile of loose blocks, a Bible lay open on the table, and a mound of vegetables surrounded a cutting board beside the sink. This was the way every family's kitchen should look.

"Have a seat." Josh swept his hand toward the bar and the table. She chose a barstool and perched on it, twining her feet around the legs.

Josh asked, "Can I get you something to drink? A Diet Pepsi? Tea?"

"Maybe just some water. I'm trying to avoid caffeine."

He filled a glass with ice and water and set it in front of her. Then he sat in a chair at the table. "Now, what did you want to know?"

What did she want to know? The big question, she didn't think she could ask—or Josh could answer. She chose an easy one. "How long have you had your little boy?"

"We adopted Navad from Ethiopia a little over a year ago. We worked through an adoption agency in Kansas City."

"How did it work?"

Josh detailed the process from their initial contact with the agency until they flew home with Navad. Bethany listened, her elbows propped in front of her.

"What else do you want to know?"

Bethany took a sip of water and swallowed. "Do you love Navad as much as you would your own biological son?"

For a long moment, the question hung like a blimp in the kitchen. Bethany wished she could grab the words and stuff them back in her mouth. She mulled over an apology, and just as she was about to say it, Josh spoke.

"I can't answer that. I haven't had a biological child. I can only tell you how I love Navad. I love him with all that I have. I would do anything for him. Do I love him as much?" Josh paused and his gaze traveled to the window and the yard beyond. When he looked back at Bethany, she thought she detected tears in the corners of his eyes. "Yes, sometimes it even seems I love him more. We lived so long without Navad, now we know how precious each day is."

Josh scooted the pile of Legos over and folded his arms on the table. "Do you have brothers or sisters?"

"No, it's just me."

"Okay. Look at it this way. Does God love you or me better?"

Bethany giggled softly. "He loves us the same. He loves everybody."

Josh nodded. "Umm-hmm. We're all different, but He loves us all. No matter how we became part of His family." He leaned back, crossing his arms over his chest. "Are you considering placing your baby for adoption?"

"Kind of. I want him or her to have a family. Not just a teenage mom who works as a waitress after school."

Josh stood and walked to a small desk. He took a piece of paper, scrolled through his phone, and copied a number on it. Then he handed her the paper. "That's the name and number of the adoption agency we used in Kansas City. They're a Christian organization, and they'll see that your baby is placed with a good family. And he'll be loved as much as you could love him—maybe more, because they have known the heartache of being unable to have a baby themselves."

Bethany stood and tucked the paper in her jean's pocket. "Thanks, Mr. Peterson. You've given me lots to think about."

Josh followed her to the door. "You're welcome any time, Bethany. Come back when Navad is home, so you can meet him."

Bethany coasted down the driveway, blinking away tears, but her heart felt lighter than it had for months.

Chapter 53

A FLASHING NEON sign promised *Cold Beer, Hot Food.* Jon steered the truck into the parking lot. When he entered, a waitress in snug shorts and a low-cut top greeted him.

"Hello. Just one tonight? Would you like to sit at the bar or a table?"

Jon gave her a nod. "A table, please."

She led him to a dimly-lit back corner and handed him a sticky menu. "This table okay?" After he gave a second nod, she continued in her perky voice. "I'm Angel. What can I get you to drink?"

"Iced tea. Unsweetened."

She sauntered away, her bleached-blonde pony-tail swinging across her back. Jon felt a jerk of sorrow. What was Bethany going to do without a job and a baby on the way? He shook his head. She wasn't his responsibility. He didn't have to take on that worry.

He opened the menu and studied it. Sounds from the kitchen drifted out. *"We need more fries." "Order up." "Hey, are we out of tomatoes?"* He was relieved to see Angel coming back.

"You're not from around here, are you?" Her full, bright-red lips smiled at him.

"Nope. Minnesota. I'd just like a cheeseburger platter. No pickles." He handed the menu back.

She took it but kept her baby-blue eyes on him. "So what's a good-looking stranger from Minnesota doing in Mitchellville, Missouri?"

Had she actually fluttered her eyelashes at him? Jon groaned inwardly and looked away. "Just traveling."

"Well, I'll have that cheeseburger out right away, handsome stranger." Her hips swayed as she moved away.

In his pocket, his phone chimed. Who could be texting him? He pulled it out and looked. A cousin in Minnesota had sent a group text asking for all her relatives to pray for her mom, his Aunt Cindy. She had just been diagnosed with cancer.

For the second time, his heart wrenched with sorrow. Not for his aunt, but Margaret, the caring woman he'd worked alongside and grown to love. He hadn't said good-bye to her, hadn't even asked her how she was feeling. Her daughter would be going back to New York. Who would take care of her? He rubbed his head with both hands. Margaret wasn't his responsibility either.

He raised his head when he heard footsteps and smelled the strong odors of grease and cooked food. Angel bent at the waist as she placed the cheeseburger in front of him. Jon averted his eyes.

"Is there *anything* else I can get for you?" Her tone and expression eliminated any mystery to the question.

"No, thanks." Jon turned his attention to the cheeseburger, and, after a moment, the waitress left.

The sandwich stuck in his throat, but he forced it down. He hadn't eaten a real meal for two days. The burger was three-fourths gone and he was finishing the last of the French fries when Angel returned with a pitcher of iced tea. He handed her his glass and she filled it.

He wasn't sure how it happened, but the next thing he knew, his lap was flooded with tea and crushed ice. He leaped to his feet gasping with shock.

Angel looked horrified. "Oh, I'm so sorry." She set the pitcher on the table and righted the glass that had tipped. She handed him a wad of napkins. "I'll get some towels." She hurried off and returned in a moment with a couple of dingy cloth towels.

Jon wiped at the wet area on his pants. "It's okay."

"I'll get you more fries and another cheeseburger." She mopped the puddle on the chair. When she looked up, her blue eyes were filling with tears.

He could handle wet jeans, but not teary eyes.

"No. I'm done." He handed her the damp towels. "Just bring me the ticket."

When Angel handed him the computerized slip, he saw the meal had been discounted. He counted out the bills, included a generous tip, and dropped them on the table. As he left, Angel approached. "I really don't make a practice of dumping iced tea in people's laps. I'd like to make it up to you. Buy you a drink? Keep you company?"

Jon gave her a tight-lipped smile. "It's really okay. It was an accident. Thanks for the offer, but I need to get some sleep." He fled to his car. Next to the restaurant stood a row of shabby faded-red buildings. The sign announced these were the "Rose Cottages." Jon parked near a door marked *Office*.

A fragile-looking man with snow-white hair limped to the desk. "Can I help you?"

"I'd like a cottage for one night." Jon assumed from the

location and look of the place that the price would not be more than he had in his pocket.

He was right. When he paid for the room, the man handed him a single key on a ring.

Stale, musty air greeted him when he unlocked the door of cabin six. He didn't care. He peeled off the wet jeans and crawled under the covers. As he fell asleep it wasn't the waitress's shapely features or even his beloved wife's that drifted from his thoughts into dreams. It was a certain green-eyed, curly-haired veterinarian.

Chapter 54

JON ROLLED OVER and groaned, ending the worst night of sleep he'd had since college days. The mattress had more lumps than the first batch of gravy Carlton made.

He looked at the jeans he'd thrown over a chair. They'd dried, but there was a distinctive tea splotch. He dug in his bag for the pair he'd grabbed from the back of his closet the morning after the fire.

As he was pulling them on, he heard a crackle in one pocket. He reached in and pulled out a twenty-dollar bill. Where had that come from? A sudden rush of memory…the day of Maple Fest…counting change…a bill floating to the floor. He'd grabbed it as he returned to the kitchen and stuffed it deep in his pocket. He'd planned to return it to the register later. The twenty dollars the cash register was short. And he'd suspected Carlton.

He sank on the sagging mattress, nearly hitting the floor. He'd spent months mistrusting Carlton without cause. Remorse flooded over him. Even though Carlton knew nothing about his thoughts, he needed to apologize.

He gathered up his clothes, jammed them into his bag, and with a last look around the room, he left. He wanted a cup of coffee, but the bar where he'd eaten wasn't open. And it didn't look like much else in town was either. At the edge of town he found a gas station offering coffee from a machine crusted with past spills. Jon filled a large cup and took it to the cashier. He laid a package of powdered sugar donuts on the counter as well.

"I need to get a tire fixed on my truck. Where's the closest place?"

"There's an Amco station in Haysville. I think they can do it." She handed him the change and turned to the next customer.

Jon sat in the parking lot sipping the stale coffee and popping the small donuts into his mouth one by one. Haysville was north. The way he'd come. The direction of Maple Grove. He had to get ahold of himself. Develop a plan. His puny savings account would drain quickly even if he stayed at the Rose Cottages.

He set his coffee in the holder and turned on the ignition. He would head north, get the tire fixed, then stop in Maple Grove long enough to pick up Maisy and contact a real estate agent to put River's Edge on the market. He could probably get his old job back in Minnesota. He and Maisy could live in a cheap apartment until the restaurant sold.

The truck moved onto the highway, and thoughts of the people of River's Edge streamed behind.

The first town he passed had a convenience store, but no service station. The next town, Haysville, appeared slightly larger. A worn Amoco sign hung in front of four gas pumps, an office, and a garage. One of the garage doors gaped open. Jon pulled up and parked. When he entered the office, a man almost as worn as the sign greeted him with a smile. He wiped grimy fingers with an equally grimy shop rag.

"Morning. What can I do for you?"

"Fix a flat tire, I hope." Jon attempted a smile.

"Be about twenty minutes before I can get to it. You're welcome to sit here in the office." The man nodded toward some shabby plastic chairs. "Got yesterday's newspaper—the Kansas City Star. Help yourself to the coffee, too. It's hot."

"Thanks. The keys are in the truck. The flat tire is in the back." Jon filled a small Styrofoam cup with coffee and lowered himself gingerly into one of the wobbly plastic chairs. He set the cup of coffee on the floor and picked up the newspaper. First he read the latest on the Kansas City Chiefs' winning streak. Then, as he turned to the front page, a section called *Living* fell out on the floor. Maisy. There was a picture of Maisy. He dropped the other sections and picked it up. It was not Maisy, but another yellow Lab that could have been her twin. This one worked as a therapy dog in one of the Kansas City elementary schools. Jon read the entire article. He folded the newspaper and laid it on the chair, wondering what his dog was doing. He pictured her playing in the yard with Josiah.

Through the window, he saw his truck being pulled into the garage. He picked up the paper again and turned to the front page. Not long after, the man entered the office, using what looked like the same grimy cloth to clean his hands again.

"You been around a construction site? That was a long ole nail that poked your tire."

Jon stood up, folded the newspaper, and left it on the chair. "I had a fire at my restaurant. My guess is the nail came from some of the parts they ripped off."

"Sorry about the fire. Can you rebuild?"

"Yeah, but I'm selling. Going back to the insurance business. What do I owe you?"

"Twenty-six dollars." The man wrote an invoice, smudging it with grease where his fingers touched. He handed it to Jon along with his keys.

Jon counted out the bills from his wallet. Then he walked into the sunshine where his truck was parked, and in a short time he was headed northeast again.

The doughnuts had long since left his stomach, and real hunger pangs hit, but Jon didn't stop. He didn't want to take the time for even a fast food drive-through. He almost felt like he was being pushed back to Maple Grove.

Shortly after noon, he pulled off the highway and onto the gravel road. His truck rumbled as he drove over the iron bridge crossing the river. He made a mental note to park on the far side of the parking lot just in case there were more of those "long ole nails."

The parking lot was full. He braked to a stop and stared. He recognized Paul's truck, Kirsten's car, Carlton's battered jeep, even Margaret's Buick—what in the world was going on? He pulled in at an angle, threw the gearshift into park and hopped out.

Walking across the yard, he could see a pile of burned appliances. The distinctive whine of a saw came from inside. He stepped on the porch as two of Paul's men shouldered their way out carrying a portion of a charred kitchen cabinet.

"Jon." One of the men recognized him. Was his name Jared or Chad?

"What's going on? Why are you here?" Jon stepped back as they passed him with the cabinet.

The man tilted his head toward the door. "Ask Paul. He's inside."

The storm door was propped open. Jon stepped inside to a beehive of activity. Down the hall in the burned out kitchen, a demolition crew was working. Carlton pulled down a sooty section of cabinet with a screech of nails ripping loose. Jon's hand touched the pocket where the twenty-dollar bill lay and guilt twisted through him.

In the dining room, Kirsten stood on a chair taking down curtains. Margaret sat at one of the tables filling cups of coffee from an urn and serving pieces of pie on small paper plates. A general hubbub of friendly chatter surrounded him.

As he stared, the room became quiet. Then Paul emerged from the storage room, his head white with sheetrock dust and a large smear of charcoal across one cheek. "Jon, my friend. Look everyone, the prodigal friend is back."

Jon stepped forward. "What...what's going on here?"

Paul gave him a gentle slap on his back. "You've made a lot of friends here in Maple Grove. We weren't gonna let a little old fire take you under. This is all volunteer labor, buddy. We're gonna get your kitchen rebuilt and the place aired out and up and runnin' again."

"But...but..." He seemed unable to utter comprehensible sentences. "Why?"

"We love you, Jon." Paul's ear-to-ear grin grew a bit more serious as he added. "And, believe it or not, God loves you too. We're just his hands and feet."

Jon's head reeled. He remembered his angry shout at God. *Show me you love me.* He had. As well as these people, his friends, those he had come to love. And he knew. He couldn't sell River's Edge or leave Maple Grove. This was home.

Just then a yellow blur tore down the stairs. Maisy forgot all her training to never be in the dining room. She danced around him, her tail wagging madly. He knelt down and ruffled her ears. She whined and licked his hand. He laid his cheek against hers for a moment. But when he stood, she whirled away. At the foot of the stairs she looked back at him. Then she dashed back upstairs.

Kirsten dropped the curtains on a chair and came to stand near him. "Josiah's upstairs," she explained. "Way too much activity for him. I told him he could play Angry Birds on my iPad. He probably doesn't know what's going on because he has his earphones on."

Bethany appeared from somewhere and helped Margaret to her feet. Leaning on Bethany's arm, she made her way across the dining room and hugged him long and hard.

"You're looking good." Jon told her.

She laughed and touched her thinning hair. "Don't lie."

"I wasn't. You look good to me. And you must be feeling okay. I see you baked a pie."

Both Margaret and Bethany giggled. Margaret spoke. "Wrong again." She gestured toward Bethany, her face glowing with affection. "You're looking at Maple Grove's newest pie baker. And—" she smiled at Bethany again, "my new roommate."

"Roommate?" Jon shook his head, confused.

Margaret nodded. "My daughter, Melanie, had to return to New York. She was concerned about leaving me by myself, so I asked Bethany if she'd move in with me. It seems she was looking for a place for her and the little one coming in April. And she's the best nurse, ever. She helps me when I need it and she lets me do it myself when I can."

Bethany seemed a little embarrassed. "It was an answer to prayer for me," she said softly.

"Sounds like a great deal for both of you. I'll have to sample your pie in a little bit. First, I need to go up and talk to Josiah."

He gave Margaret another gentle hug. Then Jon turned to Kirsten. "I have something I need to tell Josiah. I'd like you to come with me."

Her eyebrows rose slightly, but she didn't question as she followed him up the stairs. Josiah sat on the floor in the hallway, his headphones on and fingers flying across his mom's iPad. Every so often he reached with one hand to touch the big yellow dog lying beside him. When Jon stepped on the landing, Maisy stood to greet him.

Josiah looked up. He glanced back at the game, then up at Jon again. He pushed the pause button and pulled off the headphones. Then he stood and wrapped his arms around Jon for a brief hug. "I was afraid you weren't going to come back. Mom told me about the fire and then she said you left. I took good care of Maisy. I fed her a cup of food for breakfast and at five o'clock I gave her another cup for supper. I walked her every day. And I brushed her."

Jon wanted to give Josiah a hug back. But he shoved his hands in his pocket. "I'm so glad you took such good care of her. Because, while I was on my trip I did some thinking."

Josiah looked at Maisy and said softly, "A large dog's heart beats between 60 and 100 times a minute, that's about what ours beats."

Jon glanced at Kirsten's shining eyes. His heart must be beating way more than 100 times a minute. He took a deep breath and turned back to Josiah. "I think Maisy needs to stay with you. If it's okay with your mom, I want to give Maisy to you."

Josiah's head shot up, his eyes huge and staring straight into Jon's. "Forever?"

Jon nodded. "Forever."

Josiah's eyes darted to Maisy, then back to Jon's face. Suddenly he was hugging Jon, and this time, Jon hugged back. Josiah pulled away and grabbed Maisy's collar. "Maisy, you hear that? You're going to be my dog."

"Wait a minute, partner. I said if your mom thought it was okay. You need to ask her."

Josiah looked up at his mom, but his hand still clutched Maisy's collar. "I've been responsible. I can take care of her."

Kirsten still didn't answer. When Jon turned, he saw her green eyes filling with tears and as a few spilled over and ran down her cheek, his heart sank. What had he done?

"Kirsten, I'm so sorry, I should have talked to you downstairs." He laid his hand on her shoulder.

"No, it's okay, it's okay." She wiped her eyes, then touched Josiah's arm. He looked up at his mom. "Of course you may keep Maisy. But she's a gift. Tell Mr. Washington thank you."

"Thank you, Mr. Washington," Josiah parroted. When a rat-a-tat-tat of hammering exploded downstairs, he put his headphones back on and picked up the game.

Kirsten wiped at her eyes again. She walked to the window, the one that overlooked the gentle slope to the trail and the river. "I don't know what to say, Jon. You've been so kind to us. I've never seen him spontaneously hug someone before."

"While I was gone, I read an article about therapy and service dogs in school. I've always been amazed at Maisy's ability to calm Josiah. Maybe you can take her to classes and get her trained. She could even go to school with him if she had the right certifications. I think she's smart enough."

Kirsten knelt to stroke Maisy's head. "I knew you were special the moment I laid eyes on you."

Jon looked at Kirsten and knew he could say the same about her. When she stood, he reached out and she slipped her hand in his. Ever so gently, he bent and her lips met his, softly, sweetly. There was a noise outside and they looked as another burned item was hauled to the dumpster. Those were the people who cared about him and River's Edge. They were determined to rebuild it.

Just as another Carpenter seemed determined to rebuild him. He turned back to the woman whose hand he held. From somewhere deep within, he felt a shoot of new life. A tiny sprig, coming from a heart that was healing. Healing not from a place, not from fulfilling a dream, but from the only One who has the power to heal.

TO MY READERS: I pray that *Restoration at River's Edge* has blessed, encouraged, and perhaps led you closer to the One who restores all.

Your purchase of this book blesses others as well. All proceeds go to Pour International to maintain homes for abandoned babies and children in eSwatini, Africa. For more information on this organization, please go to www.info@pourinternational.org.

Other books by Susan R. Lawrence:

Atonement for Emily Adams
The Blue Marble
The Long Ride Home
Shepherd of eSwatini

I love to connect with readers at www.susanrlawrence.com